The door gave the softest creak as it slowly opened.

~⟨OO⟩~

Her body went cold. Had the last of her luck run out? Did the jailer mean to force himself on her after all?

She opened her mouth to scream just as a man's hand clamped over it. With a wordless cry, she reached up to pull the hand away, and his body blocked her.

"Julia!"

The whisper froze her.

"It's me, Sam."

She sagged back with relief and his hand slipped away. "What are you doing here?"

"Rescuing you. Don't I always?"

There was a hint of truth in his sarcastic words that offended her, but then he was pulling her to her feet. She fought to pull away, but he held her too tightly.

"Wait!"

"I'll explain everything later," he said impatiently. "Just trust me."

"Trust you!" she echoed, her voice almost a hiss. "Is this just another attempt to solidify your case? If I escape, I'll look guilty."

"The evidence is overwhelming," he told her. "If you don't escape, you'll die."

Other AVON ROMANCES

ALAS, MY LOVE *by Edith Layton*
IN THE NIGHT *by Kathryn Smith*
A KISS IN THE DARK *by Kimberly Logan*
LESSONS IN SEDUCTION *by Sara Bennett*
SEDUCING A PRINCESS *by Lois Greiman*
STEALING SOPHIE *by Sarah Gabriel*
WHAT AN EARL WANTS *by Shirley Karr*

Coming Soon

SOMETHING LIKE LOVE *by Beverly Jenkins*
WHEN DASHING MET DANGER *by Shana Galen*

And Don't Miss These
ROMANTIC TREASURES
from Avon Books

AS AN EARL DESIRES *by Lorraine Heath*
JUST ONE TOUCH *by Debra Mullins*
SOMETHING ABOUT EMMALINE *by Elizabeth Boyle*

GAYLE CALLEN

A Woman's Innocence

AVON BOOKS

An Imprint of HarperCollinsPublishers

AVON BOOKS
An Imprint of HarperCollins*Publishers*
10 East 53rd Street
New York, New York 10022-5299

Copyright © 2005 by Gayle Kloecker Callen
ISBN: 0-06-054396-5
www.avonromance.com

First Avon Books paperback printing: April 2005

Avon Trademark Reg. U.S. Pat. Off. and in Other Countries, Marca Registrada, Hecho en U.S.A.
HarperCollins® is a registered trademark of HarperCollins Publishers Inc.

Printed in the U.S.A.

10 9 8 7 6 5 4 3 2 1

To my mother-in-law,
Joanne Swenton,
a heroine in her own right.
Thank you for your incredible son
and for all the love you've shown me.

Chapter 1

Leeds, Yorkshire
September 1844

Jail was a terrible place for a woman, even a guilty one. As Samuel Sherryngton stared at the dilapidated building in a rough-looking neighborhood in Leeds, he found himself hesitating, his jaw tight from spending so many hours grinding his teeth in angry frustration. Julia Reed was in there, having spent ten days awaiting transport to trial in London, charged with treason.

He hadn't seen her since she'd been led away,

claiming her innocence with weary desperation. He still felt a pang of shock and disbelief, and a rage he sometimes wondered if he could continue to control.

How had this happened to bright and sunny Julia, the little girl who followed him through gardens so many years ago? How could she have betrayed her country, her family—him? He knew he was taking this too personally, for they had not been close in many years. But thousands of people had *died* because of her. And he'd spent the previous month of August chasing her through England, ready to intercept her before she could kill the man who would testify against her.

Taking a deep breath, he squared his shoulders and entered the jail. Even in the front office, the stench seeped out, full of hopelessness and fear.

It was easy for him to obtain permission to see Julia. A few shiny coins were all that mattered to the jailer. After agreeing to their transaction, Sam set a basket on the desk.

The man tilted back his chair and smiled wolfishly, his missing front teeth a black hole in his face. "Ye brought her food, then, eh? The wench could use some. She eats like a horse."

Sam leaned over the desk, directing some of his anger at the jailer. "You had better be taking good care of the prisoner. The charges against her have the attention of Queen Victoria."

The jailer affably lifted his hands. "Ye need

not complain about me, sir. She gets what everyone else does." Then he sorted through the basket, taking away the bottle of cider and several meat pies for himself.

"No glass in the cell, guv'nor," he said with a smirk.

Sam waited impatiently while the man unlocked the door, lifted an oil lamp, and led him down a dark passage. On either side were doors with bars as a viewing window. The air was hot, heavy, full of despondency. Someone coughed repeatedly, a deep emptying of the lungs. Another prisoner begged to ask a question, and the jailer ignored him.

"You don't have a woman's area?" Sam asked sharply.

"How big a jail does this look like?" the man replied over his shoulder. "This ain't London. And the lady got a window, somethin' rare."

At the last door, there was a feeble light from within the room, the promised window.

The jailer unlocked the door. "Ye want me to come in with ye?"

"That won't be necessary," Sam said. He stepped through the doorway and straw crunched under his feet. "Julia?" His voice sounded harsh even to himself. He'd get nowhere with her if he couldn't control himself.

She made not a sound. The door clanged shut behind him. There was a mound of blankets on the cot and a bucket in one corner.

"Call when ye need me," the jailer said. His uneven footsteps faded away.

"Julia?" Sam said again, louder, with an edge of worry he thought he'd never feel for her again.

The blankets suddenly moved, and in the dim light he watched the woman push herself slowly to sit against the wall. The white-blond hair that so distinguished her hung disheveled and dull. She wore a thin, shapeless dress, more a smock, that sagged off one white shoulder.

He should despise her for what she'd done— but something nagged at him each night as he lay sleepless in a nearby hotel.

"Sam?" Her usually expressive voice was cold.

He nodded and took a step toward her, watching as she sat up straighter. "How are you, Julia?"

She cocked her head. "Well, that's a ridiculous question," she said sarcastically.

He sat down on the edge of the cot, testing it first with his weight, to make sure it didn't collapse beneath them both. He set the basket between them.

"Food?" she asked.

"Yes."

They stared at each other in the gloom, and he saw the dirt that smudged her face, the dark shadows beneath eyes that glistened. But she didn't cry.

He almost wished she would.

"So you brought me food, Sam. Am I supposed to thank you? What more could you want from me?" She drew her knees up against her chest and hugged them to her, though it was hardly cold in this oven of a jail.

It was just another barrier between them.

"I don't know," he said, giving in to the bewildering thoughts that chased around inside his head. "This is one of the hardest things I've ever had to do."

"If you're looking for redemption, then you might as well leave."

"I don't want that."

"Then just go. Surely you'll see me at the trial in London, you and your fellow soldiers, full of enthusiasm, ready to gloat."

Sam closed his eyes and rubbed a hand over his face. "You think I'm *enthused* about any of this? This type of crime . . . I still can't grasp that you were a part of it."

She sighed again and spoke in a dull, flat voice. "Don't bother hoping that I might incriminate myself. I didn't do anything. I've already told you that. But no one will believe me."

"There's too much proof," he said forcefully.

"Sam, who could possibly hate me enough to want me dead?" she continued. "You know that's the punishment for treason. Death by beheading."

He said nothing, sickened by the thought of her baring her long white neck to a blade. She sounded so convincing, so desperate. She had always been able to appeal to his protective instincts.

What if she was telling the truth?

That was why he was really here, wasn't it? Some part of him still thought there had to be a mistake somewhere. Was he just a fool?

"I just saw Edwin Hume," Sam found himself saying against his better judgment. Hume was to testify that he'd worked for Julia, passing along information about British troops to the Russians—information that had helped ensure the deaths of sixteen thousand soldiers and their families in Afghanistan.

For a man trying to save his own neck, Edwin hadn't even been able to look Sam in the eyes. He'd taken to drinking, and would now have to be guarded to make sure he would remain a credible witness at the trial.

"He's lying," Julia whispered angrily, "but I can think of no reason why. He was part of my household, my governess's shy son. When I was young, you always encouraged me to befriend him."

"He was more of your age," Sam said briskly. "I was so much older than you. It was inappropriate for me to be your constant companion, even if it was in simple friendship."

"There were only six years between us. Not so much."

"Maybe not now, but back then—" He broke off. She'd been the master's daughter, he the gardener's son, and at the end a grown man to her fourteen years. He had realized they couldn't be friends anymore.

Julia sighed. "Edwin and I shared our first kiss."

He said nothing, though he remembered well his feelings of jealousy. That sweet kiss, not meant for him, had been the final catalyst for Sam's entry into the army of the East India Company. He knew even then that he could not stay in England and watch her grow up and away from him. Had she felt deserted? Was it his fault that she'd turned to other men?

"And now Edwin has betrayed me," Julia continued harshly, but with bewilderment. "I haven't seen him in ten years, since I joined my brother in India. I had no idea Edwin had even left England, and I certainly never saw him in Afghanistan. I can't believe that he conceived this plot against me. The man I knew would have been incapable of such a crime."

Sam thought of Edwin, a drunkard now, a man beaten by life. Was there a chance that Edwin was lying, that someone else was involved in a deliberate attempt to destroy Julia?

"Tell me this proof," she said fiercely, her fists clenched on her knees. "Explain it all to me. I was in shock when you arrested me, and I remember little of it. And the jailer just shrugs at my questions."

He didn't want to go through it all again, but . . . something didn't add up, and he had long

ago learned not to ignore his instincts. Maybe if
he said it out loud, it would come to him.

"The first thing that alerted us were the whis-
pers of treason we began to hear in Kabul,
months before the massacre. Then one of our in-
formants saw a British woman with pale blond
hair deliver a letter to the hideout of a Russian
officer."

He saw her stiffen, but her voice was brisk and
impassive. "There are no other blond Englishwomen?"

He shrugged. "He said the woman's hair was
so blond as to be white. And we already knew
you'd been in Kabul unescorted, because I had
discovered you. Your brother is a British general—
surely you can understand why you were one of
the few people with access to military information." He raised a hand before she could protest.
"In no way did we believe it *was* you just from
this meager evidence alone. But then Nick Wright
was visiting the Russian officer in an unofficial
capacity, and he saw a necklace casually left on a
table. He knew he had given it to you."

Would she deny her affair with Nick—or with
the Russian?

Her eyes grew as frosty as ice. "As I told you
when you arrested me, it had disappeared from
my jewelry box."

"You're trying to say that somebody took it to
frame you. You were living with your brother, so
he had access. Who else did?"

"Our servants. We'd brought a cook and maid from India with us. We had officers for dinner several times a week. I couldn't even begin to name them all." She lifted her chin as if to say she'd proved her point.

"As you've already seen, we have two of the letters written in your own hand, with a code added that betrays British military troop strength."

"Anybody could have intercepted those letters and added their own code."

"We have documented testimony you were seen delivering them!"

She flung her hands up. "Your witness could have been paid to say whatever the real traitor wanted him to say!"

His anger faded, replaced by tired bewilderment. "Altogether this evidence is damning, and you can't refute any of it."

"The real traitor is out there, Sam," she said passionately. "The evidence was all set up for you too perfectly."

He was being a fool, letting her sway him. But what if she was right? Could he watch her go to her grave, without being absolutely sure?

He frowned. "Tell me again why you traveled north to Leeds to meet with Edwin Hume."

She twisted to face him, her knees now on the cot, and leaned toward him. "My old governess died in her sleep, and she left possessions my brother thought Edwin would want."

He well remembered Lewis Reed, now a general in the queen's army. As young boys they'd played together, but Lewis had soon realized the differences in their stations. There had been animosity between them from then on, and Sam had been stunned by Lewis's indifference to his sister.

Yet Julia claimed that the governess's death was the catalyst for her journey. Edwin had said this story was agreed on beforehand, should their meeting be discovered. But the old woman had died only a few weeks ago. Had the story been concocted before she died? And did that mean someone had deliberately killed the governess, just to fashion an alibi? Sam needed to question Edwin further.

And if Julia had betrayed her country for money, where had the money gone? None had been found. He stared into her face, not allowing himself to believe that there was a chance she could be innocent. For a moment, her eyes caught the scant light from the window, and seemed to shine with that odd blue color of stained-glass windows that had always fascinated him.

"No more questions, Sam?" She tilted her head mockingly. "Nothing else to go over?"

He got to his feet. He was on his own trying to look deeper into her case. Everyone else believed a swift trial and execution were all that was left. He couldn't go to his compatriots, Will Chadwick or Nick Wright. Not only did they believe her guilty, but Will was off on his honeymoon and Nick had gone to offer his own marriage proposal.

They'd been three spies ordered to uncover a plot against England—maybe only a spy could discover the real truth.

And Sam was a damn good spy.

"I have to go," he said, turning to rap on the door.

She scrambled to her feet, tall in the meager cell. To his surprise, she asked, "Will you come back?"

Just an hour ago he would have refused. "I promise I will," he said, then turned away as the jailer arrived.

Julia watched the door close behind Sam and, though she hadn't thought it possible, felt even more alone than before. The jailer leered at her between the bars before he followed Sam down the hall, but she only turned her back, having learned that he was too much a coward to attempt her harm.

She went to the window and pressed her face to the bars, her only view the polluted shores of the Aire River, crowded with mills and slaughterhouses. The smell was little better out there, but she closed her eyes and inhaled deeply of freedom.

It had been ten days since she'd been cut off from the world, ten days of listening to the hopelessness of other prisoners, the occasional shouts or the quiet sobs late in the night. The despair of this place weighed on her, threatening to close her throat with the hoarse sobs she yet held back. She'd cried when Sam and Nick had first captured her, but not since. She was too numbed by all that had happened, all they'd accused her of.

She had her sins, some of which she didn't want revealed—but treason and murder weren't among them. So many people she'd known had been among the dead, their friendships lost to her forever. Her brother had been transferred from Afghanistan back to India six months earlier, and she'd gone with him, realizing only later how fortunate they'd been. Thousands and thousands of men, women, and children were killed by the Afghanis, who'd wanted the British invaders gone. Even now, the images of their faces still haunted her—the officers' wives who'd insisted on inviting her to dinner whenever the soldiers were away, the children who gathered in awe around her horse, which had been bred to be the fastest. They were all dead, slaughtered as they tried to leave the country under a peace treaty in the dead of winter.

And her own government was accusing her of causing the slaughter. Grief and despair welled up inside her again, and she fought it back, knowing she needed a clear mind.

These accusations had even cost her her

brother. They'd never been close, but she'd been certain he would answer her letter, do all within his power as a general in the queen's army to discover the true criminal. Instead, he must have believed the lies, because he'd never responded.

Her only visitor was the man who'd put her in jail.

Julia looked at the incongruous basket that perched on the cot. She shouldn't eat anything Sam had brought. He was only appeasing his guilt.

But surely good food shouldn't go to waste. She removed the cloth spread on top, surveyed the contents appreciatively, and bit into a cake dripping with a sweet glaze. She even licked her dirty fingers when she was done. There was more to eat, but her belly was already growling a warning, so she'd better take her time.

Her mind went immediately back to the things that haunted her. She'd spent her hours in jail fighting the encroaching sense of defeat by trying to figure out who had framed her for such a terrible crime. Who could hate her enough to want to see her executed? But her thoughts had gone around and around, disjointed and confused.

Had her behavior in Afghanistan made her an enemy she didn't even know about? She had lost more than her inhibitions in that foreign country. She'd forever lost Sam.

In a childhood filled with duty and distance

and indifference, her only true friend had been Sam, the gardener's son, and her escape had been the gardens. He came from a large, loving family she'd envied, had sisters she enjoyed playing with.

But it was Sam himself she'd always been drawn to. Though he was six years older, he'd always treated her with respect and friendship. But then he'd joined the army, followed soon by her brother. Her parents had died of the fever, and she was alone at fourteen years of age with only the servants, soon forgotten by even the villagers.

She had always known she wasn't like other women. Though she'd lived on a large estate, it had always felt like a prison to her. There had been no one but the servants who pitied her, yet they could not cross the boundary that divided their classes. She grew used to being alone, but gradually the restrictions chafed at her. She'd ridden her horse across streams, through forests that she pretended went on forever. But the end of her family property was as solid as an invisible boundary. She could never go farther, restricted by her age—but mostly because of her gender. Freedom had always called to her, had beckoned to her from across oceans. The globe in their family library had constantly twirled under her hands as she saw the continent her brother traveled, traced with her finger the paths he wandered.

Not that he ever sent letters himself, even then. She was just his sister, a nuisance—a dependent. But he was the key to her freedom, and she focused on him with single-minded determination, hoarding every shilling in pin money and in unused household budget which the sympathetic housekeeper passed on to her.

When she turned eighteen, nothing could stop her. She bought a ticket to the East, and even through a miserably long voyage, her excitement could barely be contained.

When she'd arrived in India, her brother had disapproved, but he hadn't sent her home. That would have meant sparing time and thought—and money—on her. Instead he made sure she knew she was always a guest, never a part of his household. She'd finally realized that her last hope of belonging to her own family—a real family—would never happen. She gave up that dream, determined to exchange it for the freedom a woman in England never had. And it had seemed to work for many years, years of travel and adventure and new cultures to explore. But even the ability to do as she pleased paled after a while when she had no one to share it with. The price for freedom—loneliness—sometimes grew too much to bear. Her disappointment occasionally made her cross the line of propriety into places she wasn't proud of.

When Lewis had been recalled to England, she'd tried to look at it as another adventure, the chance to find the companionship that had always eluded her.

With a heavy sigh, she dug into the basket and bit into a flaky meat pie.

Were her present problems punishment for the things she'd done in her past? Had God played the ultimate joke on her, allowing her to draw the notice of the Duke of Kelthorpe, only to see her chance at a family crash about her? Why had she been foolish enough to believe that she wouldn't have to pay a price for her willfulness? Even if she was proved innocent, the duke could never welcome her again. His abandonment hurt, though she hadn't loved him. She had no one left to help her—

No one but Sam Sherryngton, who'd disapproved of her in Afghanistan, who'd helped to arrest and imprison her. He might as well be a stranger now. His brown hair had just a touch of red, and she used to imagine he hid a fiery personality. But he'd always been calm and deliberate with her, even when confronted by her misdeeds. His golden brown eyes, which she'd once thought held the secrets of the earth, now betrayed only icy indifference. When he and his fellow spies had captured her, he'd remained in the background, letting Nick Wright lead in her questioning.

The shock of the arrest still hit her like a blow, and knowing Sam believed it all made nausea roil inside her. He'd *believed* the lies someone had woven about her. He'd helped track her down across England, instead of helping her. She'd spent the past ten days with his face emblazoned in her mind, full of bitterness that he'd rather see her dead than listen to the truth.

She'd been unprepared for the sight of him here in her cell, bearing food, full of questions. There'd been doubt in his eyes. Dare she hope that he would help her? Or did he want her to take him into her confidence so he could betray her?

Sam took out his frustration on Edwin Hume's door as he pounded on it for a second time. Nothing. Edwin's horse was in the stable behind the house, and he wasn't at his favorite tavern across the street. Urgency overtook Sam, making his stomach tighten, making the world around him suddenly sharp and clear. And as usual, he felt the thrill of the hunt.

He stepped behind the shrubbery and peered in the front window, shielding his eyes with his hand. He could see the deserted parlor and a corner of the dining room, and spotted the one inconsistency: a boot on its side, just in the line of his vision in the dining room.

Was there a leg attached?

He walked around the house at a quick pace until he reached the back, facing an alley. The door was ajar and so he slid his pistol from his pocket, cocked the hammer, and slowly stepped inside. The kitchen was a cluttered mess, more with empty liquor bottles than food.

And then through the kitchen door he saw Edwin Hume lying on the dining room floor, unmoving, a wide swath of blood across his chest.

Sam gritted his teeth, holding back his curse. Though he assumed Hume's assailant was gone, he went through the house quickly, methodically, until he knew he was alone. Then he stood over the body, his mind already sifting through motives and meanings.

Hume gave a soft cough, and Sam dropped to his knees in astonishment.

"Edwin?"

He shook the man's shoulder, then ripped open his shirt. Just beneath his heart, a hole in his chest oozed blood with every beat of his pulse. Sam pulled a handkerchief from his pocket and pressed it over the wound.

"Edwin!" he said with more urgency. "It's Sam Sherryngton. Open your eyes!"

The man's eyelids fluttered, but never fully opened.

"Who did this to you?"

Hume coughed again, weaker this time. His lips parted, and Sam leaned over him to catch his words.

"Lewis . . . Reed . . ."

Sam stared at the dying man. "Julia's brother was here? *He* did this to you?"

With only the barest shake of his head, Hume whispered, "Paid . . . someone. Just like he . . .

paid me. He's—" A coughing fit made blood trickle from his mouth. Arching his back with a gasp, he finished with, "—the real traitor. Tell Julia that—tell Julia—"

His body slackened as he died. Swearing, Sam sank back on his heels.

General Lewis Reed? The man had betrayed and framed his own sister?

Chapter 2

Awave of guilt made Sam close his eyes with regret. Julia was innocent. And he had helped hunt her down and put her in jail. She'd stared at him with wounded, disbelieving eyes as he let them take her away. He hadn't trusted his instincts, hadn't given weight to his doubts. Though her outrageous behavior in Afghanistan had opened her up to this kind of trouble, he should have remembered the little girl who'd shared his garden. He'd betrayed her.

A loud pounding rattled the front door until it burst open and slammed against the wall. Sam stood up as two constables entered, dressed in navy coats and top hats.

"You're too late," Sam said wearily. "The murderer already escaped."

But they drew their wood truncheons out of their coats and held them menacingly before him.

"Don't move," said the one with the extra stripe on his sleeve. "Kick the pistol away."

Sam looked down at his own weapon, which he'd surprisingly left on the floor beside Hume. Frowning, he held up both hands. "I'm no threat to you, gentlemen. I'm one of the arresting officers in the treason case this man was a witness for."

"We know all about you, Sherryngton," said the other constable, his mustache twitching, his eyes darting to the pistol. "There were rumors that you might want to help the wench, but the chief constable didn't think you'd go this far."

"And I didn't."

"The blood on your hands says otherwise."

"I was trying to stop the bleeding, for God's sake!" Sam was still too astonished to feel truly threatened.

"Maybe you were trying to clean up the evidence against you. Now kick the pistol toward me!"

Sam complied, and as the men watched it skitter toward them, he continued the kick into the one constable's face, knocking him off his feet. After blocking the blow of the other constable's truncheon, Sam punched him hard in the stomach and face. When both policemen were unconscious at his feet, he picked up his pistol, feeling his usual calm enveloping him. Keeping behind the draperies, he looked out each window, but could see no reinforcements. He left the house through the back door and mounted his horse, guiding him down the alley, toward the river and the poorer sections of Leeds—and the jail.

Julia was innocent, he thought again with a renewed sense of relief. Sam had spent over a year on the case along with Nick Wright, and they'd both been played by a master—Lewis Reed, a general in the queen's army, a man who had access to every secret the Russians needed. And he had made sure every damning clue had pointed to Julia. Sam remembered Lewis as a childhood bully, his nemesis—but a traitor?

Sam's vaunted prowess had deserted him. He'd allowed Julia to be imprisoned for her brother's crimes. And now that Sam was her only chance at freedom, he was about to be the subject of an intense manhunt.

He wasn't as worried about the Leeds constabulary as he was about his own ability to prove that Lewis Reed was a traitor while remaining in hiding. Following Lewis's trail would take time, and Julia didn't have it. She'd already been bound over for trial, and once the bill of indictment was written, she'd be taken to London—for a swift execution.

* * *

Julia was awakened from a troubled sleep by the sound of a key turning in a lock. She opened her eyes, blinking, expecting morning and a meager—though welcome—breakfast, and instead caught a glimpse of the moon between her window bars.

The door gave the softest creak as it slowly opened.

Her body went cold. Had the last of her luck run out? Did the jailer mean to force himself on her after all?

She opened her mouth to scream just as a man's hand clamped over it. With a wordless cry, she reached up to pull the hand away, and his body blocked her.

"Julia!"

The whisper froze her.

"It's me—Sam."

She sagged back with relief and his hand slid away. Though he was a vague shadow, she could see him glance at the door.

Coming up on her elbows, she softly asked, "What are you doing here?"

"Rescuing you. Don't I always?"

There was a hint of truth in his sarcastic words that offended her, but then he was pulling her to her feet. She fought to pull away, but he held her too tightly.

"Wait!"

He frowned down at her, and she lowered her

voice. She shouldn't still care about him, but she couldn't help herself. "You can't do this! They'll assume the worst of you."

"They already do. Now let's go."

"But—"

"I'll explain everything later," he said impatiently. "Just trust me."

"Trust you!" she echoed, her voice almost a hiss. "Is this just another attempt to solidify your case? If I escape, I'll look guilty."

"The evidence is overwhelming. If you don't escape, you'll die."

She knew he didn't care that she was innocent—he must not want her blood on his hands. And that was fine by her. In her desperation, she would take even Sam's help, and then leave him at the first opportunity. Without another word, she crept behind him into the corridor, noticing that the lamps were conveniently dark. She could hear the snores of the other inmates, but not the usual sounds of the jailer and his guards laughing over their nightly card game.

The three guards were sprawled across the front room, their hands and feet bound, and she found herself relieved to see that they all still breathed.

"Did you think I'd killed them?" Sam whispered.

The voice that used to be so kind now sounded flat, cold.

"After everything you've done in the last few

weeks," she said, "I could believe anything of you."

He stared at her with eyes that betrayed no emotion, then turned away. She continued to follow him, stepping over the jailer's legs. Outside, the air was still heavy with late summer heat, and the moon made her feel strangely vulnerable in the dark shadows of the alley. A horse was tethered nearby, weighted down across his haunches by bulging saddlebags.

She looked around. "Did you plan ahead and bring me a horse?"

"My intentions would have looked a bit obvious. You'll ride behind me."

She still heard that undercurrent of anger in his voice. He was risking his life for her, but only with reluctance. She had once thought she knew him well, down to his soul. But she'd been a child then. Years and lives now separated them. He had hunted her down, imprisoned her, and believed the worst of her.

He handed her a cloak, and she wrapped it around herself. After mounting the horse, he reached down for her hand. From the doorstep, she balanced on his boot in the stirrup, then swung her leg over the horse's back, fitting herself between Sam and the rear of the saddle. Without her layers of petticoats for protection, she felt ridiculous with her legs spread wide, her hips pressed to his backside. He was warmer than the night air, and suddenly she was uneasy about touching him further.

The horse broke into a trot, and she was forced to wrap her arms around Sam or risk a fall. Beneath his coat, his back stretched wide and hard. With her breasts pressed against him, she felt their peaks harden, and hoped he couldn't feel it. The hard muscles of his stomach clenched beneath her hands.

But he said nothing, only guided the horse down the alley at a brisk pace.

"We need to talk," she said.

He glanced over his shoulder. "What?"

As she leaned closer, her lips brushed his hair. A spark of electricity seemed to jump between them, and she tried to keep her voice from shaking. What was wrong with her? "We have to talk. You need to know my plans."

"*Your* plans?" he called back with obvious disbelief. "You're under *my* command now, Julia."

She stiffened and sat up straighter, wishing she could pull away from him. "I'm not one of your soldiers."

"If you were, you wouldn't be in this mess."

Before she could protest, he put a hand on her thigh. "Be quiet. There are people in the streets."

There would always be certain people who needed the darkness, and now she was one of them.

"I've thought of a place we can briefly hide," he whispered.

She raised herself up and looked over his shoulder. By the light of a dim lantern, she could see the narrowness of the street and the way the houses sagged toward one another, and smell the stench of moldering fish. Beneath the lantern, a door was yanked open, and the laughter of drunken men spilled out. This was a tavern.

Never taking her eyes off the small number of customers gathered outside, she said, "We can't go in there. I'll draw too much attention dressed as I am."

"I don't know what we're doing yet. Whatever I have to say, play along with me. And make sure to hide that distinctive hair."

She didn't like the sound of this, she thought, pulling her hood forward. The cloak smelled of Sam. Not so long ago, that would have made her feel safe. Not anymore.

Suddenly his hands drifted down her legs, and she felt her skirt slide up. A warm breeze touched her bare calves.

"What are you doing?" she hissed into his ear, wishing she could kick his offending hands away.

Before he could answer, one of the men leaning against the tavern wall suddenly lifted a hand and called a greeting out to them.

Sam pulled on the reins, even as Julia was tempted to kick her heels in the horse's flanks to escape.

Suddenly, beneath her hands she felt the change in Sam's posture. He slouched back against her, let his hand come to rest brazenly on her thigh. By the lantern light, she noticed he was wearing a plain, working-class coat and trousers, unobtrusive in this section of town.

Rubbing her leg, he said in a casual, friendly voice, "Well, men, ye know where there's a tavern with rooms to lend around here? The kind ye don't need for more than a couple hours? I picked me up somethin' pretty on me way home."

Julia felt the shock clear down into the icy pit of her stomach. Surely *she* could have devised a better plan than pretending to be a prostitute around a bunch of unscrupulous men. But Sam's hand slid up her thigh, over her skirt, and the tips of his fingers curled beneath her backside. She wanted to squirm away from him, but she remained still, playing her part beneath the lecherous, knowing stares of three strangers.

"She don't act very friendly," said one of the drunken men as he stumbled closer to the horse.

Sam chuckled. "She just don't like an audience, right, Emma?"

Suddenly he twisted and snaked an arm around her. She found herself hauled into his lap, her back and her knees supported by his arms. She caught the hood quickly, letting it reveal her profile, but not her hair. They were face to face, her hands pressed flat against his chest. To her surprise, his heart wasn't even beating quickly. She looked into his eyes and saw that every trace of familiarity had vanished, as if he weren't Sam Sherryngton anymore.

Where had he learned such skill? He was pretending, and she would have to save herself by doing the same.

She let her hands run slowly up his chest, trying not to feel every hill and valley of muscle. Unlike his, her breath was coming much too fast, whether from fear or excitement she didn't know. With an imperceptible shrug, she let the cloak slide back off one shoulder, and it took her loose dress with it, revealing the bare skin of her collarbone. Sam looked right at it, where she wanted him to, and he licked his lips.

She gave a slow, satisfied smile.

"Ye blokes better point us to a room," he breathed hoarsely.

His mouth was so close that she almost gave in to the wild impulses that so easily ruled her. But she was not that woman anymore. She wouldn't kiss him, even if it was playacting. He had only taken her from one dangerous situation into another.

There was genial laughter as the drunken men gathered around, and Julia gave them an exaggerated wink. Sam dismounted first, then reached up to grip her waist and lift her from the horse, making her feel like a dainty thing, instead of a woman who came up to the bridge of his nose and easily towered over two of the three onlookers.

"She's a long one," one of the men said with obvious awe. "Girl, can I have ye after he's done?"

"I already paid for the night," Sam said easily, settling his arm over her shoulders. After removing his saddlebag, he flung a coin to the youngest man. "Take care of me horse, and I'll see there's more of that for ye."

The man bobbed his head enthusiastically. "I'll be waitin' at the stables out back, guv'nor."

After the door to the tavern opened, the stench of smoke and cheap beer and unwashed men surrounded them as they went inside. There were other women here, too, serving drinks and letting themselves be pawed. When Julia had gotten into scrapes, she'd pretended to be a boy to avoid just this sort of thing.

One of their escorts called in a loud voice, "Tate, ye got any rooms left for the bloke here? He's payin'."

A spectacled man behind the bar looked up slowly, without interest. "Pay now, then wait in line."

There was a *line*? she thought with resignation. She'd been in worse places. But she hadn't been wanted for treason then, hadn't had an execution lying in wait for her. A single mistake now would be deadly.

She let herself brush languidly against Sam as he haggled with the barkeep over money. His hand slid from her hip down over her backside, all while he kept talking. It had been a long time since she'd allowed a man such familiarity. She'd wanted to be a different person, a better person—and instead she'd just been broken out of jail and was now posing as a prostitute. But she was free.

The barkeep pointed up the stairs, and Julia led the way. When she looked up, she stumbled to a halt. Though the rickety wooden stairs led to a second floor, there was another couple waiting at the top, pressed intimately against the wall as if they weren't going to bother waiting for a room.

Sam leaned into her and spoke in a low voice. "There are several rooms up there, and the barkeep assures me he doesn't tolerate anyone using more time than he's paid for."

Julia grimly climbed the stairs. It didn't help when Sam's hands rode her waist, squeezing.

There was no corridor to speak of, just three doorways off a landing. They were forced to wait several stairs from the top, where everyone below could see them as if they were the nightly entertainment. She could feel the pairs of eyes, some curious, some envious.

Sam stepped onto her stair, crowding her, and leaned back against the wall. She didn't look at the couple moaning nearby, only stiffened her shoulders and stared at Sam without expression.

"I've just paid for you," he murmured.

His outward expression was annoyed, though his eyes hinted at reluctant amusement. He nuzzled her neck, his mouth hot against her skin. "No one's going to believe you inspire my lust by the way you're acting."

After everything that he and his fellow soldiers had done to her, how could he expect it to be easy for her to even *pretend* she liked him? He slid his arms beneath her cloak and gathered her against him. He was wider than she remembered, hard with the muscle of a soldier.

"Relax," he whispered, pressing a kiss to her cheek. "The secret is to think like a prostitute, to become her. Such a woman wouldn't care about those men below. She'd only want to earn her money and not starve to death along with her children."

That got her attention, and she angrily lifted her face to his. Though his eyes seemed remote, his face was laughing with the faintest leer—a man anticipating satisfaction.

She leaned in and bit his ear, satisfied when she felt his jolt of surprise. "I've spent much of my life pretending to be what others wanted me to be.

You have nothing to teach me about acting."

She let her hands trail up his arms, across his broad shoulders, up his neck. As she touched his face, she felt the rasp of a day's growth of beard. Pulling his head down, she pressed his face into her neck, hoping he remembered to keep the hood of the cloak over her head. He smelled good, like soap and the outdoors. She knew how she must smell to him, and it gave her a small measure of satisfaction. She ran her hands up through his hair and arched into him. When he groaned, she felt the slightest bite of his teeth into her neck and shuddered at the surge of un-welcome pleasure.

But she was a prostitute now, and accepted his advances, although somewhere in the back of her mind the faintest warning fought to be heard. She told herself that this wasn't Sam, but a nameless customer giving her the money she needed to survive. She nipped at his ear again. With a moan, he caught her knee and pulled it up to his waist, leaning into her in a provocative manner.

But a prostitute wouldn't be feeling the excite-ment that slowly expanded in her veins until it burned through her. And he must be feeling it, too, for as she writhed against him, she felt the hardness of his erection pressing intimately be-tween her thighs. She slid her face into his neck, turned to rub her cheek against his, and before she knew it, his lips were but a breath away from hers. As they paused in stillness, his heart finally betrayed him, pounding against her breasts.

She looked up into his eyes and saw the same surprise she was feeling. And then she leaned in and kissed him, a soft gentle pressure of her lips.

Chapter 3

At the stunning touch of her mouth, Sam's world tilted and upended. He had taunted her into this, teasing, touching. Somehow everything he was supposed to be concentrating on ended up falling away beneath the onslaught of Julia's willing body. She was hot in his embrace, her mouth parted against his as she sucked on his lower lip. She knew what to do, how to touch him.

When her tongue entered his mouth, he groaned and ground his hips against hers. Far away, he seemed to hear a door opening and closing, felt the brush of people moving past them, and all he could think was that he was one step closer to fulfillment.

From below, someone gave him a push, and he caught the banister with one hand and held Julia with the other.

"Ye're next!" a man insisted. "Hurry it up!"

Dazed, Sam realized another couple waited below them on the stairs. Julia blinked up at him blankly, and he pulled her up the last of the stairs and into a small room lit only by a few guttering candles on a wooden crate. There was a chair with a broken back, and a cot scattered with dirty bedding.

She stumbled into the center of the room, then stood tall as she turned to face him. He leaned back against the closed door, staring at her for a moment. Where had his legendary control gone? He could not claim to be immersing himself in his part, not when it was Julia he'd kissed, Julia he'd spent his lifetime dreaming about, even when his dreams had finally made him bitter. And now he was a wanted man.

"Speak softly," he ordered in a husky voice, then cleared his throat. "A servant will be up with a tub, and I don't want him overhearing us."

"A tub?" She let the hood slide to her shoulders and pulled out the string that held her hair back. "It wasn't difficult to tell I needed one."

He hadn't thought how she might take his offer of a bath. He should let her think the worst of him, but he heard himself saying, "I thought it might make you feel better after your confinement."

She shrugged, and he knew she didn't believe him. He was regretting the ruse he'd forced upon her, because he was painfully aroused, and it was proving far out of his control.

"I know that this masquerade got out of hand," he said. "I couldn't come up with anything else for this situation. I didn't think you'd mind, being that you aren't a—" The word suddenly stuck in his throat as he realized what he was implying.

"A virgin?" she coolly finished for him.

"I didn't mean it the way you're thinking," he said.

"So how did you mean it?" she asked, her hands dropping to her hips, the cloak falling back from her shoulders.

"I simply meant that you're not naïve, that you've traveled enough to have seen some of society's darker elements."

"Then you're lying to yourself," she said. "And what excuse do you have for *your* reaction—that you're not a virgin?"

He folded his arms across his chest and regarded her with an equanimity he was far from feeling. "I've played all sorts of parts."

"And there's a part of you that willingly joined right in," she countered, looking pointedly at his groin.

"I can't exactly control that," he said between gritted teeth.

"You can't?" Her wide eyes blinked innocently. "But you're in control of everything else, aren't you—my pursuit, my imprisonment, and now my rescue?"

"Julia—"

There was a knock at the door, and Sam cursed under his breath as she replaced her hood and walked to the bed. She sat down on the edge, touching nothing but the cloak. Two servants entered carrying a tub full of wrinkled linens and soap, and promised to return with hot water. They leered as Julia playfully showed them her ankles. The servants returned twice more, carrying steaming buckets. Sam tossed them each a coin when they were done, and finally he and Julia were alone.

She stood up and let the cloak drop behind her. He thought she'd snap a remark at him, but suddenly she just looked tired and resigned.

"Please turn around," she said.

He nodded, then took the chair and straddled it, looking out the small window into the dark night. Clothing rustled, followed by a splash as she entered the tub.

"I shouldn't have taken out my frustration on you," she said stiffly. "You did rescue me from jail."

"I helped put you there." His voice came out

harsher, guiltier than he'd meant to reveal. "You're innocent."

She said nothing for several minutes. As he listened to the gentle slosh of water, he pushed away thoughts on what she looked like, what she was doing. Why should he so easily be seduced by her beauty, her spirit, when he was still so angry with her? He was drawn to her with the same power that had held sway over him for at least sixteen years.

"You didn't come to this conclusion about my innocence on your own," she said coolly.

He closed his eyes. "No."

"What changed your mind? Didn't you want to see me beheaded?"

"I never wanted that." He gripped the broken back of the chair until his knuckles ached. "When Nick showed me the evidence, half the reason I participated was to shove his so-called evidence in his face, proving him wrong for once." He lowered his voice. "But you seemed to be behaving like a traitor would, traveling north to stop a witness from testifying against you."

"I behaved just like myself!"

A sopping washcloth hit the back of his head. He caught it as it fell, and tossed it over his shoulder in her general vicinity.

"I told you why I went to see Edwin," she continued. "His mother had died. My brother thought it would ease the blow if I delivered her personal possessions to Edwin myself."

Sam gritted his teeth. "Did you hear what you just said? Your *brother* thought."

Julia froze, the water cooling all around her, her wet hair making her shiver. "What are you implying?" she said calmly, controlling her sudden urge to chatter her teeth. She sank a little deeper in the tub, staring at the back of Sam's head.

"It was Lewis, Julia," he said in a low voice.

"What about him?"

"Your brother deliberately sent you north to Edwin Hume."

There was a pain in her stomach she didn't want to feel, so she ignored it even as it grew deeper, harder. "Of course he did it deliberately— my governess had died."

"He did it because he knew we would follow you, that we'd assume you were determined to prevent Edwin from testifying against you, that you were going to kill Edwin for his betrayal."

She wanted to put her hands over her ears to keep from hearing the hurt he inflicted with each raw word. "You're lying," she said, barely able to catch her breath. Her shivering seemed to consume her. Lewis may not be the best of brothers, but he couldn't be capable of murder!

Sam sighed. "Julia, when I left you in jail this morning, I went back to Edwin's house to question him further. Something didn't make sense."

"You mean my innocence?" She let him hear every drop of bitterness in her voice.

"You came north for the sake of your governess, yet Edwin had claimed this was just a story you'd both worked out to explain the two of you being together. But a witness saw his face when you broke the news of his mother's death. The witness swore that, from his expression, Edwin hadn't known his mother would be dead."

"I don't know what he knew," she said angrily, rinsing the last of the soap from her body. "It's obvious he was guilty because of the way he lied about me."

"So I wanted to talk to him again, to find out the truth. When I got there, someone had already shot him."

She closed her eyes as the cold seeped so deeply into her bones that she thought she'd never feel warm again. Was there anything left of her childhood memories that hadn't been tainted? Forcing herself to stand on wobbly legs, she wrapped a towel around her, then stepped out of the tub. "So Edwin is dead."

"Yes, but he was able to speak to me before he died. He said that your brother had paid him to lie, that your brother had had him killed. Lewis is the real traitor."

She stood motionless, shivering as water streamed down her shoulders, her thoughts racing chaotically through her head. She calmly wrapped a towel about her hair. "Edwin lied to you."

"Julia—" He glanced over his shoulder at her, then looked away. "That's not something you lie about when you're dying."

"Someone who hates me enough to implicate me in such a crime would have no problem hurting me even more by implicating my brother. You've known Lewis your whole life. Surely you can see—"

"Don't you remember what Lewis was like?" he interrupted wearily. "He did his best to make his servants—to make *us* miserable. You were just a little girl, and I didn't want you to believe the worst about your brother."

Though she was unsure of the truth, she couldn't just accept such a horrible accusation about Lewis. He wouldn't allow his own men to be killed, then blame it on her. She spread the cloak across the cot and sat on it. She wore only the towel, because the thought of putting her jail smock on again made her sick.

"Sam, regardless of what you think, Edwin must have lied one last time. I'll prove it."

He turned around to face her and she let him, her back straight. His gaze dropped to her bare arms, her bare legs, before returning to her face.

"There's a dress for you in my saddlebag."

"Thank you. You'll need to turn around again. After I'm dressed, we'll discuss my plans to find the real traitor."

He did as she asked, and she rooted through

the saddlebag. He'd brought a dress, a chemise, even petticoats and drawers, but no corset—not that she'd complain. And the dress even buttoned up the front, so she wouldn't have to ask for his help.

She fastened the last button beneath her chin. "You can turn around now."

He came toward her, and though he was leanly muscled, his size seemed to take up so much room. He caught her by the upper arms and gave her a little shake.

"You have to live in the real world, Julia. This is not some afternoon excursion you can plan. You're wanted for treason, and the government will send every police officer it can after you."

"Then why don't you just leave me?" she said angrily, pushing away from him. "This isn't your concern, is it?"

"I'm making it my concern. And besides, you may be wanted for treason, but now I'm wanted for murder."

She stared up at him. "What are you saying?"

"Two constables found me standing over Edwin's body. They think I murdered him to keep him from testifying against you."

"You didn't kill him, did you?"

Even as she said it, she knew he wasn't capable of such a thing, but a strange look flickered in his eyes.

"I didn't—but when I discovered what he'd

done, it crossed my mind. I had to do a lot of things to survive in the East, Julia. Don't underestimate me."

There was a threat implied there, but before she could think of a response, he began to stuff her jail smock into the saddlebag.

"We're leaving," he said. "I'm going to find you a place to hide. I'll come back for you after I've proven your innocence."

"No!" She grabbed his arm and pulled him around to face her. "This is my life and I will not hide! I need to prove to everyone that I did not let all those people die."

Chapter 4

ᴄᴏᴏᴏᴏᴏ

Sam looked at the stubborn expression on Julia's face and knew that if he left her alone, she would be recaptured. She thought she was a grand adventurer because she'd sailed down Indian rivers and climbed Afghani mountain passes, but she knew nothing about life on the run, what it took to stay alive when there were men who wanted her dead.

Yet, if she remained with him where he could keep her reasonably safe, she would be repulsed by the methods he might have to employ. He tried one more time to talk her into hiding, but she would have none of it. He was reluctantly grateful that she wasn't a missish girl, pampered and spoiled. She would accept whatever difficulties their journey presented. Of course, that was why she was in so much trouble.

"Now you listen to me, Julia," he said in a low voice, wishing he could tower over her, but settling for leaning toward her.

She lifted her chin stubbornly.

"If you're to remain with me, you will do *exactly* what I say."

"But I have the right to disagree with you."

"You have that right. But if I say 'not now,' you keep your mouth shut and follow my orders."

She wore the faintest smile, and laugh lines waited about her eyes for her good humor. At twenty-eight, she was not a girl fresh from the schoolroom, but there was a wisdom in her expression that was uncommon for young Englishwomen. Of course, the Englishwomen with whom he'd come in contact had mostly been the wives and daughters of officers or civil servants. Even in India, they were sheltered from the native people, still playing their society games.

But Julia had lived parts of her life outside the boundaries of convention, and it was for that reason she was easy to implicate in treason. Sam had discovered she was in Afghanistan when he caught her sneaking back into the British encampment outside Kabul, dressed as a boy. After that, whenever he was in Kabul, he had looked for her, followed her on more than one occasion to protect her. And that was how he discovered she had shared a bed with Nick Wright, Sam's good friend, the man who eventually arrested her. Sam had even introduced them to each other.

It shouldn't still hurt him, but it did.

Her white-blond hair was drying now, softening, curling as it fell to her waist. It was the most distinctive thing about her, the easiest way for people to identify her. Yet if anyone was close enough, it was her eyes they remarked on next. They were wide with life, the brilliant color of sapphires. He still could not look at those precious stones without thinking of the wonder of Julia.

"Very well, I'll obey you," she said, as if she were granting him a royal favor. "But know that it doesn't sit well with me. You had me imprisoned—"

"Julia—"

"And yes, although you've helped me escape, you now want to blame everything on my brother. I'll go along with you, and perhaps we can prove he is innocent."

There was a sudden, impatient knock on the door, and they both turned to stare at it.

"What is it?" Sam demanded, sounding angry, sulky, as he tried to show that he'd been interrupted at an inopportune time.

"If ye're not gonna use the room—"

"I paid for the night!" he shouted, then looked around, spotted the chair, and sent it crashing into the door.

Julia rolled her eyes as her lips twitched up at the corners.

When there was no answer, he fell backward to sit on the cot. The old wood gave a loud squeak.

"No wonder they couldn't tell what we were about," he murmured, then bounced a bit for some rhythmic squeaking.

"Stop that," she said, attempting a stern frown.

"We've got to give them a show. Sit down with me and we'll talk. You have no choice, since I ruined the chair."

She narrowed her eyes as he bounced some more. "I'll get seasick with all that jostling."

"You get seasick?"

"Of course not!"

"I didn't think so. So are you going to stand all night?"

He saw a trace of weariness before she hid it behind a grimace as she stared at the cot.

"Sam, those sheets are disgusting."

"I'm sitting on the cloak."

"I don't know—"

He caught her around the waist, and though he meant to pull her next to him, somehow she ended up in his lap. She cried out, and the wood gave a mighty squeak.

"Ah, that sounded just right," he said, trying to ignore the warmth and weight of her.

She folded her arms across her chest, sat stiffly for a moment, and then finally eased her back against him. He hated that she could probably feel the pounding of his heart.

"I'm not hurting you?" she asked. "I'm not the most delicate of women."

"You're not hurting me."

But he'd better start thinking of something else or she'd know just what she was sitting on. He gave a couple more bounces to satisfy the tavern customers, and she slapped his arm.

"I have several plans to prove your innocence," he said. "After we mislead our pursuit for a bit, we need to return to Misterton village and your family estate. Lewis went there immediately when you both returned from India. And your governess was murdered there as well."

"Murdered?" Her body stiffened, and she glanced over her shoulder at him with shock and horror.

"It was the perfect excuse to send you north, wasn't it? And a little too convenient that she happened to die just then."

She looked away from him, every line of her body mutinous. "She was very old and very frail."

"Then that made it even easier for the killer."

Her gaze snapped back to him. "I can't believe Lewis did this. But I'm letting you do as you wish to prove that it wasn't him. Maybe Edwin hired someone to kill his mother. You only have one witness's word that he looked surprised to hear that his mother was dead."

"Too hard to believe." Sam tried to imagine Edwin Hume as a criminal mastermind. All he could remember was the pathetic drunkard the man had become. But Julia wasn't ready to understand that yet. "I'm assuming Lewis did this for the money. Did he have much?"

"His government salary was enough for us to live on there, but more than once he complained to me about how expensive it was to keep up Hopewell Manor." There seemed to be a longing in Julia's voice when she mentioned her home, but it was quickly masked. "I rather got the impression that he was in debt. But many people are, without resorting to treason," she added severely.

"Of course."

"And— Never mind."

He frowned at the back of her head. "What are you thinking, Julia? Just say it."

With a sigh, she said, "I didn't have much of a dowry. But what I had, I discovered that Lewis had spent. But—"

"Yes, I know, that's not proof he's a traitor. Just the bullying, selfish ass I always knew he was." He lowered his voice, angry that he still had to resist the temptation to lean closer and smell her hair. "But you didn't need a dowry to attract a husband, Julia."

"Of course I did," she scoffed. "I knew early in life that my meager dowry could hardly overcome the deficiencies of my unusual looks and my less-than-impressive bloodlines."

"You didn't have a dowry when you attracted the Duke of Kelthorpe," he said.

"He didn't need one."

She sounded sad and confused, and he found himself bitterly wondering if she loved the duke. It seemed like every man had had a chance with her but himself.

"Somehow, he liked me for who I was, the experiences I'd had," she continued. "But that's over now, isn't it?"

"We're going to prove you innocent."

"Yes, we are, but that won't matter to the *ton*."

"Perhaps the duke won't care what they think?"

But she gave him a glance that said they both knew the truth. "Even if he doesn't, the rest of his family will. I'll never see him again."

"You don't know that." He should ask if she loved Kelthorpe; it was on the tip of his tongue, but he just couldn't say it, and certainly didn't want to hear the answer.

She remained silent.

Sam pulled her back more comfortably on his chest. "So if your brother received money from the Russians, he would need to hide it. He couldn't just deposit it in his bank accounts, for that would be too obvious. And since he went to Hopewell Manor first, the money might be there."

She suddenly yawned, then apologized for it. Her head finally rested back on his shoulder, and he could feel the silkiness of her hair against his cheek. The fresh smell wafted over him, and he thought of summer gardens, and Julia with roses in her hair. He painfully needed to adjust himself, or twist his hips away from her—something. How was he going to concentrate on his mission if he had to constantly control himself when he was around her?

She yawned again. "You won't find any record of money, but we'll look for it, see if he's paid off any debts."

"Good girl," he said.

"I'm not a girl, Sam. I'm an old spinster."

She was half asleep as she said it, and he couldn't help his faint smile.

"We're going to have to hide all the 'old spinster' that's so evident in you. How do you feel about disguises? They're my specialty."

But she didn't answer, just rubbed her cheek into his neck in her sleep. Tilting his head, he could see the slope of her nose, the curve of her brown eyelashes.

And suddenly he remembered a scene such as this in his childhood. Julia had only been six to

his twelve years, and she had begun to follow
him about, asking the names of the flowers in
the garden. He liked her directness even then,
and thought she was a fearless little girl. He
hadn't known that she was briefly escaping her
home and the indifferent way she was treated by
her family. Only months after they'd begun their
friendship, she'd come running to find him digging out a new flower bed in a remote corner of
the Hopewell gardens. She'd been trying to hide
from the wrath of her brother, and since Sam
knew all about Lewis's pettiness, he'd taken the
little girl under a trellis, where ivy grew in pro-
fusion to hide them. She'd sat in his lap and
shivered, and wouldn't tell him why, until finally she'd fallen asleep.

Just like this.

The urge to protect her had blossomed then,
and hadn't waned throughout the years of his
adulthood. She still needed him. He would
make everything up to her—his doubt in her
innocence and his gathering proof of her treason. She would know safety for the first time in
her life. And then when they were separated
again, as they had to be, maybe he'd find some
peace.

Julia stirred, then came abruptly awake. She
was confused for a moment, having felt so safe
and warm. The window showed the early light
before dawn, but there were no bars, only glass

with a crack running through it. And she felt safe and warm because—

Sam.

She glanced over her shoulder and he was watching her solemnly.

"Sorry to wake you," he said. "We have to leave."

His arms were about her, his chest had been her pillow, and his hard thighs supported her. She flushed and rose quickly to her feet, straightening the plain gown, trying to fix her wild hair.

"I think you said something about disguises," she said.

He stood up slowly, then lifted his arms over his head and stretched. She could see the buttons of his shirt pull as his chest expanded, and she felt a flush of awareness. She had slept in his arms, something she'd never done with a man before. It felt almost as intimate as—

She turned away, not wanting him to see her reddening face. She didn't want to be attracted to him now, not when he'd helped accuse her of treason. She needed her anger as a barrier between them.

"We'll definitely be hiding that hair of yours, but not today," he said. "Today we want to be seen."

She gaped at him. "But . . ."

"I have a plan."

An hour later, she stood at Sam's side, in line for tickets at the Leeds railway station. The building was barely larger than a wooden shack beside the train tracks, with several benches inside for waiting passengers. A railway employee sat behind a desk slowly counting money and handing over paper tickets.

Julia bit her lip and forced herself to keep her gaze on the people in front of her. She felt exposed, her hood swept back off her shoulders, her blond hair a blazing beacon of guilt. She fought the urge to look for the constables who must surely be searching for her now. Sam had insisted he'd tied the constables up tightly, that only this morning might the men be discovered and the alarm given.

But wasn't the train station one of the first places they'd look for her?

Then it was their turn before the railway employee's desk. She kept her hands folded to hide their trembling. When Sam began to speak she flinched, even though he was soft-spoken, subservient—with a hint of a lisp, she noticed with amazement.

"Please, sir, we need to purchase two tickets to Edinburgh, Scotland."

The man carefully sorted through piles of tickets, and she wanted to scream her impatience.

"Ye'd best hurry," the man finally said, his speech as slow as his movements. "This train is about to leave, and there won't be another till the mornin'." He slid two tickets toward them, then searched for change.

She gritted her teeth, trying to keep her composure. Sam had chosen their destination deliberately so they wouldn't have to wait long at the station.

"Any baggage?" the man asked.

Sam hunched his head between his shoulders. "We sent most of it on ahead, sir, with my wife's brother. Will that be all right?"

The man only shrugged.

Sam took Julia's arm, and she silently let him lead her out onto the railway platform. A large black engine sat on the tracks, metal gleaming, steam hissing as if with impatience.

Once again, she forced herself not to look behind her, even though the hairs on the back of her neck prickled with awareness. "Do you think they—"

"Shh."

He steered her into the first railway car with wooden benches. She was grateful he'd had enough money for a second-class carriage, rather than the open boxcars where they'd be exposed to wind and rain. He'd had to sell his horse. She had a feeling they would miss the animal soon enough.

The train finally got under way, and she breathed a sigh of relief. "We're safe," she whispered to Sam.

He gave a small shake of his head and spoke softly without looking at her. "Yes, the constables would have set upon us by now, but they're not all we have to worry about. The true traitor won't want you to escape and discover the truth."

She bit her lip, absurdly grateful that he hadn't said "your brother." Her stomach clenched all over again. "So do you think we're being followed?"

He only shrugged.

She turned and looked out the window, trying to focus only on the flat plain of southern Yorkshire, its fertility being harvested on every farm they passed. She had seldom traveled by train, and it was still rather stunning to see the countryside fly by so quickly. Her body was constantly jostled, and the rumbling of the wheels on the track seemed loud not only in her ears, but vibrating through her chest.

They reached the city of York in a little over an hour, and while the train stopped for passengers, they slipped off. Julia's hair was now completely covered within her hooded cloak. Sam bought new tickets returning south, and this time he was a bombastic Scotsman, his auburn hair a little wilder, his brogue as pronounced as any Highlander. She wanted to cringe as his conduct drew attention to them, but since he seemed like such an utterly different person, maybe that was the point. Who would think a wanted man would behave so flamboyantly?

They had to wait several hours at the York train station, which was a much larger stone building. She surreptitiously watched him as he charmed old ladies, chucked babies under the chin, and in general made himself a pleasant distraction. His ready smile was still so handsome that she felt like a young girl again, and remembered how painfully enamored of him she'd once been. She'd been so naïve about men.

He bought chicken pies from a vendor, and they stayed within the station, surrounded by passengers for protection. Once on the train, it was several more hours before they reached Rotherham, a town less than thirty miles from Hopewell Manor.

They purchased another horse, this one more worn with the years, but still capable of carrying two people. In the dirt alley outside the livery stables off High Street, Julia watched while Sam swung up into the saddle and reached down for her. She stared at his outstretched hand, her fists on her hips.

"You cannot be serious," she finally said.

"Why? We rode this way yesterday."

"And it was uncomfortable. I can't imagine riding thirty miles like that."

"So you'd rather walk?"

The livery worker was leaning in a doorway laughing at her predicament. She understood that their finances were limited, but she'd have taken a donkey over riding with Sam again.

But there would be no donkey. She roughly

took his hand and let him pull her up, holding her hood over her hair. Before she could squeeze herself into the saddle behind him, the horse tossed its head and gave a little sideways dance that made her clutch Sam's shoulders.

With an amused voice, he said, "Stop moving and he'll calm down."

Once more she was forced to plaster herself against Sam. As she struggled to make herself comfortable, her hand brushed his heavy coat pocket.

"What's in here?" she asked, giving a tug on his coat.

"A pistol. Someone's already tried to kill you once."

She closed her eyes and involuntarily her hand went to her throat. She remembered vividly being under arrest, held in Edwin Hume's house. A man had overcome her guards and dragged her away. She hadn't understood who was rescuing her, but when she found herself outdoors, she'd panicked and run.

And when he'd gotten her far enough away from the house, he'd grabbed her around the neck to strangle her. She was only still alive because Nick Wright had saved her life. The real traitor had obviously wanted her dead before any trial could happen.

How had she forgotten that it wasn't only the police force who wanted to capture her? She'd never had a mirror to see the bruises, but she'd felt them as she'd lain awake in jail, her throat aching.

As the sun was setting, they left Rotherham heading east into the darkness. Julia had traveled with armies, and knew the dangers that could await her in even England's peaceful countryside. Especially now when she had both sides of the law chasing her. As the last stone farmhouses faded away behind her, her anxiety rose so high that she hadn't even realized she clutched Sam's waist until he shifted forward away from her.

"You're holding on a bit tight, Julia," he said, glancing at her over his shoulder. "Afraid you're going to fall off?"

"As if you could even match me in horsemanship," she scoffed, loosening her grip.

He hesitated, still trying to study her face. She looked away.

"I'll keep you safe," he said in a low, intense voice.

Safe? She'd rarely felt that in her life. She shrugged with bravado, even as her throat tightened with suppressed tears. She didn't trust herself to speak.

When he finally turned forward again, she bowed her head and heaved a tired sigh.

A few miles later, twilight hovered over the land, and the trees began to thicken, hiding the square pastures scattered across the plain. Between each trunk darker shadows lay, and she felt like there were eyes in there, watching her. Sam straightened his coat until his pocket was tugged forward. She sat up straighter to see his hand resting on the hidden pistol. So he felt uneasy, too?

Suddenly there was the crack of a gunshot, and with a cry she flung her arms around him as the horse reared up, its neighing like a scream.

Chapter 5

Julia knew she wasn't hit by a bullet, but was Sam? He flung himself off the horse, pulling her with him, just as another shot went off. This time she could tell they were being attacked from the left side of the road. Sam pulled her toward the right, keeping the horse between them and their attackers. His pistol was in his hand, but she knew he wanted to see her behind cover before he worried about returning fire.

They heard running steps only a moment before the horse shifted sideways as someone used the far stirrup to vault over and knock Sam to the ground. Julia looked frantically for the weapon Sam had dropped, but she couldn't tell where the pistol had gone.

Someone caught her arm from behind, whirling her about to face him. It was a man all dressed in black, with something obscuring his face. She brought her foot up and kicked him hard between the legs. When he staggered back, clutching his injured anatomy, she looked at Sam, who was delivering a solid punch. She flung herself to her knees in the brush, continuing her search for the weapon.

"You bitch!"

She looked over her shoulder to see her assailant stumbling toward her. Her hands closed on a long, hard stick, and she swung it up. It caught him on the side of the head, knocking him to his knees.

Where was the pistol?

She saw Sam with his hands around his attacker's neck. The man fought furiously, pulling at Sam and kicking out with his feet. Sam's expression was almost impassive except for the wild light in his eyes. Then he heaved the man off the road, headfirst into the brush where he lay unmoving.

The other man was staggering to his feet. Sam pushed her aside and threw himself at the last assailant. The two men rolled over one another, and she followed them, holding her stick and looking for the best chance to strike. Then Sam ended up on top, straddling his opponent, with a rock in his upraised hand. The man kneed him in the back, sending Sam sprawling.

The assailant got to his feet and fled to the trees on the far side of the road. In the near-darkness, they couldn't see what he was doing. They ran across the road, then had to stumble back as a horse broke through the scattered bushes. It took off at a gallop back toward Rotherham, their last assailant riding low over its neck.

"Where's my damn pistol?" Sam shouted.

But before he could go search for it, they heard the frantic whinnying of a riderless horse just as it plummeted through the trees at them. She flung herself aside as Sam reached for the dangling reins and pulled the horse up short. The animal jerked angrily on the reins, then finally quieted.

"Are you all right, Julia?" he asked, breathing heavily, wiping sweat from his forehead.

She slowly got to her feet, feeling exhaustion surge through her now that the danger had passed. "Just bruised. I'll be fine." She put a hand on the horse's neck, trying to calm it. "I assume this is the other man's horse?"

"Evidently."

He looked down the road, but already their attacker was swallowed in darkness. Softly, Sam cursed. She couldn't see his expression well anymore, just the dark shadows beneath his eyes and the deadly line of his tightly pressed lips. There would be no full moon to guide them tonight—or to lead their attacker back.

"You handled yourself well," he said.

She searched his eyes skeptically, but he appeared sincere. "Thank you. Perhaps we'd better tie up the other man."

They walked side by side across the road, leading the horse. She watched as Sam knelt down beside the unconscious man. After a moment, Sam sat back on his heels.

"He's dead. He must have broken his neck when he fell."

She didn't even feel pity. "We'll have to bury him."

He nodded and rose to his feet.

"Those weren't constables," she said.

"No. The traitor finds your death even more desirable now. He'll know soon, if he doesn't already, that I'm the one who's protecting you."

"And he should be worried?" A poor joke on her part, but she had to do something to lift the terrible feeling of desperation.

But Sam only stared at the still body of their assailant. "He already is. And he'll soon know where we're going."

"He can't know for sure. We could be taking a circuitous route south."

He glanced at her. "We'll have to be very careful."

Their horse, though not well trained, had lazily remained nearby, munching grass. Now he lifted his head and whinnied at the other horse. In a moment, they were bumping noses down in the grass.

Julia was glad the body had seemed to fade into the dark shadows of approaching night. "Do you have a shovel somewhere in that pack?"

He shook his head. "We'll make a rock cairn just inside the woods, and I'll come back later to bury him."

"We can't look for rocks tonight."

"No. Let's cover him with branches for now, and we'll make camp just down the road."

The darkness was almost complete by the time they'd covered the body, and with only a quarter moon, they couldn't travel far. They walked down the road leading the horses, looking for a stream that might widen into a clearing. Eventually, they settled for a break in the trees, and what seemed like a faint path. She followed Sam in. Tall weeds brushed her skirts, and the horses nickered softly in distress.

She understood how they felt. It was ghostly walking through the dark, with only Sam's back to guide her.

Eventually the trees thinned out, and they heard the faintest sound of splashing water. She licked her dry lips with relief.

"Ah, my memory didn't betray me," he said with satisfaction.

"You've been here before?"

"I often took that road with my father when I was a lad. But it's been almost fifteen years. I guess the deer don't change their paths much."

While he saw to the horses, she carefully followed the sound of water in the darkness, tripping once in a hollow, then another time over a fallen tree limb. Finally, when the water had grown louder, she knelt down and crawled forward until the uneven ground fell away. Her hands splashed into a stream up to her wrists. With relief, she cupped water and drank deeply.

"I wouldn't have let you remain parched with thirst," Sam said. "I have wine and cider."

"You should have told me! I had already convinced myself I could survive the night without anything."

His muffled "hmph" spoke volumes. He must be offended by her implication that he was unprepared. She had to remember, he was a man who'd done more with his life than simply be a gardener.

A few minutes later, she heard the sound of a match striking, then saw the faint light of a single candle. She wouldn't give him the satisfaction of admitting how impressed she was by his preparedness. Instead, she reached down for the branches she'd stumbled over earlier. Soon they had a small fire going just a few feet from the stream.

She sat on a blanket, her cloak protecting her

back, while the front of the garment was parted to let in the warmth of the fire. She sighed with satisfaction and closed her eyes.

When she felt his presence beside her, she looked in his direction, only to see him opening several wrapped packages.

She rolled her eyes. "Oh, all right, I will graciously admit that you're well prepared."

"Graciously?"

She ignored his dry tone. "So what do we have?"

Soon she was munching on chicken, bread, and cheese, washing everything down with cider.

Sam watched her the whole time, but while she pretended not to notice, she felt his eyes upon her in the strangest, unsettling way.

"You did well today," he finally said.

"For a girl?" she countered.

"For an untrained woman. You didn't lose your head. They could have killed us both, if you hadn't disabled the one."

"But I didn't kill him," she said grimly.

"Do you wish you would have?" he asked.

She heard his astonishment. She'd never had to kill anyone, but she certainly had no qualms about it if it would save her life. "I wanted to do my part."

When her stomach was pleasantly full, she threw another log on the fire, then set about braiding her hair into a long plait suitable for sleeping. Sam watched her in a way that reminded her of how she used to watch *him*. But she'd been a girl then, and surely her glances were innocent. She didn't know what he was thinking when he looked at her.

Did he think her a woman duped by her brother? Too stupid to believe the truth he was convinced he knew? But how could it have been her brother who'd tried to have her killed?

As if he could read her mind, he suddenly said, "Tell me about your life with Lewis for the last ten years."

Julia sighed. "We could talk all night."

"I'm not going anywhere." He leaned closer. "I need to know everything you can remember that might help me."

She stared into his eyes, golden brown with sincerity, and tried to read the truth there. Fourteen years ago, she hadn't cared how old he was, or that her parents would object. She had thought she'd seen emotions in his eyes that might mirror her own tender feelings for him. But then he'd left to join the army so suddenly, and she'd been alone.

She was still alone—she had to remember that.

Sam watched Julia's face as she talked about her awkward relationship with her brother. As if she didn't want him to read her emotions, she often looked down into her lap, where she picked at a stray thread in the plain gown. Much as she tried to insist that her freedom mattered more than her brother's indifference, he heard a wealth of pain in her voice, especially when she grudgingly reminded him that Sam himself had never answered her letters.

How could he tell her that he had ached for her friendship when he was so alone in a foreign country? She couldn't understand what it was like to know that he had no chance for anything with her beyond a stilted acquaintance. So he had protected himself by distancing her, perhaps preferring not to realize that he might have hurt her. She'd been only fourteen when he left—he'd thought she would soon be anticipating a future marriage like every other young girl, preparing her trousseau, polishing her dancing skills. He couldn't have known that her parents would soon die, leaving her even more alone.

But he still had every letter she'd ever sent him, even though he had never replied.

He had so many questions, ones he knew she wouldn't answer. Why had she no fear for her own safety, no care for her own reputation? Had her family's indifference scarred her so badly? If that was true, he shouldn't be so angry with her—but then, she should have been intelligent enough not to cross certain societal boundaries. Instead she'd flung herself over them.

The only new information she provided about her brother was that he requested his transfer away from Afghanistan. If Sam could eventually procure Lewis's military records, he'd learn the details.

He sighed. "Let's forget about this for tonight. We're both tired and cold and we need to sleep."

"I'm not cold," she said stiffly, stubbornly, even as she clutched her cloak tight.

He threw the last few logs on the fire. "Well, I'm cold. Lie down and I'll lie behind you."

"You will not touch me."

"You slept in my lap last night and didn't have many qualms about it. Tonight you're returning the favor by keeping me warm."

Sam let Julia fume in silence while he went to get the other blanket. He'd prefer her to be angry with him than worried about who might be following them. He didn't think their attacker would return without first reporting to Lewis. So they were safe. For now.

He stood above Julia, who sat wearing a mutinous expression. He pulled her blanket out as wide as it would go, nearly toppling her. But she held her ground and glared at him. She had no one else to focus her anger on right now, so he accepted it without comment. But he wasn't going to freeze. He lay down behind her on his side, curling his body around her hips and thighs where she sat. He felt all of her stiffened pride.

"You know," he said casually, "if you lie down, you'll have both me and my blanket to keep you warm."

She remained silent for a long time, until there was a distant rustle somewhere in the undergrowth. She pulled her cloak even tighter like a fortress wall, then reclined to her side regally, leaving an inch between them. He spread the blanket over them, then slung an arm over her waist, unable to suppress a shiver. He tucked his knees behind hers and pressed his chest to her slim back.

With a sigh, she finally relaxed. "Since you're so sensitive to the cold," she said over her shoulder, "however did you manage traveling with an army? My tent always had a canvas wall thrown up around it, because God forbid a soldier should see me in the evening. But at least it kept out most of the drafts."

"You'd be surprised how warm a horse is."

She gave a little shudder, and he realized it wasn't from the cold, but from trying to hold back laughter.

"At least we're dry," he said.

"God, yes. I was constantly damp on so many journeys. I couldn't decide if that was worse than traveling in the heat."

"I preferred the damp. Must be my English roots. Go to sleep, Julia," he added mildly. "Tomorrow will be a busy day."

He thought she might ask for specifics, but she only sighed and squirmed a bit as if trying to get comfortable. He bore this stoically as he lay with his head on his arm. She finally settled into the same position, leaving her arm along the length of his, almost touching. Her backside curved into his hips, and he tried to think of tomorrow's journey, rather than show her once again just how uncontrollable that part of his anatomy was.

She fell asleep before he did, and as drowsiness stole over him, he memorized the feel of her long body, the softness of her skin, the weight of her backside nestling into him. His arm lay across her, his hand touching hard earth. Gingerly, he pressed his palm into her stomach, his thumb and forefinger just touching her ribs. Several inches either way and he'd be in paradise.

Chapter 6

❧

In the morning, Julia awoke first and found herself on her back, stiff from lying on the ground—but not cold. She tried to tell herself it was due to the cloak wrapped around her and the blanket on top, not to the tall man stretched out beside her. She felt the weight of his bent arm across her stomach and chest. As she took a deep breath, she realized exactly where his hand rested, and she froze so as not to awaken him.

She gave a silent groan and tried not to feel his hand on top of her breast. He wasn't cupping her—there wasn't enough of her to cup, especially when she lay on her back. A cloak and a dress and chemise still separated them. Even if he was awake, he might not realize where his hand lay, she thought with grim amusement.

Then the humor of the situation vanished in a flood of memories of the last few weeks, of her arrest and imprisonment. Someone wanted her dead and buried, and the truth along with her. Sam was giving her this last chance at freedom, she thought, willing away tears. If she couldn't prove her innocence, she would have to flee the country—or die.

One step at a time. Today they would reach Hopewell Manor. The sky above was gray, but did not seem to threaten rain. Perfect traveling weather.

Holding her breath, she gently pushed his hand down to her stomach.

"Good morning," his voice rumbled in her ear.

She wondered if he realized where his hand had been, but all he did was reach up and lazily scratch his bristled chin. His eyes were too close—everything was too close. She quickly sat up, giving a shiver at the loss of his warmth.

"I thought military men awoke at dawn," she said.

"Only when our horses wake us up."

She arched a brow at him as he rolled onto his back with a groan.

"Too long in one position," he said.

"What's for breakfast?"

"A woman after my own heart."

Instinctively she smiled at him. "Remember

when we used to—" But she faltered abruptly as nearer memories rushed back.

He lay still, looking up at her. "You sometimes used to meet me in the garden, carrying your breakfast in a little handkerchief."

"And I always had something extra for you." She turned away, embarrassed. "I must have been such an annoying child."

"No," he said quietly.

"But you were working."

"I enjoyed answering your questions. You were a bright light of inquisitiveness on cold mornings like this."

"The garden seemed so much more interesting than my governess's lessons."

And then she remembered that her governess was dead, maybe murdered. There was an awkward silence as Sam slowly stood up. He reached down for her, and she allowed him to help her to her feet.

"If you'll excuse me for a moment," he said, and disappeared into the woods.

Men had matters of the body so much easier than women. She stomped into the woods opposite the way he had gone. When she emerged a few minutes later, he was frowning at her.

He put his fists on his hips. "When you weren't here when I returned, I thought—"

"That ladies don't need privacy in the morning?" she interrupted. "Do I need your permission for that as well?"

"Of course not. But next time, at least tell me which way you're going."

She hadn't thought of that. "Very well," she said, trying for contriteness.

He shook his head, then glanced at the horses, who grazed side by side in the grass. "Now let's examine our new acquisition."

"Before we eat?"

"There might be even better things than the cold meat and cheese I'm carrying."

Though the horse ended up having nothing but a decent saddle, the animal was a welcome gift all by itself. She would control her own mount—if nothing else in her life.

She sat down by the ashes of the fire to munch her cheese, only to see Sam staring at her strangely. Before she could question him, he dropped to his knees at her side and spread wide her skirts on the ground.

Indignantly, she began, "I don't see what—"

And then he put his fingers through a bullet hole, which had blackened a small ring of fabric near the hem.

She gaped at it. "It appears my luck isn't all bad."

He gave a low whistle. "And here I thought you wouldn't be a good luck charm."

Julia shoved another piece of cheese into her mouth before she could respond to that. Was he actually being nice to her this morning? Or was it some kind of truce?

He rose to his feet and looked back down the path. "Would you rather wait here while I see to the body?"

She wiped the cheese crumbs from her hands. "No. I can help. And besides, you aren't going to bury him next to the road, are you?"

"I was going to pull him into the woods."

"But you need rocks, which are here at the stream. Let's bring him here."

Between the two of them, they dragged the dead man to their camp. The streambed and banks yielded enough rocks, and once the assailant's face was covered, she had an easier time finishing the work.

"Was there anything in his pockets to identify him?" she asked, settling the last rock in place.

"Nothing." Sam straightened and wiped his arm across his forehead.

"Then are you finally going to show me what's in that other saddlebag?"

He glanced at her. "Disguises."

Sam watched Julia's expressive face, which was full of wariness and the interest she couldn't hide.

She sighed. "From our time at the tavern, I already know how good you'll be at this."

Eventually he would tell her about the five years he'd spent disguising himself every day. But he still felt the ungentlemanly need to tease her. "I could tell from the tavern that you'd be good."

She drew her breath in quickly and glared at him.

He knew damn well what she was thinking, but all he did was cock an eyebrow and say, "You understand how to adopt a role."

"Oh," she said, her face flushed. "I rather had to, didn't I?"

He shrugged.

"So what will I do that will so completely disguise me from servants I've known my whole life?"

"You mean the servants you haven't seen in ten years?"

"I saw them for a week last year. But you understand my meaning."

"We're going to change your hair," he said with satisfaction.

"The color will still—"

"That's one of the things we'll change."

After only a brief hesitation, she met his gaze levelly. "What do you have planned?"

Reluctantly, he admired her poise. "You'll be a brunette. I bought a chicory paste back in Leeds. We'll let it sit in your hair a few hours, and then you won't even look the same."

She wet her lips and straightened her shoulders. "A paste? Will it be difficult to work into my hair?"

"Probably. But we have no choice."

"I have an idea that will make it easier. Do you have a knife?"

He studied her for a moment, then reached down for the knife in his boot.

She gave a brief smile. "Why didn't you use that against our attackers?"

"It was in my saddlebag then. I thought the pistol would do well enough. So what are you going to do with it?" he asked as he handed it over.

Before he could even move, she pulled the plait of braided hair over her shoulder and sliced it off below her ear.

Sam's mouth dropped open, but he couldn't help himself. A woman's hair was often her pride, and he hadn't imagined she would do something that drastic.

Yet he noticed that after she dropped the braid into the bushes, she tried to clasp her hands together to hide their trembling.

"How are we going to excuse your hairstyle?" he asked, watching as she spread her fingers through her uneven hair. "All women wear their hair long."

"It needs to be shorter so I can pass as a man."

Inside him a stillness blossomed, as he remembered the first time he'd seen her all grown up, in a Kabul bazaar. At first, he'd only noticed her as a tall, thin boy, dressed in trousers with a patched frock coat over a shirt. She'd roamed between the stalls, gaping at the Russian slaves for sale beside the melons and iron hinges.

In a low voice, Sam said, "Do you remember

when I thought you a soldier's son escaped for a day of adventure?"

She lifted her chin. "I would have succeeded in my ruse but for that monkey trying to pull off my cap."

"A strand of your hair fell almost to your waist. You're lucky all the men were too distracted by the screeching monkey." He smiled. "I noticed your eyes next, as richly blue as a gem in the queen's crown. I thought the shock of recognition would kill me."

"Is that a compliment?"

"Just a fact. And then my shock gave way to fear."

"A big man like you, afraid?" She was laughing at him.

"They would have stoned you if they'd discovered you were a woman."

Her smile faded, leaving only a trace of defiance. "Then you followed me, scaring me even worse. That was cruel of you."

"You would have run if I'd confronted you in the bazaar. I hadn't meant to frighten you."

"So instead you grabbed me in an alley." She pointed at him accusingly.

"But I saw you safely back to the encampment that day—not that you paid attention to my warnings."

After all these years, he could still see the myriad of expressions that had crossed her face when she'd recognized him, from wistfulness to sadness to regret. And then the unkindest one of all—polite disinterest.

He knew she'd been angry that he'd left Hopewell Manor so abruptly, and angry that he hadn't wanted to continue their friendship while in India. And when he'd caught her dressed as a boy again, things had gotten even worse.

"Julia, you passed as a boy once or twice for an afternoon. This will be days, maybe weeks, around people who know you."

"And they won't expect me to be a man, now, will they?" She held out the knife. "Finish what I've started. Make me look presentable."

He would have argued further, if only it didn't make such perfect sense. And she would blend in so well with his disguise.

But could she carry it off?

He took the knife from her, feeling her smooth, cool hands, which looked decidedly unmasculine. Stepping nearer, he tilted her face up so he could study the way her thick hair fell. Luckily he'd had the experience of cutting his own hair a time or two. He cut to a length just beneath her chin, a rather longish look for a man, but one that might grow out easier for a woman. Her hair hung straight, but he suspected, once washed, its gentle curls would surface.

She tentatively ran her hand through it. "Do I look like a man?"

He gazed down her body, from the small swell

of her breasts, to her full hips which held out her skirt. He cleared his throat. "No."

"Not in these clothes, of course," she said, rolling her eyes.

"And not with that hair color. I'll get the chicory paste."

They knelt by the bank of the stream, and he worked the thick, oily paste into her hair while wearing leather gloves to protect his own skin. He was careful not to get much of the dye on her scalp. When he was done, he rinsed the paste off the gloves, laid them out to dry, and then sat back on his heels.

He stared at the oily brown mass that was her hair. "Now we wait two hours for the dye to work."

With a sigh, she leaned back on her hands.

He watched her contemplatively for a moment, wanting to ask how she had met the Duke of Kelthorpe, the man she'd almost married, but he couldn't think of a way to make it relevant to Lewis's guilt. Yet it was important in her journey north last month, so he approached it that way.

"On your way to deliver your governess's personal effects, you went to Kelthorpe's weekend house party first."

"The duke was counting on me," she said.

Sam noticed that she was no longer meeting his gaze. "You were betrothed to him?"

"Not quite. Why must we discuss this?" she

asked coldly. "Isn't it enough that he'll never see me again?"

This morbid, jealous curiosity of his was getting him nowhere. "I just need to put motives with actions for what you were doing last month. You must understand that to us you looked guilty of treason. A man named Campbell was going to bribe us not to expose you as a traitor."

She jumped to her feet. "I've never heard of this man!"

"He's already dead. But there were other men who seemed to be acting on your orders, trying to kill Nick, Will, and me. Do you remember Jane Whittington from Kelthorpe's house party?"

"She was engaged to William Chadwick, one of your *friends*."

She stressed the word with a distaste that was almost amusing.

"They're married now, but they were almost killed after meeting you. We had you watched the whole time you were at Kelthorpe's, and during the hunt, you disappeared for several hours. Campbell was on the grounds at that time, so we assumed you'd met with him and given the order to have Will killed."

She paced, her movements stiff. "I had to meet a messenger from my brother." And then her eyes went wide as she realized what that could mean. "It had to be a coincidence. Lewis was warning me in a letter to behave, that Kelthorpe was our best hope."

"You mean his best hope to get rid of you," Sam said, getting to his feet. "Why didn't the messenger just come to the house to speak with you?"

"I don't know!" She whirled toward him, her face as white as the rag they'd tied beneath the dripping dye. "But you're deliberately making this seem sinister."

"It *is* sinister; our lives were in jeopardy. Jane almost didn't survive a poisoning attempt."

"It wasn't me!" she sobbed.

He grasped her upper arms. "I know that! I believe you."

For several minutes she struggled to recover her composure, but he didn't move away. She wiped tears from her eyes and swayed. Somehow she ended up leaning against him, and it seemed so natural to put his arms around her.

He found himself wiping a tear from her cheek. "I don't do this to hurt you, Julia, but to save you."

"I know."

She gave a final sniff and stepped away from him. The day seemed to grow chillier without her.

Sitting down facing each other again seemed too intimate, so Sam casually walked to the stream and drank water from his cupped hands. Julia leaned back against a fallen tree, half sitting, bracing her hands behind her. This pose made looking at her breasts far too easy.

He picked up a pebble and flung it into the water. As he moved farther upstream, he caught a glimpse of something shiny in the weeds, and realized it was Julia's braided length of blond hair. It lay forgotten, like her femininity would soon be.

He pretended to reach for another rock, and this time fisted his hand about her hair. He turned his back and slid it into the breast pocket of his coat. He was a fool.

Chapter 7

Julia struggled against a feeling of over-whelming sadness and defeat. Her backside was numb from the rough tree bark and her scalp itched unmercifully. "What will we do if we can't find the traitor?" she finally whispered.

Sam stopped his pacing and looked at her. She tried to read his face, but his expression was one of resolve and self-confidence. And for a brief moment she could have kissed him for it.

"We'll find him," he said firmly. "And if not, we'll leave England."

She glanced at him speculatively. "We?"

"I'm wanted by the law just as you are."

"All because of me," she whispered.

"Then it makes us even, because you're partly here because of me."

"But mostly because of a traitor."

He nodded his agreement. They spent the rest of the two hours in uneasy silence, while she considered the enormity of the challenge ahead of them.

As he rummaged through his saddlebags, he said, "I found the soap to wash out your hair, but I seem to have forgotten towels."

"Heavens, you're not completely prepared?"

He rolled his eyes good-naturedly. "Do you mind if I use your petticoats, since you won't need them?"

She turned her back and reached beneath her skirts to untie the laces at her waist. Two petticoats fell to the ground, and she felt cooler—and much more naked—without them. Somehow her drawers didn't seem like enough protection—from what, she didn't know.

"Do you have clothes in there for me?" she asked as she set the petticoats beside the stream.

He donned his gloves again. "No, since I didn't anticipate you changing genders. When we reach Hopewell Manor tonight, we'll go see my sister Frances. She'll be able to find appropriate clothing for you."

He spread a blanket on a small rise beside the stream. "Lie down here, with your head leaning over the embankment. As I rinse your hair, the water should drain back into the stream and not on you."

Feeling self-conscious, she sat down beside him and lay back, her head dangling awkwardly until he cupped it with his big hand. She felt strangely vulnerable, yet safe at the same time, because he was Sam. He used an empty cider bottle full of water, refilling over and over to rinse through the thick paste that coated her hair. He was so close above her, intent on his work, eyes narrowed with concentration. It felt strangely . . . arousing to be lying beside him as he bent over her. He immersed his hands in the soap, then began to lather it into her hair, and with relief she closed her eyes.

His fingers on her scalp moved in slow circles, cleaning, soothing. It had been so long since anyone had touched her hair, held her in such a gentle manner. He rinsed, then added soap again, all the while cradling her head with a tenderness that made her feel safe, and more relaxed than she'd felt in weeks. When his fingers stilled, she opened her eyes.

He was looking down at her wearing an expression she couldn't decipher, while his hands cupped her head. They stared at each other, caught in a moment that seemed almost familiar, yet completely new.

He cleared his throat. "I think we're done."

She was almost disappointed. He helped her

sit up, then wrapped her head in petticoats. The first one was stained brown when she removed it, but the second petticoat she applied was mostly wet.

"How do I look?" she asked, fingering through her hair and pushing it back from her face.

"Macassar oil will help hold your hair back. I'm sure my sister can procure us some. You definitely look different," he added.

She spent the rest of the morning cutting and scuffing her nails, then learning how to walk like a man. Sam explained that she couldn't just count on the clothes to disguise her, since they'd be with people who knew her. He reminded her to take long strides, and to stop wiggling her hips. He insisted she even needed to have her chest bound, as if there were much to hide. He taught her how to bring a gruffness to her naturally deep voice, and reminded her to mimic the servants' manner of speech.

"The secret is to think like a man at all times," he said. "Think about your profession and the reason we're there."

"Those are two different things, aren't they?"

"No. Didn't I tell you how we're going to disguise ourselves?"

She shook her head.

"Sorry. We're going to masquerade as the police."

"The police!" Julia repeated, feeling anxiety tighten her throat.

"Perfect, isn't it?" Sam said eagerly. "We'll be investigating the case against the notorious traitor and escapee Julia Reed."

"But—but the police will surely have already interviewed the household in the two weeks since I was arrested."

"Yes, but now that you've escaped, the Leeds police force has sent detectives—us—to investigate further, and to be prepared should you show up at the estate. And while we're on official business, we can also be looking for the true traitor."

It was a rather brilliant idea. It allowed them to ask a lot of questions without anyone being suspicious.

"But what if the real police decide to investigate?" she asked.

He frowned. "I'm hoping they believe they already have enough information. They might very well drop in to see if you've returned home, so we'll have to trust my sister to deal with them."

"I wish we didn't have to involve Frances in this."

"There's no help for it."

"Could it be dangerous for her, or others in your family?"

She could tell by his expression that he'd been worrying about the same thing.

"I hope I can protect them. I think we'll try to keep your identity a secret from everyone but my sister. And you know the traitor won't give up. He'll be sending more men against us. I can only hope he's so worried about his reputation that he won't risk attacking us directly in a public place." He scrutinized her appearance. "Besides, we'll have the protection of the apprentice officer Julian."

"Who?"

His smile was faint. "You don't remember when I used to call you that?"

Tentatively, she shook her head.

"I used it the first time I came upon you dressed as a boy."

"Of course! I was never so frightened in my life when a man seemed to be calling my name in the middle of the bazaar." She still remembered the shot of terror, the feeling of being surrounded by men—then the thrill of a challenge. The "thrill" part was always what got her into trouble.

"I didn't call your exact name. And you *should* have been frightened."

"If it makes you happy, I'm *still* frightened. I want to be able to protect myself, and not be such a burden on you. Do you have another pistol in that bottomless saddlebag?"

"Maybe. Can you still load and shoot it?" His face clouded. "But of course you can. We found one strapped to your thigh when you were arrested. Another bit of evidence that didn't look good for you."

"So I'm not supposed to protect myself when traveling alone?"

Sam put his hands on his hips and studied her. "Did Lewis teach you to shoot?"

"No. My father did."

"The proper Mr. Reed?" he said, eyes widening. "I never would have thought it."

"Just before my parents died, when Lewis was talking about leaving, my father decided I might need my own protection. I put my skills to good use in India, where I used to hunt jackal."

He gave her a smile and a shake of his head, then reached into his saddlebag and took out a bundle wrapped in an old rag. Within was a pistol, which he handed to her. "There's powder and shot in the pouch. Load it while I get changed. I'll inspect you later."

His words sent a shiver through her, the same shiver she'd had while sleeping curled against him. But she only nodded and seated herself on her blanket, watching surreptitiously as he pulled out a carefully rolled bundle of clothing.

"Where did you get the uniform?" she asked.

"One of the constables at the Leeds jail was about my size. He was kind enough to loan it to me."

"You mean unconscious enough."

He grinned.

His smile could still make her blush, as if she were a shy fourteen-year-old again. But they were rare smiles now, given by a man who'd seen too much of the world. What had he been doing in Afghanistan? Why had he not worn a uniform whenever she saw him there?

He disappeared into the trees, and when he reappeared, she had a momentary fright, as if a stranger had discovered their little camp.

For he didn't even *walk* like the Sam she'd begun to know again. He had a very slight limp, so faint that it seemed he was recovering from an old wound. He wore a navy blue frock coat, with pewter buttons down the front, and tails that hung almost to his knees. His shirt and trousers were white, as were his gloves, and he wore a leather stock tied around his neck so high that it brushed his chin. A black top hat completed the ensemble. He'd combed his hair forward, until strands hung haphazardly down his forehead. Four days' growth of a beard helped hide him. She'd never kissed a man with a beard before.

Inwardly, she groaned at her own thoughts.

"So what do ye think?" His voice had a touch of a lower class accent that made him sound like a man who'd overcome a poor background.

"You look . . . professional."

He walked toward her with that strange gait, his shoulders rounded, his face fixed in a rather dazed smile.

"So what kind of a police officer are you?" she asked.

"A small-town constable who's intelligent, but

has learned to hide it well." He looked down at the pistol in her hands. "May I?"

She held it out, and their skin brushed as he took it from her. She wanted to rub her hands together as if she could erase the strange feeling. He checked the priming pan and the flint, then pronounced himself satisfied.

There were roads to Misterton that were infrequently traveled—deer or sheep paths, really—and Sam was amazed that they hadn't changed in so many years. Julia rode astride her horse wearing his old coat, shirt, and trousers, rolled up for length. She looked like a little boy dressing in his father's clothing. Until they could procure more suitable garments at Hopewell Manor, it would have to do. He found himself glancing over often, hoping to catch a glimpse of her ankles.

After they'd spent several hours riding in silence, she cleared her throat. "Sam, when I was at Hopewell Manor last year, I was told that your father had died. It must have been difficult being away at such a time."

"It was. I had almost decided to resign my commission and return home, but his death made things difficult for my family financially."

"But your brothers—"

"I brought in more income than any of them. So I stayed in the army."

She looked as if she suspected there was more to the story, but he ignored her unspoken questions.

"Is your mother well?" she asked. When he nodded, she continued, "It seems a shame not to tell her you're home. She must miss you terribly."

"It won't be for long. Did you see my brother Henry? He's now the head gardener."

"I know. He was with you often when I was young."

"Yes, but he was too shy to talk to you, the master's daughter."

"He always had something else to do when I came by," she said, smiling. "I used to think he hated me."

"He just didn't know what to say."

"I once tried to corner him to demand the truth. He blushed and stammered so much, I knew he couldn't possibly hate me."

"Of course not." He pushed a low branch out of the way. "You must have spoken to Frances last year."

"She makes a very capable housekeeper."

He smiled, caught up in fonder times. "I always thought she was planning her married life from the time she was ten."

"I understand her husband died."

He sighed. "Only a few years after they married, and they had no children." He still had the letter she'd sent him, smudged with her tears.

"But she's young," Julia said reassuringly. "Surely she'll find another husband."

"She said she's in love with a memory now, and no other man will do. She immersed herself in the estate, and became housekeeper a couple years ago. She loves the freedom she has to run the place, since Lewis is so seldom there."

They both stayed silent as a shepherd crossed their path, herding ten sheep. The boy doffed his cap to Sam's uniform with respect and curiosity, but Sam only gave him a brisk nod and motioned him to keep going.

When the horses were trotting again, Julia said, "I remember your twin sisters well, because they were my age. How are they?"

"Alice and Abigail are both married to tenant farmers on the estate. Numerous children, though I've lost track."

"You're not very good at the nieces and nephews."

"I've never met any of them," he said gruffly. He heard the emotion in his voice and knew she must have, too.

She glanced at him sympathetically. "This will be a difficult homecoming for you. You won't be able to tell any of them who you are. Which of your many siblings have we forgotten to discuss?"

"The youngest, George and Lucy. And I don't

have any idea what they're doing. We'll have to ask Frances."

There was an ache in his chest that wouldn't go away when he thought about his youngest siblings. Would they even remember him? Lucy was only six and George eight when he left home.

When they were having a luncheon of bread and cheese beneath an oak tree, he asked, "What do you want your name to be?"

Her face sparkled in the dappled shade of the tree, and he wanted to stare at her.

"What would you name me?" She frowned and chewed her stale bread slowly.

"How about Walter? A solid, normal name. Walter . . . Fitzjames."

"Constable Fitzjames," she said, nodding. "What kind of man should I be?"

"My new recruit, looking to me for every bit of my knowledge."

"And won't that make you feel wonderful," she said dryly.

Sam forced himself to look innocent. "I will be the senior officer here, not quite the chief constable, but close enough. You don't make a move without me, do you understand?"

"Yes, Constable," she said, sighing loudly. "What about your name?"

"Joseph Seabrook. It's a name I haven't used in a long time."

She scrutinized him suspiciously. "What do you mean by that?"

He considered lying to her, but what was the point? She could hardly be in any more danger knowing the truth about him.

"I had plenty of different names the last five years," he said. "Nick, Will, and I were agents for the Political Department of the East India Company army."

"You mean . . . spies?" Her eyes went wide, and she didn't bother to hide her shock. "So that's why I never saw you in a uniform."

"I followed you several times in Kabul disguised as an Afghani to keep an eye on you."

"How—how dangerous for you!" Her cheese lay uneaten in her lap as she stared at him. "But what did you do? Where did you go?"

"I can't talk much about it, but I traveled extensively through India, Afghanistan, and Turkistan." He looked up at the sun, already beginning its downward curve. "I can answer your questions at another time. We're going to reach the estate after dark as it is. I'd rather be settled in a hiding place until we can awaken Frances."

Julia tried not to stare at Sam like he was a stranger. It had always been difficult for her to picture gentle, considerate Sam as a soldier, but now to imagine him impersonating other people, perhaps living another life for weeks or months at a time—well, she was just stunned. She really didn't know anything about him anymore.

Except how excited and nervous he made her

feel whenever he was too close. And he was often too close, helping her saddle her horse, or taking the remains of their luncheon out of her hands to put away in the saddlebags. He was taller than she was, broader, every way a man. She watched him mount his horse and set off, and everything inside her fluttered.

Her feelings for him were a weakness she couldn't afford. She knew the secrets of what went on between men and women. In Afghanistan she'd become a different person, wild, desperate, doing things she knew were dangerous. But after every daring adventure, morning would always come, leaving her hollow, depressed.

If her brother had found out—or anyone else—her reputation would have been ruined. But a reputation hadn't seemed to matter when she would never be able to marry. Lewis would not have given his approval if she'd found a husband in a lower social class, and men of her own class were looking for a dowry more than a flesh-and-blood woman.

And now Sam was back in her life. Unlike with other men, she wanted the comfort of his embrace, and something more, the tenderness that only he had ever made her feel.

But he still treated her like a wayward little girl who got in his way, and whose problems he would have to reluctantly fix. And she didn't know how to make things different between them—or if he would want something more.

Chapter 8

Every bone and muscle in Sam's body ached, a feeling he was long used to. His backside was damp, though he hoped the blanket kept the dirt away from his white trousers. What a ridiculous color for a uniform. He and Julia were crouched behind the ornamental shrubbery that decorated either side of the gate at the main entrance to Hopewell Manor. It had to be well after midnight, but he couldn't read his pocket watch in the darkness.

Julia sat beside him and dozed, her arm pressed to his, giving a soft snore once or twice. She hadn't been a burden so far, much as he'd been worried about such a thing. The bravery he'd seen in her as a little girl had only blossomed.

But now would come the true test. Could she pass as a man in front of a whole household?

But she was a woman—how could anyone not see that? He himself could think of little else but her soft curves and the kissable shape of her mouth.

When he'd judged it late enough, he shook her gently to awaken her. Her head, which had been bobbing forward, now fell against his shoulder. He couldn't see her face, but he felt the warmth of her breath.

She murmured, "Is it time, Sam?"

He resisted the urge to run his fingers across her cheek, to feel the fullness of her lower lip. "It's time. We'll have to scale the wall first."

She sat up and moved away from him. "I know the perfect spot."

"You do?"

"One of the servants' children showed me, and how to scale it. I think it was your sister Abigail. Follow me."

He put his hand out to see where she was going, and ended up with his palm flat against her backside.

"Sorry," he murmured.

She didn't say anything, just wiggled out from behind the shrubbery. They followed the wall until they reached an old beech tree towering skyward. He watched in surprise as Julia, just a vague outline of shadows, nimbly climbed from branch to branch, until she was sitting on top of the wall. He joined her, then took her hands and lowered her over the side. He jumped down beside her and they both remained still, listening. He clasped her hand and she returned a warm squeeze.

They followed the long brick wall to the servants' wing, where the window trim became less decorative. She showed no hesitation at all as they walked past one dark room after another, until she reached a set of double-wide windows. They hunched down.

She let go of his hand and leaned nearer to him to whisper, "This is it. Her private sitting room is next door."

"I'll go in first. Will you be all right out here until I call you in?"

She gave a quiet laugh. "I just spent ten days in jail, Sam. The outdoors is feeling pretty wonderful about now."

Very gently, he threw a scattering of pebbles against the window, sounding like hard raindrops. When nothing happened after several minutes, he tried again.

Suddenly the window opened wide, and moonlight glimmered on the barrel of a pistol.

Sam pushed Julia flat against the wall. "Frances!" he whispered loudly. What if it wasn't her?

They heard a gasp, then a woman leaned her

hands on the window frame and stuck her head out. "Samuel? Is that you?"

He slowly stood up, both hands raised, and turned to face her. "It's me."

She gave a strangled cry, reached out to enfold him in a hug, and pulled him half over the windowsill.

But he didn't mind. She was warm and solid, and still smelled like baking bread—like home.

"Oh, Sam," she whispered as she pressed a kiss to his cheek.

"Hello, Frances. Can I come in now?"

"Oh, oh yes, please!"

She backed away from the window, and as he climbed in, a candle flared to life beside her bed. He quickly closed the curtains, but left the window open so Julia could listen.

Frances was still tall and thin, and it made him sad to see that life had etched lines in her face. But her hair was still that reddish blond that he used to tell her looked like washed-out blood. It tumbled down around her shoulders, and she clutched a shabby dressing gown at her waist.

She stared at him, smiling, and he grinned back.

With his chin he pointed to the dressing table, where the pistol now lay. "Worried about intruders out here, are you?"

"More than one man has tried to enter my bedroom window," she teased. Then she murmured his name again in wonder and flung herself into his arms.

Sam hadn't realized he would feel so moved to be home again, to be hugging one of his sisters. Memories crowded in on him, of simple family dinners, stories as they gathered around the hearth each night, laughter shared. He had spent fourteen long years away and missed so much.

Frances took a step back and turned him into the light, holding on to his upper arms while she studied him. "You look so different, Sam."

"Good. I'm counting on it."

She frowned at him. "What does that mean?"

"I'll tell you everything I can, all in good time."

She hesitated, then nodded slowly. "Since when did you become a constable?"

"Actually, I'm not. I'm still with the army. But no one can know who I really am."

"But—"

"There's so much to tell, Frances. Why don't you sit down?"

He waited as she sat in a wingback chair near the window. She let go of him reluctantly, as if he might disappear.

"Julia Reed is in trouble," he said.

"I know," she answered in a solemn voice. "General Reed sent word when she was arrested, in case newspapermen visited us."

Sam felt tense just hearing that name. "Have any?"

"No, but General Reed assured me that the government was trying to keep everything as quiet as possible. But a constable was here asking questions, and he said he might return with more."

"Did he specify when?"

"No."

Damn, another thing to be worried about. "Did Lewis say he was leaving London?"

Her brows lowered. "I'm not sure that's any of your concern, Sam."

"I've made it my concern," he said tersely. "Is Lewis coming here?"

"No," she finally said, watching him too closely. "He has business in London. Sam, you need to explain yourself, and what all these questions have to do with Miss Reed."

He held up a hand. "Now, don't be upset." Opening the curtains, he whispered out the window, "It's all right."

Julia stood up, gave him a reassuring smile, then accepted his help climbing into the room. When he brought her into the light, Frances stared, but there was no sign of recognition on her face. Julia only looked silly in his baggy garments. Frances glanced at him in confusion.

"Frances, this is Julia Reed."

His sister's eyes went wide for only a moment, and then she looked troubled. "M-miss Reed, we were told you were in jail."

"I was," she said softly. "But *he* had something else in mind."

Frances's lightning gaze landed on him. "Samuel Sherryngton, what have you done?" she demanded in a hoarse voice.

He was grateful when Julia remained silent. "I was one of the officers who tracked down evidence that branded Julia a traitor. Then I discovered we were wrong. I couldn't let her wait in jail while I proved the truth. They were going to behead her."

"So you took her from jail!" Frances cried, then clapped a hand over her mouth and sank back into her chair, her face a pasty white.

"What choice did I have? The real traitor made it appear that I'd killed a witness who would have testified against Julia."

"You're wanted for"—Frances lowered her voice—"*murder*?"

He nodded. The silence was tense, uncomfortable, but he had anticipated Frances's reaction. Now he could only hope he'd been right about her response.

"Why would you bring her here?" his sister whispered. "Surely her own home is the first place they would look for her." Her shocked gaze kept darting to Julia.

He sat down opposite Frances and took her clammy hands in his. "No. They wouldn't assume a criminal would be stupid enough to go home."

"Well, you can't hide her here—it is too dangerous!"

Julia sat down on the arm of his chair, her backside pressed into his arm. "I don't want to hide, Frances, you must believe me. But I'm innocent. Sam thinks he has an idea who committed the treason."

"But why here?" Frances asked desperately.

Sam grimly said, "Because I think Lewis Reed betrayed his country, and framed his sister for the deed."

He hadn't thought his sister's face could get any whiter, but it did. When her eyelids fluttered, he said, "Julia, get her some water." He patted her hands and murmured her name. The blow must be enormous, considering so much of his family's financial soundness rested with Lewis.

Frances tried to protest, but when Julia found the water pitcher and brought her a glass, she gladly drank it.

Then she stared at the two of them with deadly earnestness. "Tell me everything."

When he was finished laying out all the evidence against Julia, and now against Lewis, Frances was silent, her gaze distant with thought.

"So you see why we're here," he said gently. "I need to discover proof that Lewis is the traitor."

Julia sighed. "And I still hope he's innocent. Will you help us?"

Frances shook herself back to awareness. "What do you need me to do?"

He let out a breath in relief. "Let us stay here, masquerading as constables, while we search for evidence against the true traitor."

"You can't possibly fool our family about who you are!" Frances said.

"You said yourself that you didn't recognize me. I've been gone fourteen years."

"But Henry—"

Sam raised a hand. "I probably can't keep the secret from him, so if necessary, I'll tell him. But no one else."

"What about Lucy?"

Their youngest sister? "I was going to ask you about her and George."

"George is away working on railroad construction up in Scotland. But Lucy is here, living in this very house! She's been learning a maid's trade for the last year. She hadn't found anyone she would marry, so she wanted to support herself."

"Relax, Frances," he said. "She won't remember me. She was six years old when I left."

"But she'll certainly keep me on my toes," Frances countered. "I'll have to be even more careful not to speak familiarly with you."

"I'm a police officer. I can talk to you as much as I need to."

Frances sighed in defeat. "How will we begin this charade?"

"Tomorrow Julia and I will show up at the front door and ask permission to remain and look for evidence. Of course, you won't be able to refuse. Give us rooms, some of the adjoining ones."

"Adjoining!" Julia said, getting to her feet and moving away from him. "That can't be necessary."

"You think I trust that you won't get yourself into trouble trying to prove me wrong about Lewis?" He looked back at Frances. "Adjoining rooms. So we constables can work without disturbing the rest of the household."

A frown never left Frances's face as she seemed to be committing everything to memory. "What will you do then?"

"Look for clues. We'll have to search Lewis's bedroom, of course."

"You can't mean that," Frances said worriedly.

Sam tensed. "Why not?"

"He is my employer, and this is his household. I'm already betraying my loyalty. Is there no other way?"

"Eventually I'll have no choice."

"Only if everything else has failed," his sister pleaded. "If he's innocent, I'll never be able to forgive myself for violating his privacy. And how would it seem to the other servants, who look to me to keep order? And surely Jenkins, the butler, would tell General Reed. That man is a great snoop."

Sam didn't say anything more about Lewis's

bedroom, knowing that he'd search it without telling her, if necessary.

"Can't you . . . talk to people?" Frances asked.

"We will. Are there any servants still around from when I used to work in the garden?"

She frowned and considered. "There's old Tom in the stables. He's been grooming the horses for thirty years."

"I remember him."

"So do I," Julia added dourly. "He never allowed me to ride Papa's stallion. Said it was not ladylike. I kept away from him as much as possible."

"Then that will be at least one person who won't recognize you," Frances said. "And then there's Mrs. Bonham, the cook."

"The cook?" Sam said. "Wasn't she a kitchen maid before?"

"She's been promoted. She won't be happy you're here. She'll have to serve a meal in the dining room, instead of just the servants' hall."

"We don't want to arouse suspicions," Julia said. "Maybe we should just eat with the servants."

"No," Frances said. "You're guests. General Reed wouldn't like it if you weren't treated well."

Sam arched an eyebrow sarcastically.

Frances ignored him. "Mrs. Bonham is crafty, and has such a good memory that she's even recognized cows sold off the estate years be-

fore. You'll do well to stay away." She smothered a yawn.

Sam got to his feet. "We should let you sleep. I
only have one more request of you. Julia needs a
young man's clothing."

With a discerning eye, Frances looked Julia up
and down. "We have livery garments, but you
wouldn't want to match the servants. There are
trunks of General Reed's clothing from his
youth stored in the attic. You both wait here—
and make no noise!"

She lit another candle, then picked it up and
swept from the room.

When Julia covered her face with her hands,
Sam was surprised to see that she was trembling.

"I hate to do this to her," she whispered.
"What if she's caught?"

He listened at the door and was satisfied with
the silence. "It would be easier for her rather
than us to find an explanation for roaming the
house at night."

When Frances returned, she carried a worn
portmanteau stuffed full, which she proceeded
to dump onto her bed. "I hope something in here
fits you." She pulled Julia to her side and began
to hold up various trousers to Julia's waist. "I
even found two pairs of serviceable boots."

Julia blinked repeatedly. "You are too good to
me, Frances. I don't know how I'll ever repay
your kindness."

Frances waved off her concern, but she

seemed to be looking from Sam to Julia and back more than was necessary. He quickly glanced out between the closed curtains, while Julia busied herself laying out clothes. He didn't know what Frances was thinking, but under her penetrating stare, he found himself remembering with guilt the kiss he'd given Julia under the guise of playacting.

When they'd finally assembled two pairs of trousers and drawers, three shirts, a checked waistcoat, a plain brown frock coat, and a soft hat with a floppy brim, Sam professed himself satisfied.

"One last thing before we leave," he added, beginning to feel annoyed at Frances's close examination. "I need a piece of white cloth a couple yards long, only a foot in width."

His sister looked puzzled. "I'm sewing new shirts for the footmen. I have material in my sitting room." When she returned and handed Sam the folded cloth, she asked, "What will you use this for?"

He watched Julia blush as he explained their need to hide her "womanly attributes."

When they stood at the window, prepared to leave, Frances softly asked, "Where will you go for the night?"

"We spent last night out in the open," he said matter-of-factly. "We'll be fine."

"But it's begun to rain," Frances said, opening the curtains.

Sam quickly blew out the candles, leaving them in darkness. The three stood silently looking out on the faint mist of a rain shower.

"There used to be an old gardener's shed," he said, "abandoned after Father built a larger one. Is it still here?"

His sister shrugged. "I never heard of one being destroyed."

"Then we'll go there. Up with you now, Julia."

He boosted her onto the windowsill and she jumped out, landing softly. He followed her, and with a last wave for Frances, they set off across the garden.

The old gardener's shed was partially hidden by a trellis affixed to it, and was overgrown with ivy, so that it seemed part of the plant rather than a building. Sam pulled vines aside, then pried open the door. Julia ducked beneath his arm to get inside, and he followed, smelling musty dampness and dirt. He pulled the door shut and they were alone in the darkness.

Chapter 9

❦

Julia stood still while Sam dug in his saddlebags and found his matches and candle.

"Do you think the horses will be all right until
morning?" she asked, as a flame flared to life.

His eyes reflected the light just above her.
"They're hobbled well off any trail. They'll be
fine for a few hours. It'll be dawn soon enough."

The small shed contained only two stools—
one teetering on a broken leg—a dusty work-
bench, and several stacked wooden crates. She
heard the steady drip from a leaky roof, but it
must be in a corner, for she saw no wetness on
the packed earth floor.

He went to the only window, which was covered by a shutter, and pushed it more securely in place. "We don't want the light to show to anyone who happens to step outside for air."

"At this time of night?"

"You never know. Now let's get you out of those clothes."

She understood his purpose, had even undressed in the same room as him before, but it didn't stop the small shiver that moved through her. She turned her back to him, removed the coat, and slowly unbuttoned the shirt. The shed was so small that he was practically at her back, and her too-long trousers brushed his lower legs.

Angry with herself for feeling embarrassed and shy, she knew there was no place for such foolishness. "Can you turn your back?" she asked when her trousers started to sag.

"I already have."

The shirt and trousers dropped to the floor and she kicked them aside. She had left her chemise on earlier in the day, so that Sam's shirt wouldn't leave her chest so transparent. Just as she held up one of the new shirts, Sam spoke.

"Wait. I have to show you how to cover your chest."

"Not likely," she scoffed, "considering I'll be doing that over bare skin."

"Leave your chemise on, and I'll show you over that."

"All right," she said with reluctance.

They both turned to face each other. She noticed that he was careful not to look down her body, but when he held up the white cloth, she knew he'd soon not have a choice.

"Lift your arms," he said softly.

When she did so, he reached on either side of her, pulling the cloth snuggly around her back.

"I'd rather not pin this in place," he explained, "for fear of you feeling a prick at an inopportune moment."

She nodded, keeping her gaze averted as he worked.

"As you wind the cloth," he said, "spread the material down your torso, so it isn't all bunched in one place."

"That might make me look more womanly than I normally do."

She raised her gaze to his, expecting laughter, but he was looking at her strangely as he tucked the material in at her back. Standing within the circle of his arms, she stared helplessly up into his face, wanting him to kiss her, wanting the comforting touch of him for all the wrong reasons: because she was scared and lost and so dependent on him. His eyes shone with a compassion he normally didn't allow her to see. His lips were slightly parted, and when he glanced down at her mouth, she almost gave in to her desires and kissed him.

But she'd be using him.

She pulled away, and his arms fell to his sides. "Done?" she asked with false cheer.

He rubbed his hands on his thighs. "Yes. Will you be able to repeat it?"

"Of course. And I'll go to Frances if I need help," she added pointedly.

A faint smile crossed his face, and then he turned his back. "Go ahead and change."

For a moment, she let herself admire the width of his back, the muscles she'd pressed herself against more than once. It would take all her determination to resist her feelings for him.

Did he desire her as well? Oh, she'd aroused him once or twice, but they'd been close together in the most intimate fashion. It wasn't *her* he was responding to, but a female body.

Wasn't he?

She turned her back and quickly removed the binding and pulled off her chemise. Shivering in the dampness, she wound the cloth over her naked chest, and thought she'd done as good a job as he had. She exchanged her drawers for a man's pair, then added shirt, trousers, waistcoat, and coat to complete the ensemble. She was trying to tie her shirt collar into place when something occurred to her.

"Sam," she said, turning around, "we forgot a cravat."

He started to face her. "I have an extra—" He broke off and just stared at her.

"What's wrong?" she asked, looking down at herself. "Did I put the clothes on incorrectly?"

"No . . ." Then with firmness he repeated,

"No. I guess I just didn't imagine you'd be able to look more like a young man than you had in Afghanistan."

"Really?" she said, smiling with pleasure. "So you can't see my chest?"

"No, the binding actually makes you look broader. It's a good thing you're a robust woman."

"Robust?" She narrowed her eyes.

"Of—of course, I don't mean anything bad by that," he stammered. "It's just lucky that you're not petite like some women are."

"Hmm." She let him tie a black cravat into a bow at her neck. "I suggest you bring out the blankets so we can have at least a couple hours' sleep."

He looked relieved by the change of subject. "We'll want to be out of here just before dawn."

"Will you be able to wake up in time?"

He nodded. "Something I learned how to do in the army."

So much of who he was, was wrapped up in the army. And now he'd jeopardized it all just for her. How would she repay him? How would she live with herself if she'd permanently damaged his reputation?

They lay down side by side, taking up all of the small floor. This time they didn't touch, just tolerated the warmth their bodies gave to the shed. But their arms were so close that when she rolled over in the cramped space she brushed against him.

She couldn't fall asleep. "Sam?" she whispered.

"What?"

She braced her head on her arm and looked out into darkness. "Was this shed in use when you worked here?"

"Only when I was young. Your father gave mine permission to have a new one built, nearer the main garden."

"Then why didn't anyone tear this down?"

"Probably used it for storage when necessary. It doesn't seem as if my brother even remembers it's here."

"Did you use it?"

He paused. "What do you mean?"

"Sometimes I'd come to look for you, and no one could find you."

"I used to do my schoolwork in here," he admitted. "If I tried to study at home, inevitably I'd have to help my parents with the younger children."

She deliberately lightened her tone. "And you didn't like to do that?"

"I helped them whenever they asked. But when my chores were done, I needed time alone."

"And I had *too much* time alone," she said, imagining him as a young boy, grateful for the quiet, working studiously to better himself.

"We lived very different lives," he said.

She didn't want to think about that. "So tell

me—as you grew older, surely you used this shed for other things."

"Just my studies."

"You must have brought a girl or two here to be alone. Isn't that what boys do?"

She heard a rustle in the silence, and wondered if he was looking toward her. Then she felt the slight puff of his breath and she shivered.

"No."

He spoke simply, and she believed him. "Why not? Were there other places a boy from a large family could be alone with a girl?"

Again he hesitated. "I never met any village girls I wanted to be alone with."

Sam didn't know what ridiculous impulse had made him say such a thing. He should have said girls had chased him his whole life. But after everything he'd done to her, he couldn't lie.

"There were some very pretty girls in Misterton," she said. "None of them appealed to you?"

"No, which is one of the reasons why I went into the army. I thought that by traveling, I'd meet other women." That was certainly what he'd hoped. But he'd never had a serious attachment, because no one had ever matched Julia. "You need to sleep. You have to have all your wits about you to carry off this masquerade."

"All right," she murmured.

It didn't seem to take long before she was breathing deeply, evenly. He called her name, and when she didn't respond, he gently touched his fingers to her hand. Such soft skin.

He must have finally fallen asleep, for suddenly he awoke, thinking the air smelled of the freshness of the coming day—and hope. And then he realized why he felt at peace: Julia was wrapped in his arms, her bent knee covering his hips, her head pillowed between his shoulder and chest. In the faint light coming from the cracks in the door, she looked dark and tousled, not like herself at all.

But she certainly felt like Julia, and his body was letting him know what he wanted to do with this woman in his arms. He should have changed her position; instead he foolishly called her name.

She came awake immediately, looking up into his face with surprise.

They broke apart as if lightning had struck them.

"It's a good thing we'll have our own beds," Sam muttered.

She only nodded hastily, pulling her frock coat tighter about her chest.

They waited in a copse of trees outside the gates of Hopewell Manor for several hours. Once the sun was sufficiently up, Sam went through his saddlebags and produced a small wooden box.

"Is there anything you *don't* have in those

bags?" She practiced walking between the trees, swinging her arms in a manly fashion.

He thought he'd be amused at her attempts, but she had taken to the movement rather easily.

"This is something I always carry with me to help disguise my features," he said.

He opened the box and showed her several glass vials and a small brush.

"Cosmetics?"

"Very good. Now come here and sit in the light."

"Are you sure this is necessary?" she asked.

She sat on a fallen log beside him. The sun through the leaves shadowed her face in light and dark.

"We'll have to repeat this every day," she cautioned.

"It will help with your disguise. We can't have you too pretty."

"I'm not pretty."

He glanced at her, startled. He saw that she wasn't searching for a compliment, had even spoken matter-of-factly, as if she'd accepted such a ridiculous thing long ago.

"Your opinion doesn't count," he said.

"Why not?"

"You can't be the judge of your own appearance."

She laughed. "Sam, you say such silly things."

He loved to watch her smile. She had even teeth and such a natural sparkle in her eyes that matched the prettiness of her mouth. He continued to look at her, until she finally pointed to the cosmetics box.

"Do we need to add water?" she asked.

He quickly looked back at the box. "No, only to wash out the brush."

He opened one vial and shook a touch of black powder into his palm. "I'm going to give you faint shadows under your eyes." He dabbed the powder on her skin with his finger. She looked up at him with fluttering eyelashes, whose length he hoped no one noticed.

When he was satisfied that her eyes didn't seem to sparkle so much, he applied more of the powder on her cheeks and jaw, using the tips of the brush to give the faintest speckled effect.

"This is for the shadow of a beard," he explained. "Try to touch your face as little as possible."

When he put the cosmetics away, he brought out a bottle of macassar oil and showed her how to work it into her hair. Soon her hair was swept back off her face and behind her ears, leaving a straight part at the top of her head.

Sam stepped away with relief, already dreading having to touch her every morning for this process. He studied her carefully. "Your lips are a little too pink, but there's not much we can do. When you smile, don't show your teeth. That should help."

She groaned and threw up her hands. "How

will I ever do this, Sam? There's so much to remember!"

"As I told you before, you need to become the character, to think only as he would."

The horses had grown restless, and when Sam and Julia finally mounted, it took several minutes to calm them down.

Once Julia signaled that she was ready, Sam said, "Here we go."

He watched her straighten in the saddle and throw back her shoulders. Then he took the lead, checking carefully that there was no one on the road before he led them out of the trees.

The gates were wide open during the day, and just as they entered, a boy emerged with a small flock of sheep. Sam nodded and touched his top hat, while the boy just gaped, probably at the constable's uniform. Last time Sam had been home, Misterton only had a sheriff, a local who volunteered his time.

Sam wanted his presence well known, and this would certainly start things rolling. If he was lucky, someone would come forward with evidence.

Lucky, but not likely.

The gravel road wound through gardens he still remembered vividly. There were glades of rhododendrons, scarlet geraniums, and vivid blue lobelia. His brother hadn't changed much in the design, only adding the occasional exotic plant to make one startled and surprised.

The road separated around a large fountain, and he took the opportunity to glance back at Julia. She was seated rigidly, unsmiling, her whole demeanor the height of seriousness.

He barely held back a smile.

By the time they reached the front portico a young groom was waiting near the stairs. They dismounted and handed over the reins. Sam watched Julia adjust her hat, then look out across the estate curiously as if she'd never seen it before. Good.

He took the marble stairs slowly, thoughtfully, no detail escaping his notice. He raised the door knocker and let it drop loudly.

"Ready?" he whispered over his shoulder.

"Ready."

General Lewis Reed stared out over London from the third story of his town house, feeling as if the whole city were stretched out at his feet, when all he wanted to do was retreat into the obscurity of Hopewell Manor. He had just attended another dinner in his honor, another night wearing a false smile painted on his face.

Patience, he counseled himself, as he'd often had to do these last few months. It would all be worth it in the end.

There was a scratch on the door, and a maid informed him that a soldier waited in his study with a message. As Lewis descended to the first floor he wondered how much longer he had to wait before he could safely resign his commission and be done with the military.

But the soldier waiting in his study was Clive Randolph, and the man was in Lewis's employ now, not the military's.

Lewis closed the door behind him. "Is there news about my sister's trial?"

Randolph shrugged. "There'll be no trial until they recapture her."

Lewis gripped a chair back and took a deep breath as all his worries intensified. "How the hell did she escape?"

"She had help. Sam Sherryngton, one of the soldiers who'd helped capture her in the first place. Seems he didn't believe she was guilty after all."

He remembered Sam as a boy who didn't understand his lowly status on the estate. "When I heard he was involved," Lewis said between gritted teeth, "I knew it boded ill. He was always too concerned about Julia. But I never thought he'd commit a crime for her. I assume you followed them."

"They almost gave us the slip by heading north," Randolph said. "We were covering the train stations, when there she was, that hair as bright as day. Seemed like she wanted to be seen, you know?"

"Get on with it," Lewis said curtly.

"We almost missed the switch—I caught it, of course. Albert would have continued on to Edinburgh," Randolph said, shaking his head as he smiled in triumph.

"They switched trains?"

"Headed south again. We couldn't approach them on the train or in town, so we attacked outside Rotherham."

"Did you kill them?" Lewis knew it was too late to be squeamish about another murder, but she was his sister. Yet her death would solve so many problems.

"No. The bloke killed Albert."

"Damn." Lewis paced to the window and back. How had everything become so complicated? All he'd needed was a little money to hold on to his estates. He'd never thought that his information sold to the Russians would lead to a massacre.

"I thought you'd want to know they were headed for Hopewell Manor."

Lewis swore and came at the man until he backed up against the wall. "And you left them there?"

"You told me to report to you."

"Get back there! Don't leave again until they're dead. But I don't want the staff harmed in any way. Lure them outside before you end it. I don't need any more talk about my family than necessary. And remember, if I'm caught you'll go down with me."

Randolph nodded coolly and headed toward the door.

When the door closed behind him, Lewis sank into a chair and covered his face. Everything was spiraling out of control. He had never planned to frame Julia, but she was such an embarrassment to his orderly life that it had proven the perfect opportunity to steer the blame away from himself. He was trapped into ending this violently. He couldn't alert the police to her whereabouts, for fear they would investigate her theories.

She'd left him no choice.

It was her own fault that she had to die.

Chapter 10

After knocking on the door of Hopewell Manor, Sam resisted the urge to glance back at Julia. He could only trust her now.

The door slowly creaked open, and the butler, tall and imposing with his powdered hair, embroidered coat, and formal knee breeches and stockings, nodded his head. Sam knew there would be no respectful bow; Sam and his assistant were obviously not gentlemen.

"May I help you, Constable?" the butler asked.

"Why, yes, sir, ye may. Is General Reed at home?"

"He is not. Would you care to leave a message for him?"

"No, sir. I'd like to speak to the person in charge. Is that you?"

The butler showed only a moment's distaste before his face became a blank mask once again. "If you would wait in the entrance hall, I'll send Mrs. Cooper, the housekeeper, to you."

He ushered them inside, and Sam looked around the hall, for in truth he'd never been in the formal area of the manor before. Even though the master wasn't at home, everything gleamed in the daylight, from the marble table-tops to the intricately laid tiles on the floor. The sculpted ceiling was arched high overhead, the two full stories of the house.

While they waited, he glanced at Julia, but her gaze was fixed forward without expression. What must it be like for her to come back here, a place where she'd never been made to feel comfortable? And now she was a wanted criminal. Hopewell Manor might hold the only key to her freedom—or it would be the place she was captured. And it had been *his* idea to bring her here. He wasn't used to questioning every decision he made, but with her life on the line, it was a constant challenge to bury his doubts.

Frances strode in, her large key ring jingling at her waist, her expression pleasant. "May I help you?" she asked, as the butler withdrew from the hall with a bow.

"Yes, ma'am. Ye'd be Mrs. Cooper the house-keeper?"

She nodded. "Is there a problem, Constable?"

"I'm Constable Joseph Seabrook, and this is my assistant, Walter Fitzjames. Surely ye already know about Miss Reed's troubles."

"Yes, another constable came to speak with us soon after she was arrested."

"Well, ma'am, she's escaped the jail. My chief constable in Leeds sent me here for a further investigation. If I can uncover enough clues, it might lead me to her. Ye haven't seen her, have ye? Or a bloke by the name of Samuel Sherryngton?"

Her eyes narrowed at him. "I've seen neither of them, Constable. And as the butler Jenkins must have told you, General Reed is in London, and not due here anytime soon."

Sam was impressed by how well Frances was handling her role. She was making it easy for him to concentrate on his own character.

"That's all right, Mrs. Cooper, because we're mainly here to talk to the staff, to examine the house and the grounds, to get an impression of Miss Reed's life."

"She spent much of the past ten years abroad, sir. I'm not sure what you'll find."

Sam grinned genially. "Ye never know, ma'am, and with the help of a good woman like you, we may finish our investigation in only a few days."

Her eyes widened nicely. "A few days! That is quite an imposition, Constable. I'd need to see your orders."

He heard Julia betray herself with the faintest gasp, but if anyone else had overheard, they might think she was just affronted by Frances's request.

"I've got them here, ma'am." He brought out folded papers with the correct wax seal that he'd stolen from the Leeds office.

While Frances looked them over, Sam turned to Julia and said, "Now, see, Fitzjames, how important it is to prepare? What would you have done in this situation if ye'd forgotten the papers?"

"Yes, Constable, sir," Julia said gruffly.

When Frances looked up, Sam shrugged and nodded his head toward Julia. "Fitzjames is a recruit in trainin', Mrs. Cooper. I'm doin' my best to help him learn the business."

Frances handed him back the papers. "Let me show you into the drawing room, and I'll send for some tea."

The drawing room was immense, running down the front of the manor, with groupings of settees and chairs and little tables scattered everywhere. Huge crystal chandeliers were hung from elaborately decorated ceilings. Frances pulled a discreet cord, and while they were seating themselves on overstuffed chairs, a maid entered pushing a well-laden cart before her. The maid was dressed in a plain gown and white apron, and beneath her cap was a brilliant shock of red hair.

Was this his baby sister Lucy? He tried not to stare at her too eagerly, so he complimented her on the generous spread of cakes, all while studying the fine freckles across her nose, and the way she snuck a peek at him with intelligent brown eyes. She looked much like his childhood memories of his mother. He felt his throat tighten up with emotions he wasn't used to feeling, and forced himself to look back at Frances. She was simply staring at him, but he saw understanding in her eyes.

Once Lucy had finished setting the repast on the low table, Frances said, "That will be all, Lucy."

"Yes, Mrs. Cooper."

She bowed her head and left the room. Yet she cast one inquisitive glance back over her shoulder—at Julia. Was the girl suspicious already?

As Frances filled their teacups, she said, "Constable Seabrook, I noticed you have a slight limp. Are you in pain, sir? I could send for the local physician."

"No, thank ye, ma'am. It's an old wound, one that acts up on me on occasion, especially when I spend long hours in the saddle. But I thank ye for your kindness."

Even though the door was now closed, Sam wouldn't break character, for servants had a habit of listening at keyholes. He could see Frances clutching the arms of the chair, her work-roughened hands white at the knuckle. She opened her mouth and he quickly shook his head, knowing damn well that she was going to speak too freely.

Frances nodded, then took a sip of her tea. She began her words on a sigh. "You said you'll be staying a few days, Constable. Do you have lodgings in Misterton?"

"We came right from Leeds, ma'am, and haven't gone into the village yet. But I wonder if ye might have spare rooms for us here. It will make our work go much faster."

Frances regally inclined her head, and Sam wanted to smile at how she'd taken to the formality of her position.

"Of course I can offer you rooms, Constable. What else can I do for you?"

"Give us the freedom to wander where we will on the estate, Mrs. Cooper. The investigation will be smooth if I don't constantly have to run to you or Mr. Jenkins for permission."

Frances eyed him sternly over her cup. "You will not disturb the master's private apartments without me accompanying you."

He glanced at Julia, who didn't even raise her gaze to this squabble between brother and sister. Sam narrowed his eyes at Frances. "I promise I'll come to ye first."

Her acquiescence could cost her her position, he knew. He wasn't here to ruin things for his family. He promised himself to do his best to find other means to clear Julia first.

"I'd also like a list of the staff, their positions,

and their length of service. This will help me when I question them."

She nodded. "I'll have it for you by the end of the day."

"Could ye spare a servant to show us about? I wouldn't want to inconvenience someone as important as yourself, ma'am."

"It would not be—"

"This is certainly a comfortable estate, ma'am. Would there be a lot of tenant farms?"

Before she could get out more than a nod, he continued. "We'd appreciate a list of tenants, too."

Frances broke in before he could ramble on. "I can't see why a list of farmers is necessary. This investigation is about Miss Reed, isn't it?"

"And why she might commit such a crime, Mrs. Cooper. It helps to know what motivates a criminal mind."

"I can't believe Miss Reed is a—"

"Are you gettin' all this, Fitzjames?" Sam called, turning to find Julia frozen with her teacup to her mouth. Her finger positions looked decidedly feminine. He glared at her and lifted his own teacup silently. She quickly adjusted her grip.

"Did ye forget your notebook again, lad?" he continued, shaking his head. To Frances he said, "I've instructed the lad to take notes, but hunger got the best of his stomach, I guess."

Julia indelicately stuffed an iced cake in her mouth.

Frances sighed. "I shall notify you when luncheon is ready, Constable. But first I'll show you to your rooms so you can refresh yourselves."

"Refresh ourselves?" Sam echoed. "We surely don't need a bath, however kind ye are to offer one."

Frances grimaced. "I—I meant if you'd like to change clothes, or perhaps rest before the meal."

"Rest?" he said, standing up. "In the middle of the day? Surely you yourself are too busy for such a thing."

"I am a servant, sir," she said between gritted teeth. "But guests are treated differently in this household."

"I am but a servant, too, Mrs. Cooper, though of the town of Leeds. But go ahead, show us to our rooms. We'll—what was the word?—*refresh* ourselves."

Julia watched the very interesting emotions that played across Frances's face as the housekeeper finished the last of her tea. Sam's behavior was enough to drive anyone to madness, with the annoyingly slow speech, and the way his thoughts rambled from one to the next.

Frances seemed to be escaping as she swept open the drawing room doors, only to find another maid dusting a table nearby.

"Florence," Frances said, "didn't you already dust the hall this morning?"

The girl's face flamed beneath the curls escaping her cap. "I—I remembered I forgot this table, Mrs. Cooper."

"Finish it quickly and be about your duties."

The girl made a few last swipes at the table with her cloth, then hurried down a corridor.

"Do you have luggage you wish the footmen to bring up for you, Constable?" Frances asked as she led them up a broad staircase.

As they passed marble statues in recesses along the stairs, Julia remembered them as being some of her favorite hiding places for her treasures. Her snooping brother had never found these. Every time she thought of Lewis, she was shocked anew at Sam's accusations. Until there was proof, she just couldn't believe it yet.

The farther away they were from the rest of the staff, the more she felt the tension begin to seep away. It was stressful to constantly worry that any gesture, any misspoken word, could mean her discovery.

Sam was telling Frances about the portmanteau and saddlebags left with their horses, but Julia paid little attention. She tried to remind herself that this was home, this life she was fighting to preserve, but the manor had felt more like a museum than home. Home had been in the garden, where she might see Sam.

But that was a lifetime ago. Where was home now? Hadn't she been struggling her whole adult life to find it? And she was farther away than ever.

They'd stopped at an ornate door, and Sam was frowning as he ducked his head inside. "Mrs. Cooper, we'd prefer rooms together with a door in between, if ye've got them. We've got much work to do, and don't want to disturb the household."

Julia stared from one to the other, wondering who would win this battle of wills: Sam, who wanted to keep close watch on her, or Frances, who struggled with the impropriety of it all.

The siblings glared at each other, until finally Frances said stiffly, "Very well, the next set of doors is a small suite, a sitting room with a bedroom on either side. Will that do?"

"Immensely," Julia said, glad that they would have neutral meeting ground in which to work.

Brother and sister turned to stare at her and she tossed her head. "I'll have many notes to transcribe, Constable, for us to keep a good account of our investigation."

One corner of Sam's mouth turned up in faint amusement.

Inside the sitting room, she tried to remember the last time she'd been in this suite. She'd explored every aspect of the manor when she was young, but since nothing had ever changed, she'd grown bored with that quickly. Her mother had never been the kind of woman who felt the need to redecorate every year.

Frances stepped close to Sam, and he held up his hand.

"No," he murmured. "I'll approach you when I feel it's safe." In a more normal voice, he continued, "What a fine room this is, Mrs. Cooper. I see there's a desk. Could we have another for Fitzjames?"

"I'll have the footmen do as you request."

"So then I can come to you for our tour?"

"Sir, I believe you mentioned assigning another member of the staff to—"

"But ye know everythin' worth knowin', don't ye, Mrs. Cooper?"

"Of course, sir."

When Frances finally left, she seemed glad of the escape.

Julia frowned. "Can we talk freely, Constable?"

"Find your book and take notes of our conversation with the housekeeper, Fitzjames. I need to take a look about the room." In a lower voice, he added, "And make sure your penmanship is not feminine."

For the next hour, she watched in amazement as Sam searched every foot of their suite, top to bottom, running his fingers along trim, patting patterned wallpaper as if it might conceal something. Every piece of furniture was moved aside to see what was behind it.

"What are ye lookin' for, sir?" she finally asked, when he stood in the center of the sitting room, his frock coat thrown haphazardly on a chair, his shirtsleeves up to his elbows.

"The opportunity for someone to spy on us,"

he answered, rolling down his sleeves. "And it seems that it's impossible, unless someone is listening at the door, though there are three of them. If we speak quietly, close to the windows, we should be safe."

He motioned for her to follow, and then parted the draperies, looking out on the garden that stretched out below. She heard his swiftly inhaled breath.

"Do you see your brother out there?" she asked softly.

He shook his head. "I was thinking about last month, when I followed you here. I forced myself not to look for any of my family. All I did was scale the wall at night and watch you through the windows."

She put a hand to her throat. "*Watch* me?" Had she changed clothes before an open window? She should be dismayed at the thought, but she found the concept of Sam staring at her naked body far too intoxicating.

He smiled. "Your room is on the second floor. Trust me, I did not scale the *building* to keep an eye on you. I just wanted to make sure you were here for the night." He turned back to the sunlit view. "But I never got a chance to look at the garden."

She moved up beside him, and shielded her eyes from the glare of the sun. "How does it make you feel?" she asked.

"In some ways like home. I know every inch

of the grounds, every type of soil and plant—except the interesting new ones Henry has since added." He rested his head on his forearm, leaning against the glass pane. In a husky voice, he continued, "And in other ways, it was my prison."

She remembered her feelings of abandonment, of desolation when he'd first told her he'd be leaving. "You never wanted to be here," she whispered.

"That's not true. It is, after all, the place in which my family still happily resides. Right now, I'd give almost anything to announce who I am, then just sit in my mother's kitchen talking to them all."

"But because of me, you can't."

"I've done a lot of things in my life because of you."

She inhaled swiftly, the shot of pain from his words almost more than she could bear.

Then she saw he was watching her too closely. "Don't look like that," he said. "I'm not wanted for murder because of you. I was fulfilling my assignment when that happened. It's not your fault."

"Then what do you blame me for?" she cried.

He covered her mouth and looked to the door. With the other hand he pulled the draperies shut, leaving their corner suddenly dim. Her eyes went wide as she realized she might have betrayed them.

He didn't move away from her. To her shock, his other arm came around her waist, and the hand at her mouth went slack. He let his fingers touch her lips, slide along them from corner to corner.

Julia felt as if the floor tilted beneath her, and she had to clutch his arms for support. This was Sam, touching her, holding her, fulfilling so many dreams she'd once had. But they were both adults now, aware of consequences she'd never had to consider. And there was a desperation in his eyes she'd never seen before.

"I don't blame you for my behavior, Julia," he murmured.

His arm tightened around her; his body became a supple wall against hers. She could feel his every breath, the pulse of his heartbeat, and her own heart answered the rhythm.

"Then what have you done because of me?" She spoke against his fingers, but he didn't move them, seeming to absorb her breathless words.

"Fourteen years ago, I left Hopewell Manor because of you."

She was unable to think of a response, not when he seemed to be almost pressing her to him, his hands sliding down her back, and his fingers dangerously close to the swell of her backside.

But he didn't explain. Instead he lowered his head and kissed her, a brief touching of parted lips that was nothing like the rough kiss they'd shared in the tavern.

It was the kiss she'd dreamed of as a young girl following him about the garden. A delicate thing, a worshipful thing. His mouth was soft. He kissed the pout of her lower lip, the bow shape of her top lip, even one corner. The brush of his mustache and beard should have tickled, but instead added to the experience. She moaned at the feel of his hand sliding slowly down her body. Wearing trousers instead of layers of skirts, she felt the indentation of each of his fingers as he cupped her backside and squeezed.

His other hand feathered gentle caresses down her neck, and then gently he slid his finger beneath her collar.

Her eyes, at half mast in wonderment, opened wide. His own did the same.

Suddenly he was stumbling back from her, and she reached out a hand for him. She was cold without him, bereft, puzzled.

He turned his back on her, his head bowed. "What the hell am I doing?" He straightened and stiffly said over his shoulder, "That was wrong of me. You're under my protection, and this was an—an assault."

"Assault?" she echoed in a trembling whisper. "How can something that felt so wonderful be an assault?"

"You're not thinking clearly," he said harshly, finally walking back to her. He seemed remote, as if he towered over her in his anger. "You're dependent on me for your freedom—it's only natural that you'd feel . . . close to me."

"You think this is something that just magically appeared inside me these last few days?" She went to touch him and he stepped back, leaving her hand awkwardly in midair. "Surely I showed you, when I was young, how I felt about you."

"The important phrase is 'when I was young.' You were fourteen when I left, Julia," he said heavily.

"Some girls are married at fourteen. They know their own minds."

"Not many, and not anymore."

"Country girls—village girls."

"But not daughters of the gentry. And certainly not to men like me."

She shut her mouth in consternation, for the black look he wore said he would not be reasonable. He put his coat back on, and took care fastening each pewter button. She suspected he was delaying having to look at her.

Straightening her own coat, she felt the empty ache in her breasts. What had happened here? What did she have to do with his departure from her life all those years before, and why wouldn't he explain it?

Chapter 11

Frances did not come for them herself. She sent Florence instead, who left after bringing hot water and clean linens and soap. Julia watched with dismay as Sam closed his bedroom door on her, and she reluctantly retired to her own chamber.

Florence came back for them a half hour later, and led them down through corridors Julia found herself remembering as they went. Images of her childhood flashed in her mind, and the memories were sad. The formal dining room was immense, and the table had been set up with only two places at one end. Two footmen of matching height, wearing the ornate livery and

powdered hair of their service, stood beside a
sideboard with covered platters of food.

Sam stared about him, looking rather
awestruck. Then he cleared his throat. "Florence?" he called before the girl could leave.

"Aye, sir?"

"We don't need to eat alone. Where is everyone else eatin'?"

She blushed. "We have no other guests, sir.
The servants even now sit down to their meal in
the servants' hall."

"Then take us there. We'll get to know everyone."

The footmen betrayed no expression, but Florence looked aghast. "Mr. Jenkins would not
have it, sir!"

"Mr. Jenkins isn't the one dinin' alone, now,
is he?"

"He often takes his meals alone," she protested.

"Well, I don't. Lead on, Florence."

Julia slid silently in line behind them. She
knew Sam wanted to eventually talk to all the
servants, and this was one way to begin encouraging their trust.

But she also suspected he didn't want to spend
any more time alone with her than he had to.

The servants' hall was low-ceilinged and overheated, full of the smells of cooking and hard-
working bodies. The laughter that had escaped

out the door as they approached died into silence at their appearance.

Frances sat at one end of the table, Mr. Jenkins at the other, with at least two dozen servants on benches between them, women on one side, men on the other.

Frances shot to her feet. "Is something amiss, Constable?"

"Of course not, Mrs. Cooper. Fitzjames and me didn't know what to do with ourselves, all alone in that big room. We convinced Florence to lead us here."

The girl shot a pleading look at Frances, who calmly nodded.

"Sit down and enjoy your meal, Florence." She turned to all the avid faces around the table. "Everyone, these gentlemen are Constable Seabrook and Constable. . . ." She turned to Julia. "Forgive me, sir, but I've forgotten your name."

"Walter Fitzjames, ma'am," Julia said. Her voice came out hoarse and uncertain, and her face heated as she became the focus of every pair of curious eyes. She wanted to look away, but instead forced herself to meet every gaze. No one showed anything but curiosity.

Frances turned back to Sam. "Constable, please sit in my place."

"I won't have it, ma'am. I'm but a workin' man, though I'm a guest here. Surely someone can push aside and make room for us."

There was more room than it appeared, and Julia found herself seated with Sam on one side of her and a footman on the other. She did her best to remain shy with her eyes downcast, since she was frightened to death with so many people staring at her. Though Frances said only a few servants remained from ten years before, the rest had seen her but a month ago, or maybe even during her childhood, if some of them were the children of local farmers.

She let the conversation resume and swirl around her, concentrating instead on holding her shoulders back, as if the awkwardness of the position would make her look more like a man. Sam made himself jovial and rather silly, and it seemed to relax everyone. His beard had filled in, and she was beginning to wonder if even she would have recognized him, acting as he was. She was amazed at how easily he made himself fit in, and then she remembered what had never occurred to her when she was younger: he'd been a servant. He'd repeatedly made clear that he didn't want to hear about her long-ago feelings for him, and had said women of the gentry didn't marry men like him.

Did he see himself as *only* a servant? It seemed impossible that Sam, so larger than life when she'd been a child, might really think so little of himself.

When the conversation around the table sank into a lull, Sam cleared his throat and slowly looked at all of them. "Constable Fitzjames and meself are here on business, as ye probably guessed. Ye know that your mistress has been arrested. Fitzjames and me want to sit down with ye one by one and talk. We'll ask questions, and ye can answer as best ye can. All we want from ye is the truth, and we'll be satisfied."

"Well, I believe none of it," one old man said gruffly.

He was dressed in old breeches and a patched coat, and Julia was certain that the smell of horses was coming from him.

Sam regarded him with interest. "And your name, sir?"

"Don't call me sir. I'm but Tom, the head groom. I been here goin' on thirty years, and ye'll never make me think that slip of a lass is a criminal."

Julia fumbled for her notebook and pencil in her pocket, hoping she could force away the sting of tears. She wrote down his name, position, and comments.

Sam nodded. "I need to hear things like that, too, Tom. We can talk more later."

Tom only harrumphed and ate the last of his pork roast. "I'll be goin' back to the stables," he said as he pushed to his feet.

He almost moved the bench out from beneath all the men. Everyone but Julia was used to it, for they righted themselves easily, while she barely caught herself from falling to the floor.

Sam nodded and stepped back over the bench to stand. "I thank you all for answerin' our questions. We'll start the interviews tomorrow." He turned to Frances. "Now, Mrs. Cooper, about that tour ye promised us."

Mr. Jenkins stood. "One of the footmen will gladly escort you, Constable."

"It's Mrs. Cooper that knows everythin' goin' on in the house, sir. Are ye ready, ma'am?"

Frances wore a faint blush, and Julia saw that several of the maids whispered together and smothered giggles. She wondered what that was all about.

It took several hours for Frances to show them through the manor. Sam found himself watching his sister with admiration. She'd earned her position through skill and knowledge, but she obviously loved this house. He hated to make her feel that her livelihood was threatened. But what would happen to the estate once Lewis was arrested? Sam was certain the man hadn't named Julia as his heir.

He couldn't believe his own stupidity where Julia was concerned. He'd kissed her, given her reason to think there could be something between them. Standing so close to her, he'd been unable to stop himself from taking her in his arms. Had he no self-discipline left at all?

She'd tasted of sweetness and warmth—and the forbidden. He'd succumbed once, like a fool, but no more.

And just when he thought he'd banished her from his mind, Frances led them into the gallery, where ancestral portraits frowned down on them. At the end, caught in a stream of sunlight, was Julia's portrait, life-sized, the image of a girl on the threshold of womanhood, looking out across the room with a wistfulness that he well remembered.

The three of them paused beneath it in awkward silence. Julia looked up at the image of herself with a bitterness that pained him, as if she were no longer that girl—or maybe wished she never had been. They went back downstairs without speaking of it.

They stepped out between glass doors onto the terrace and walked across until only a stone balustrade separated them from the expanse of the garden spread out below. He inhaled deeply, and the sweet odor of hundreds of varieties of flowers struck a deep, satisfying chord within his soul.

Sam casually glanced around to see if they were alone. In a low voice, he said, "Is Henry here?"

"He should be," Frances whispered. "Of course, he'll be the one to give you the tour of the grounds. There he is."

Off in the distance, Henry rounded the bend of a path, pushing a wheelbarrow. Frances lifted her hand in a gesture that was part summoning, part waving. Henry waved back, left the wheelbarrow off the path, and started toward them.

For the first time, Sam felt nervous. He was going to try to fool his brother, but if he couldn't, he didn't want Henry recognizing him in front of witnesses. He almost thought it would be better to tell Henry the truth outright.

But then the competitive part of him resurfaced, as he remembered that he and Henry had challenged each other to everything from footraces to weeding. He wanted to see if he could pull off the masquerade.

Like Sam's own, Henry's hair was more brown than red beneath his cap, long to the collar yet neat. His workman's clothes, though pressed, were dirty from the day's labor. He was much larger, broader than Sam remembered. Time hadn't touched his brother in harsh ways, and Sam was glad of it.

Henry came up the curved stone staircase, tipped his hat to Frances, then, squinting in the sunlight, stared frankly at Sam and Julia.

"Henry Sherryngton, head gardener, this is Constable Seabrook and Constable Fitzjames."

Sam reached to shake his hand, but Henry hesitated and said, "My hands are stained from a day's work, sir."

"Honest work, sir," Sam answered back.

They shook hands, and Sam saw with relief that no light of recognition appeared in his brother's eyes. Sam hid a smile as Julia fumbled with her notebook to avoid shaking hands.

Frances looked from one to the other in a

wide-eyed fashion and quickly said, "Henry, the constables will be spending several days with us."

"Is this about Miss Reed?" Henry said.

"It is, Mr. Sherryngton." Sam deliberately slowed down the speed at which he spoke. "We need to interview the staff and tenants, get more of an idea why Miss Reed would turn to a life of crime."

Henry looked skeptical, but all he did was nod. "If you'll follow me, sirs."

Sam glanced at Julia, who was looking at him with wide eyes. "Have ye been takin' notes, Fitzjames?"

"Of the tour, sir?" she asked in a husky voice.

"Especially of the tour. I want a list of all outbuildin's so we can examine them later."

"Yes, sir." She buried her face in her notebook.

After Frances returned to the manor, Henry led them off across the grounds, showing them stables and barns, dairy and brewery. Sam enjoyed just listening to his brother talk. Henry even slowed down his pace when he noticed Sam's limp.

Two young children ran up a path, calling, "Papa! Papa!"

Even though he'd known his little brother was a father, Sam watched with astonishment and quiet envy as Henry knelt to hug his children, telling them he'd be home for supper soon. Sam berated himself for the emotions he couldn't control. He'd freely chosen his life, and couldn't—wouldn't change it now.

He realized Julia was studying him too closely, only her watchful eyes showing above her notebook. Sam calmly returned her stare, and she finally looked away.

When they reached the newer gardener's shed, Sam assumed that Henry would simply point it out as they walked by. Instead, his brother led them inside. When Sam and Julia followed into the dim interior, the door suddenly slammed shut behind them.

Sam whirled and found Henry standing with his back to the door, his arms crossed over his chest.

"What the hell is this about?" Henry demanded.

Sam raised an eyebrow and drawled, "I thought I made everythin' clear, Mr. Sherryngton."

"Don't 'Mr. Sherryngton' me—*Mr. Sherryngton.*"

Sam heard Julia take a quick breath, but all he did was study his brother's face. "Hello, Henry," he said softly. "Would you mind keeping your voice down?"

Henry scowled and stepped forward in an obvious attempt to intimidate Sam. "I'll say it again: what the hell are you doing, trying to be somebody else? Being a Sherryngton's not decent enough for you? We haven't seen you in fourteen years, your letters stopped coming almost a year ago, Ma cries her eyes out every night—"

Sam raised a hand, determined not to let his hurt show. "Enough. If you'll be quiet, I'll tell you everything."

Henry frowned back and forth between the two of them, showing no recognition of Julia. Sam would leave it that way, if he could.

"How did you recognize me?" he asked.

"Your voice," Henry said angrily. "And your eyes, too. Now it's time for you to answer my questions."

"I'm not sure why you didn't receive my last letter, but I just returned to England a few months ago."

"And only now can you manage to get yourself home?"

"Henry, I've been on assignment for the army. I couldn't desert my mission. We were following a traitor from India—"

"Julia Reed?" Henry interrupted.

Sam sighed. "Yes, but I've recently discovered she's not guilty. Now I'm trying to prove it."

"And this can't be out in the open so you can see your own family?"

Sam briefly explained his own murder charge, and his brother looked horrified.

"By God, leave the country!" Henry whispered hoarsely. "You'll never be able to prove yourself innocent. I'd rather never see you again, as long as I knew you were alive."

"I can't desert Julia."

Henry threw up his hands. "You've got to let go of this pathetic fascination with her!"

Sam momentarily closed his eyes. He could feel Julia staring at him, her notebook forgotten.

"Be quiet, Henry," he said in a grim voice.

"Not until I make you see reason."

"She is a friend in need. I'd do this for anyone else."

"But you didn't *arrest* anyone else," Julia mumbled, then seemed to realize her mistake.

Now Henry's attention was diverted, and he stared hard at Julia, before he finally gave a low whistle.

"Miss Reed, I presume," he said.

"Henry," she answered with a nod.

Henry sighed. "You weren't going to tell me about . . . this?" He pointed helplessly at Julia. "Does anyone else know?"

"Just Frances."

"Frances! You chose her instead of *me*?"

Sam had to laugh at the echoes of childhood rivalry in his brother's voice. "We had to. We had no men's garments for Julia to wear. But you can't discuss this with Frances. You can't even talk to us, unless I initiate the conversation. I can't risk discovery. It'll mean death for both of us."

Henry stared at them, swallowing hard.

"Someday you'll have to tell me how you got yourself involved in this." He glanced at Julia. "Although I have a good idea."

"No, you don't," Sam said firmly.

"So I can't tell Ma."

"No!"

"She'd keep it quiet. It would be such a relief for her."

Sam winced. "I hate causing her pain, but I can't risk how she'd look at me if she knew. Tell no one, Henry, not even your wife."

His brother nodded solemnly.

"You have beautiful children," Julia whispered.

They both stared at her.

"Thank you," Henry said.

Sam could only wonder. Julia was twenty-eight years old, well past the normal age for marriage, with no dowry, and now a terrible reputation. He wondered if she had hoped for children, and if there was still a chance that if Sam cleared her name, she might find happiness.

Without him.

The thought gave him no peace.

Chapter 12

❦

After supper in the servants' hall, Julia and Sam found themselves treated to a rendition of songs by two of the maids. It was very obvious to Julia that the household staff got along well, obviously better than when she'd grown up here.

When the impromptu concert was over, Sam ordered her up to their sitting room to work on her notes for the day. She noticed that Sam stayed behind to talk to Frances in front of the rest of the staff. He was obviously trusting in the fact that no one would think it unusual that an investigating constable would want to speak to the woman in charge of the manor.

Julia trudged up to the second floor, then pretended to get lost so she could ask a passing footman the way. She silently congratulated herself on her cleverness. Someone new to the household would think the corridors a labyrinth.

But once she was inside the sitting room, she put her back against the closed door and allowed herself to slump. She had never imagined how hard it could be to pretend to be someone else. And to think that Sam had spent years doing this.

She wondered if, in his place, she would somehow have lost herself, but Sam didn't seem to have. She admired his strength of character, his certainty in the way he'd chosen to live his life.

His confidence was reassuring at the same time as it was deflating. She would never be any good at this. What if they never cleared her name? She would spend the rest of her life running, hiding under assumed identities. And she would have cost Sam his own freedom. How long would it be before he resented her?

There was a tentative scratch at the door. Julia checked her cosmetics in the mirror, then went to answer it. Sam's sister Lucy stood there, a sheaf of papers held in her hand.

"Might I come in, Constable?" she asked without any of the shyness she'd had before.

Julia had no choice but to step back and motion her inside. She left the door open.

Lucy looked around the room inquisitively, then turned to face Julia with a smile. "I brought the staff list Mrs. Cooper prepared, Constable."

"Thank you," Julia said.

Lucy handed her the papers, drawing it out a bit so she could look into Julia's face.

Julia felt her smile freeze. Was Sam's sister . . . flirting with her?

"Mrs. Cooper said to tell you that she'll have a list of tenants from the steward by tomorrow." Lucy smiled, her face full of innocent curiosity. "Sir, do you mind me asking where you're from?"

Julia laid the papers on the writing desk, glad to put distance between them. "I grew up in Leeds, Miss Lucy."

"Oh, you don't need to be formal with me, sir. I'm just Lucy. I grew up here on the estate. My papa was the head gardener, and now my brother is."

"If we have questions about the estate, we'll know who to ask."

"Good." Lucy scuffed her toe on the carpet, then looked back up. "Would you mind telling me your Christian name?"

Julia cleared her throat. "Uh . . . Walter."

"What a fine, strong name . . . Walter." Lucy smiled.

Julia smiled back, remembering to keep her mouth closed. She needed to be rescued!

And as if on cue, Sam limped through the door. "Why, good evenin', Lucy."

Julia saw the way his eyes had lightened upon seeing his sister, although his expression switched quickly to politeness.

The girl blushed. "Evening, Constable Seabrook. I've brought you the list you needed." With a curtsy and a smile, she said good night, then turned to the door. She came to a halt and looked back again. "Would either of you gentlemen require a bath after your long journey?"

It seemed like such a foreign luxury, yet the thought made Julia glow on the inside.

Before she could speak, Sam said, "We're not used to bein' waited on, Lucy. Ye could tell us where to fetch the hot water, and we'd do it ourselves."

Julia waited breathlessly for the maid's response.

"Nonsense, sir!" Lucy said, waving her hand in dismissal. "There's only one hip-bath in this wing, so which of you would like to be first?"

Julia didn't even let Sam speak. "Constable Seabrook has work to prepare for tomorrow. Ye can put the hip-bath in my room, Lucy."

The maid nodded and left.

Sam closed the door behind her, then looked at Julia. "Lining up the women already, are you?"

She groaned, and motioned him to come to the window with her. In a low voice, she said, "This is—terrible! I feel like I'm leading her on!"

"It can't be helped. And I'm sure a bath is

worth it." He shook his head. "You acted as if I would deny you one."

"Well, I couldn't be certain," she said primly.

"I imagine you'll soak forever."

"Only until I'm well pruned." Tentatively, she added, "Sam, what should I do about Lucy?"

"About her . . . interest in you?" he asked with a grin.

She nodded.

"I hope we won't be here more than a few days, so her feelings won't be hurt. But until then, her infatuation may prove helpful."

"Helpful?" she repeated, aghast. "I won't play with your sister's emotions."

"I'm not asking you to. But she might feel free to tell us things that go on in the manor. Don't encourage her—don't say anything. We'll see what happens." He went to the desk and picked up the papers. "It seems we have about twenty servants to interview. It might take two days."

"You don't want to start searching for clues?" she asked, coming closer to him, letting herself admire the way he stood, the ease of command that seemed to come so naturally to him.

"Witnesses give very good clues. Someone might have seen something suspicious when your brother was here."

She wandered the room, lighting more candles, putting her notebook on the new desk that had been brought in during the day. She couldn't help thinking of the clues she'd learned today about Sam. What had Henry meant by Sam's "fascination" with her?

Sam certainly didn't seem fascinated now. He threw his coat and hat across a chaise lounge and settled down in a deep, cushioned chair with his papers.

She might as well not even be in the room. What about that kiss? Did she even dare to ask him?

In the end, she was a coward. She let him keep his silence, and when Lucy ducked her head into the sitting room to say that her bath was ready, Julia gladly closed herself into her own private room. Lucy had placed the hip-bath on towels in front of the hearth. She'd lit coals in the grate for warmth, and left candles burning about the room.

Julia silently locked the door to the hall, then stripped off her garments and sat down gratefully in the tub. The water only came to her waist, but it was hot and welcome. She managed to wash her hair, amazed at how easy it was with its short length.

When she was clean and shivering, she couldn't help thinking of her own tub in another wing of the house, deep enough to sink to her shoulders. Such luxury was something she hadn't experienced much in the last ten years.

Reluctantly, she dried herself off and dressed in a clean shirt and trousers. Her hair hung in waves about her face, but she wasn't going to oil it before bedtime. The same with the cosmetics. She would just have to avoid seeing Lucy. So she padded barefoot into the sitting room and found Sam at the desk, writing. She curled up in a chair and watched him. Whenever he glanced at her, she pretended she was reading from a book she'd found on a bed table.

With a simple "Good night," Sam retired to his own bath, which Lucy had had moved to his room. A disappointed Julia went to bed, where sleeping alone suddenly seemed foreign, unwelcome. In just a few days, she'd become accustomed to awakening in his arms.

Running away with him to the Continent suddenly didn't seem so terrible.

They woke up early so Sam could enhance Julia's manly appearance for the day. Though he saw the shadows under her eyes that didn't need much cosmetic help, he didn't ask her how she had slept. He had to discourage the intimacy she seemed to so easily inspire.

After breakfast, he was given permission to use the library to interview servants. He studied the room thoughtfully, as Julia stood close by, watching him.

She was never far away, never far from his thoughts, especially last night in his lonely bed. But now she looked confused as she watched him place two comfortable chairs facing each other. He explained about making a subject feel comfortable enough to relax and speak freely.

"And who will we be interviewing first?" she asked, seating herself behind the desk, picking up her pencil, and opening her notebook.

"Mrs. Cooper. Might as well start at the top."

"Yes, sir."

Frances fiddled when she was finally seated in her chair, as if Sam were going to attack her. She had dark circles beneath her eyes, and he knew the enormity of this task was taking a toll on more than he and Julia.

"General Reed and his sister returned to England last year, Mrs. Cooper, and Hopewell Manor was the first place they came to. Can ye tell me what went on the week they were here?"

As he'd suspected, Frances had little to say that was of any help, as she tried to recall what parties the Reeds might have attended.

"Now let me turn to Mrs. Hume's death. She was the children's governess?"

Frances nodded. "When she was too old to work, we asked her to remain with us."

"Was General Reed here when she died?"

She looked puzzled. "Yes, he was. He'd come up alone from London for a day or two to take care of business."

Sam felt a surge of triumph. Lewis had been in the manor when the old woman died, had gone back to London, then later sent Julia to the estate to take the old woman's possessions to her son in Leeds. He must never have told Julia where he went when he left London. All to fit in with the scheme he'd set in motion, making her look guilty of treason.

And if Lewis had been here the night of the woman's death, then Sam had to find a way to tie them together. Frances explained that Mrs. Hume hadn't been ill before she died, and was simply found dead in her bed.

"Mrs. Cooper, I understand from my many interviews with his sister that the general was . . . low in his finances."

Frances stiffened, but said nothing immediately. If it wasn't true, she would have denied it in a heartbeat.

"As you can see from the condition of the estate, sir," she said with a telltale quaver in her voice, "he managed to keep things together regardless of occasional . . . circumstances."

"Such circumstances bein' when your wages were late?"

Her lips pressed together and she sighed. "Yes, sir. But it was never for very long."

"And how long was that?"

"Usually just a few weeks. Twice he was about three months late. But, Constable," she hurriedly added, "he was halfway around the world. Things happen."

She glanced at Julia, who had her head lowered as she continued to scribble her notes.

"Did ye know, Mrs. Cooper," Sam said softly, "that the general spent his sister's dowry? She had nothin' to bring a husband in marriage."

Frances's eyes grew anguished. This time Julia raised her head and slowly nodded.

"When Miss Reed discovered what he'd done," Sam continued, "he told her he didn't want to lose this estate."

"But he's been back in the country for a year now, Constable. He's been able to make everything right."

"Were debts suddenly paid off, or was it a slow process?"

"It took almost the full year, Constable, before the general was caught up."

Damn. He'd wanted to hear that Lewis had magically come up with a vast sum of money.

Frances slumped back in her chair, and Sam knew he was destroying his sister's security bit by bit.

But he'd do worse to prove Julia's innocence. Inside him rose a growing impatience he wasn't used to feeling, a tightening in his gut that made him edgy, angry. If Lewis Reed walked into the room, Sam didn't know if he could keep from hitting him.

There was a brisk knock on the door, and his brother Henry ducked his head in.

"Begging your pardon, Constable, but might I have a word with you?"

Frances got to her feet. "I'll see you at luncheon, gentlemen."

After she had gone, Henry carefully looked out into the corridor, then closed the door and approached the desk.

Sam frowned at such suspicious behavior. "Is somethin' wrong, Mr. Sherryngton?" he asked.

Henry folded his arms over his chest and suddenly looked reluctant. "Sir, you'll think me foolish, but I thought I saw someone sneaking over the wall into the gardens at dawn this morning."

Sam narrowed his eyes. "You think?"

Henry shrugged. "The sun had yet to rise and shadows were everywhere, but . . . yes, sir, I think someone came in over the wall. Normally I'd assume it was an errant footman from the household, or one of the grooms."

"Thank you, Mr. Sherryngton," Sam said. "I'm sure it is nothin' to worry about. But I'll stay aware."

"You'll stay aware," Henry repeated.

There was a teasing smirk in his voice that Sam fondly remembered.

"It still seems strange, Sa—Constable," Henry said, "to think that we have *you* to watch over us."

Sam arched a brow at him, then, at a muffled sound, turned to find Julia coughing intently into her hand.

"Mr. Sherryngton," Sam said, "do ye doubt my trainin'?"

"No, sir, it's just difficult to imagine. But I'd better get back outside."

"I'm sure the geraniums need ye to watch over them," Sam called.

He heard Julia gasp, but Henry only grinned, and Sam grinned back. For a moment, it was as if they were young again, teasing each other one moment, then the next moment ready to defend each other against the world.

After Henry had left, Julia just stared at Sam wide-eyed.

"What?" he said.

She raised both hands. "Nothin', sir." Then a wistful expression came over her face. "That was just . . . nice."

He rolled his eyes, then turned thoughtfully toward the door. "I think I'll go have a walk and stretch my legs, Fitzjames, while ye organize your notes and ponder other questions we could ask."

"I assume ye'll be in the garden, sir?"

"You assume correctly."

As Sam walk purposefully toward the door, Julia called, "Might ye need me to watch your back, sir?"

He cast a wry look over his shoulder and left the room, although he could hear her faint laughter. He walked through long corridors, which grew narrower and darker as he entered the rear of the manor. He stepped outside to find the sky overcast and threatening rain. He headed down a path he knew would circle the gardens, covering as much ground as possible. He passed Henry's two assistants on their hands and knees weeding, and they tipped their hats as he limped past. His ears remained alert and his eyes scanned for unnatural movement. Soon the foliage grew a little wilder, blocking out more of the sky. He turned a corner, and a shovel hit him across the head.

After Sam left, Julia stifled her laughter. They should not be joking about so serious a subject as a villain's pursuit, but she'd explode if she couldn't relieve the tension somehow. She shivered as she remembered the kiss he'd given her yesterday. She wasn't going to think about the other way to relieve tension.

She bent over her notes and began to rewrite them in a neater hand. As she considered what Frances had said, and what information they might retrieve from the other servants, she didn't notice time passing until the mantel clock struck. Sam had been gone almost an hour.

Slowly, she closed her notebook and pocketed it. Why had he not returned yet? A frisson of nerves darted up her spine, and she told herself she was being foolish to worry. What could happen in a lovely garden during the middle of the day?

She walked through the silent house, then out onto the terrace. A brief gust of wind reminded her that autumn was not far away. Even the birds seemed silent because of the impending storm. She experienced a strange feeling of being watched, but she turned in a circle and could see no one in the windows, no one approaching from one of the paths.

Just as she left the stairs and stepped onto the grass, she heard a shout.

"Go back!"

She froze as Henry and Sam emerged from a thicket. Sam had his arm around Henry's shoulder, and seemed to be having trouble walking. But he was looking right at her.

"Get up on the terrace!" he called.

Rain began to fall in a soft wave, its coolness startling her. She took the stairs backward, her gaze glued to Sam. He winced as Henry guided him up the stairs.

"Guard your face from the rain," Sam said in a low voice as they caught up to her.

She was shocked when he gripped her arm and dragged her along with them, as if he didn't trust her to follow. She kept her head low, and blotted with her fingers at the occasional stream of rain down her face. All she would need was to have a servant see her "whiskers" smeared.

When they got inside, Henry took them directly to Frances's deserted sitting room. He lowered Sam to a chair, and Julia watched his pale face with concern.

"Constable?" she said softly.

"I'm all right. Just a bump on the head. Tell everyone I tripped."

Henry nodded, but Julia continued to study him. "You didn't trip," she said.

"No. I was hit with a shovel. Luckily, Mr. Sherryngton came along."

"So Mr. Sherryngton wasn't imagining things in the shadows," she continued.

"It seems I wasn't." Henry frowned as he poured water in a basin and wet a cloth. Handing it to Sam, he said, "Didn't mean for you to be the target, Constable."

"Don't worry, Mr. Sherryngton," Sam said, wiping his face, then pressing the cloth to the side of his head. "I think my assistant and I are the only targets he wants. And look, I'm not even bleeding." He held up the cloth for their inspection. In a low voice, he told his brother about their assailant who had escaped three days before. "He must have received his orders and come back to carry them out."

"He didn't kill you," Julia pointed out.

"No, but I believe there's no point killing only me. Maybe I was the bait."

"I see," she murmured, looking out the window, thinking of the dangers that now lurked outside her home. "His plan worked, for I was just coming to find you."

"You won't be doing that again," Sam said darkly. "You're not to go outside without me."

"Is even the manor safe?" Henry asked.

Sam frowned and was silent for a moment. "You'll have to alert your assistants and the grooms. Tell them we're worried we might have a thief about. I'll have the footmen take turns prowling the house at night. That should dissuade our visitor, at least temporarily."

"I just don't want anyone else hurt because of me," Julia whispered.

Chapter 13

Throughout the morning, Julia watched Sam at work as he interviewed the next five employees. He had insisted he was fine, that he was capable of sitting and asking questions.

Sam was certainly full of patience. She couldn't understand how he was able to project such a calmness to each of the people they interviewed. Always, the "subject" (as Sam liked to call them) came in nervous and worried, and by the second question, Sam had them distracted with his rambling thoughts about the estate. It was a skill long practiced.

A skill she wanted to try.

And then it was time to interview Lucy. Before

Sam's sister arrived, Julia came around the desk.

He looked up from the papers in his lap with wariness, then held up a hand. "The headache is almost gone. I'm fine."

"I'm glad to hear it. But that wasn't what I wanted to discuss." She took a deep breath and spoke firmly. "Constable, I feel I've learned some of your skills by watchin' ye. *I* would like to interview the next subject."

His stare was understandably hesitant. "Fitzjames, I don't think—"

She leaned over him, and his words stopped with obvious surprise. This was the first time she'd used her femininity—hidden though it was—to try to persuade Sam. "Give me a chance," she whispered. "This is my life. I'm not used to feeling so helpless."

So close up, his brown eyes seemed lit with tiny pricks of golden light, exotic, enticing. He scrutinized her and she allowed it, trying to forget her pretense as a man, and to use every bit of her womanly appeal with just the desperation in her eyes.

"Very well, Fitzjames," he murmured.

She noticed his gaze had dropped to her mouth. She slowly licked her lips. Sam arched a brow, his expression so calm it disappointed her.

"Such blatant enticement is not necessary," he said, as if they were discussing the weather.

"Then why is there a sudden bead of sweat on your temple? It's not warm today."

He frowned and opened his mouth, but there was a soft knock on the door.

She straightened, then pointed behind the desk. "Time to take notes, Constable Seabrook."

He sighed, but stood up to follow her lead. When Julia called for her to enter, Lucy came strolling in, looking more subdued than she had the last time Julia had been alone with her.

Lucy cleared her throat. "Before we start, I'd like to know how my brother became part of this."

"Beggin' your pardon?" Julia said, unprepared and unsure of what to say.

"My brother Sam. Frances just told me this morning that the police think Sam is a murderer."

"He did help Miss Reed escape," Sam pointed out in a neutral voice.

"That is just foolish! Anyone who knew him would know he's not capable of murdering anyone. I may have only been six when he left, but I remember him."

"What could you possibly remember, Lucy?" Sam asked.

Julia knew him too well not to hear the emotion he disguised.

"He was . . . kind, and very patient, which is hard when you have so many brothers and sisters. He always had time for me."

Sam cleared his throat and looked down at the papers on his desk. "Our job is to find them both

and bring them to trial so the truth can be un-
covered. Any way ye can help us would be
greatly appreciated."

"You mean help you put my brother in jail?"

He sighed. "Or maybe help us discover what
really happened. We're only lookin' for facts, not
mindlessly placin' blame where it might not belong."

Lucy looked away and quickly swiped at her
eyes. "How can I believe you? Frances said that
when the last police officer was here, he made it
sound like there was no question of Miss Reed's
guilt, like she was some . . . immoral person."

Julia's stomach tightened, and she told herself
it was only what she'd expected.

"But she's not like that!" Lucy insisted.

Sam said, "She left here ten years ago. And
you remember that about the daughter of the
house?"

"She would . . . talk to me, after her brother
and my brother had left. I know I was still a
child, and she was almost a woman, but she
missed my brother terribly, and talking seemed
to help."

There was an awkward pause, during which
Julia steamed with mortification.

"They were good friends," the girl continued.
"And then Miss Reed's parents died, and she
was all alone here but for the staff. Frances said
no one was surprised when Miss Reed up and
left to follow her brother."

"Lucy, would ye mind if I ask ye some questions?" Needing to change the subject, Julia used the same relaxed, friendly tone Sam did. She started out worrying about the deepness of her voice, and how far apart to keep her legs, and where to put her hands, but soon the role consumed her and conversation about Hopewell Manor flowed.

At first, Lucy didn't have anything new to add. When the topic reached the governess, Lucy was much more knowledgeable than the others had been.

"Mrs. Hume was such a dear," the maid said. "I often took tea in her room in the afternoons, when she wasn't feeling able to be up and about."

"Was she ill often?" Julia asked, remembering Mrs. Hume from her youth, when the woman had seemed full of boundless energy and enormous patience, especially when dealing with Lewis.

"For an old lady, she was seldom ill at all," Lucy said. "But her bones were old, she would say, and sometimes didn't want to carry her about."

"So you weren't expecting her to die so suddenly."

Her face clouded with sadness. "Not a bit. Just that afternoon I'd walked with her through the garden. I was even going to wish her a good night before I went to bed, but she already had a visitor, and I didn't want to disturb them."

Julia kept her smile pleasant, although her insides seemed ready to crawl out. "Who was the visitor, Lucy?"

"Why, the master himself, come to see how his old governess was doing."

Julia's smile suddenly seemed frozen, as if her lips would never come apart. Something heavy settled around her heart, squeezing. She hadn't wanted to believe the truth about her brother.

But right now she had a job to do. She ignored every confused thought and concentrated on the maid. "Lucy, at what time in the evening did General Reed visit Mrs. Hume?"

"Almost midnight, which I found strange, if you're asking my opinion. *I* knew that Mrs. Hume usually went to bed late. He must have known that, too."

"Did he see you?"

"No, sir. I was coming 'round the corner just as he went inside. He had a wine glass in his hand, which he almost spilled on himself as he tripped going in the doorway."

He was drunk, Julia thought desperately. He didn't know what he was doing, whose room he was entering.

But no man could be that drunk. He'd spent his whole life at Hopewell Manor, and he knew it as well as she did.

She just had to know the truth.

Sam suddenly spoke in his calm voice. "Lucy—"

Julia held up a hand and shot him a cool glance. "If ye don't mind, sir, I can handle this."

He sat back in his chair and gravely nodded at her.

She took a deep breath and let it out slowly. "Lucy, how long was the general in Mrs. Hume's room?"

"I don't know, sir. I went to bed myself."

"Was anyone else with ye when ye saw him?"

"Why, yes, sir, Florence."

Two witnesses.

"We both backed down the corridor the moment we saw him," Lucy continued.

"And in the morning the governess was dead."

"Yes, sir." Lucy's lower lip trembled, and she blinked her eyes. "I found her when she didn't come down for breakfast. She looked like she was asleep, but . . ."

When she trailed off and sighed, Julia said, "I'm sorry we have to remind ye about such a sad day. But this is important. Was anythin' out of place in her room?"

Lucy frowned. "I don't think so."

Julia rose to her feet. "That will be all for now, Lucy. We'll break for luncheon."

Sam came around the desk. "Lucy, could ye please send two trays up to our sittin' room in half an hour? Fitzjames and I have much to discuss."

Julia felt like fragile glass, with a small fracture beginning to spread its destruction. She stood stiffly, waiting for Lucy to leave.

When the girl was gone, Sam said, "What can I do to—"

She stalked away from him, not knowing what she meant to do, only that she couldn't remain in this room. She carefully opened the door, feeling as if she had to control her every movement, or she would be flinging aside everything in her path. She knew Sam followed her, but it no longer mattered.

Lewis had betrayed her.

She covered her ears with her hands as if she could make the terrible thought go away.

But it performed its own echo inside her, hastening the shattering of glass that was her soul. She picked up her pace, knowing she couldn't remain in a public place much longer. She wasn't sure where her steps were taking her. She could only look at the marble floor.

She briefly felt Sam take her arm, slow her down enough to whisper, "You're almost to the family's private wing."

She'd been heading toward her old bedroom, as if she were still a child escaping the pain of her family's indifference. She swung about awkwardly and took a different staircase, until she found herself outside their sitting room.

Her hand reaching for the door looked like

someone else's, as that terrible voice in her head became louder and louder.

Lewis betrayed you. Lewis betrayed you!

And then she was inside, and when Sam closed the door she should have felt better, safer, and instead she felt like she couldn't breathe. She ran to the window, fumbled for the latch.

"Julia, what are you doing?" he whispered behind her, his hands on her shoulders.

"Need—air. Oh, God, I c-can't breathe—" She was gasping, tasting tears she hadn't known were streaming down her face.

Her fingers jerked on the window latch, tearing part of her thumbnail. She stared at the welling blood, feeling like her lungs would soon burst.

Then he had the window opened, and she gulped the cool breeze like a dying fish finally immersed in water.

A sob broke from her, and she knew it was only the first of many. She covered her mouth, trembling, panting, and then Sam's arms were around her. He was trying to protect her, but nothing could stand between her and the sure knowledge that her brother was a monster.

"Oh God, he killed people," she whispered hoarsely, her face pressed into his shoulder. "He—he did these terrible things, betrayed us all, and—and—"

She cried, her face buried against him, trying

to hush the emotions that poured out of her. Her brother hated her so much that he'd rather see her dead than admit his own crimes. He'd deliberately made it seem like she'd committed them, as if he'd thrust a knife into her himself.

"Julia, I'm so sorry," Sam whispered into her hair.

"You were right, all along you were right."

"I take no satisfaction in it, you know that."

"I didn't want to believe it from the beginning. He's my brother and I guess I always hoped . . . How can he—how can he live with himself?"

"Money is more important to him than human lives. Even when he was a child, none of us mattered compared to his status, his position. You felt the brunt of this, Julia."

She hiccuped on a sob, buried her suddenly cold hands beneath his coat for warmth. Gradually her cries ceased, and she felt hollow, numb, every other emotion driven out except for grief, as if her brother had died. In a sense, he had.

She looked up into Sam's face. "Tell me we'll make him pay for his crimes."

With his palms, he wiped the wetness from her cheeks, then cupped her head and solemnly said, "If it's the last thing I ever do, I'll see him beheaded for what he's done to you."

"Not just to me," she cried softly. "His information murdered thousands, some of whom he'd c-called 'friend.' "

But Sam's face was lined with the pain he felt just for her. He'd been the light of her childhood, and now the only man to believe in her innocence, to risk even his life to prove it.

She kissed him desperately. Surprised, he stumbled back and fell into a wingback chair. She followed him, straddling his lap, holding his face against hers with a desperation she couldn't begin to understand. She had nothing anymore but him, no one to want her but him. If she died, only he would mourn. The rest of the world would believe themselves better off with her death.

And with only a maid's word as evidence, she was lost.

He reared his head back, then grabbed her shoulders and held her away. "Don't assume the worst, Julia," he said, breathing heavily. "This desperation isn't what you want—"

"I want you."

Her strength seemed bottomless as she knocked his hands away and rested full against his chest where he lay back in the chair. He smelled of sunshine and flowers and freedom, a man of the gardens who also knew the worst of the world.

"I'm not asking you to love me!" she whispered. "Just make me—make me—"

"Forget?" he demanded, his eyes full of compassion. "For minutes, even an hour, you might be able to put it all from your mind, but afterward, you'd feel even worse, for you'd only be using this as—"

"You mean using *you*, don't you?" She sat up swiftly, mortified to find that she was still crying, even as she felt his hips between her thighs. "That's what I always do, don't you know that?"

"Julia, that's not what I said!"

She flung herself off him and turned about in the center of the room with no idea what to do next. "All I do is use men, whether it's for sex or for proving my innocence."

"You're not using me."

Her angry glance could have stabbed him. "I've used men before you—why should you be any different?"

He said nothing, just looked at her with sad eyes.

"I don't want your pity!" She needed to yell the words, but settled for a hoarse whisper. "Lewis uses people for money, I use men for—for—"

"Wanting to be close to someone is no crime."

His words made her ache, made the tears threaten again. "It is when you know you don't mean it in a permanent way. But I did it anyway. Do you think Lewis is punishing me?"

She turned to Sam in anguish, but stepped back when he would have come nearer.

"Maybe I deserve to be punished," she said. "I was angry with Lewis—angry with you, though years had passed since I'd last seen you."

He closed his eyes and lowered his head.

"I wanted something to make me feel alive, because I wasn't ever going to have the family I'd always wanted. And this—officer made me feel . . . beautiful, like a woman should feel. What could a few stolen nights matter? There would never be anyone to marry me."

"Julia—"

"No, you have to hear this! I let him—I let him . . . have me. I knew it wasn't love, I pretended that didn't matter. He was kind to me. It only lasted a couple days, until he left Kabul. And then there was Nick—"

She saw the wince he couldn't hide, knew how much she'd hurt him. But she was still in the past, remembering Nick's passion. "I was still so angered by your indifference, so I used him, too. But I thought I was finally coming to my senses, realizing this pattern I had where men were concerned. I was using them out of revenge, not passion. I stopped things between Nick and myself, and I think I even hurt him, but I had to make things right. I vowed I would never use a man so selfishly again." With her eyes, she willed Sam to believe her as she said, "I met Kelthorpe, and was shocked to discover his interest. I would have been a good wife! He was my security, my peace, and I would have made him happy, so he wouldn't know I was still just using him. I would have *made* myself love him!

"And now you," she added brokenly. "When

my world falls apart, look what I do, how I treat you. . . ."

He put his hands on her upper arms, and it was too much effort to hide how she flinched.

"We all do things we regret," he said gently. "You're in pain, and it's normal to try to escape it. I don't feel used," he insisted with a firmness that made her heart break. "Don't castigate yourself anymore because of me."

He tried to hold her, and she resisted, worried that she would embarrass herself even further. But he was so warm, and she was trembling with shock and sadness, and something too deep to even be grief. She sagged into his embrace.

"It will get better," he murmured, his lips so close to her ear.

His chest vibrated with his deep voice, lulling her into that hollow, aching feeling of nothingness.

At a soft knock on the door, she stiffened.

Sam cursed and pulled away. He looked down into her face. "That must be Lucy with our luncheon. You can't be seen like this."

"I know." She wiped at her cheeks, knowing she was making it worse. "I'll wash up and . . . fix things."

"Will you come back and eat with me?"

She shook her head. "I couldn't eat anything. I can't even go back down with you."

"Then don't. I'll tell anyone who asks that you're resting because you don't feel well."

"Fine." She pulled away from him, suddenly desperate to escape his compassion.

"Julia—"

"No, no, it's all right. I—I just need to sleep."

She closed her bedroom door and rested against it, listening to the murmur of voices in the sitting room, and then finally silence.

She pressed her cold hands to her face in pathetic astonishment at everything she'd just revealed to—done to Sam. She wouldn't blame him if he finally deserted her.

But it was his fate on the line, too; Lewis had made sure of that.

She knew she wouldn't be able to sleep. After touching up her cosmetics as best she could, she waited a half hour until Sam went back down to his interviews, then slipped from her room.

She didn't know where she was going. When she saw the occasional servant, she tried to look busy, striding quickly like she had a purpose, casting her gaze down so they wouldn't see her red-rimmed eyes.

She found herself in the family wing, where the halls echoed with emptiness. But it had always been empty here, devoid of happiness or hope or the togetherness of family.

She came to a stop in front of Lewis's suite, which her parents had once used. He'd had his things moved in when he and Julia returned from India.

Slowly, she opened the door. The room was

awash with sunlight, gleaming dust-free, as if waiting for Lewis to come home.

She had to make sure he never got the chance to do that. She wanted . . . justice, even more than revenge, she tried to tell herself.

But whom was she kidding? He'd betrayed her, sent people to kill her, and this hatred that burned inside her would never be quenched.

The door suddenly opened, and Julia whirled around to see Frances, whose face was set in stern lines.

"You promised you would not disturb the general's room without notifying me," Frances said.

She sounded as betrayed as Julia felt, and Julia wanted to laugh at the absurdity of it.

"He's guilty." The words came out of Julia's mouth, shocking them both.

The housekeeper gasped and leaned back against the door, closing it. "You said you might be able to prove him innocent."

Julia shook her head, and it felt as heavy as a piece of old, cracked marble. "I wanted to believe that. I can't anymore. My only relative is a murderer."

"Miss Reed—"

"I'm Walter Fitzjames!" she said, knowing that she sounded crazy. "I can't be his sister anymore."

"But—Constable, what happened? Sam—Constable Seabrook has said nothing to me."

Julia walked to the window and peered out,

trying to remember how the garden gave her peace. It was elusive. "Your own sister was the key. She saw Lewis go into Mrs. Hume's bedroom late the night she died."

Frances's eyes went wide. "He—he never—"

"He never showed any interest in Mrs. Hume, I remember. She was just a servant, a hated teacher who was making him think about useless subjects like mathematics, when all he wanted was to be on a battlefield like his tin soldiers. Do you know he couldn't even remember her *name*? She lived under his roof his entire life, and she was . . . nothing to him." Her words trailed off into grief again, and she angrily dabbed a tear at the corner of her eye. "He killed her. All so he could have a reason to send me north, to make it look like I was the traitor. He had me carry her possessions to her son in Leeds. That was the only reason Mrs. Hume had to die. You could almost say it was because of . . . me."

Frances came to her and spoke in a stern voice. "His actions were his own, regardless of the motives. You were innocent."

"I don't feel innocent." But she did feel angry, and she let the rawness of it flow through her, burying everything else. "He's not going to get away with this."

"Do you have any more proof than Lucy's word?"

"Florence was there as well. They both saw

him. And Edwin Hume told Sam that he'd been hired by Lewis."

"But Edwin is dead."

"Yes. Another murder on Lewis's head. But there's the money with which my brother slowly paid off his debts. Where has that come from?"

Frances was obviously at a loss. "He is home from foreign service—perhaps he has investments he's able to tend now."

"Then those investments should have prevented his debts in the first place. No, I know he had little money—before. Eventually, we're going to find where he's hidden what the Russians gave him. And that will be all the proof we need."

Chapter 14

Besides Florence, who echoed everything Lucy said, Sam found no other interesting information on questioning half the staff. He'd thought maybe Mrs. Bonham, the crafty old cook, might have remembered him, but in the end, she'd answered his questions without recognition. It would take another full day to interview everyone, and he hadn't even started on the outside staff.

He wanted to go up to Julia, but felt he should eat in the servants' hall again, to keep up appearances. To his surprise, Julia joined them, and a feeling of relief overtook him. He hated to think of her crying over that bastard of a brother.

She looked composed, as if she hadn't spilled some of her darkest secrets to him hours ago—secrets he hadn't wanted to hear, but in the end was glad he had.

It had hurt to imagine her with other men, but somehow, knowing that she'd been confused and unhappy seemed to bring out his protective streak again. Her family had damaged her, left her ripe for seduction by men who cared only for pleasure. And he was throwing his good friend Nick into that group, too.

But he himself wouldn't become just another man to her. She didn't deserve to be hurt, and neither did he. When this was over, she'd go back to her life, and he'd go back to the military.

And then he thought of her kiss, the way she'd been so hungry for him that she'd knocked him off his feet. Even now he wanted to shudder with how difficult it had been to resist pulling off her clothes and giving in to something he'd dreamed about for what seemed like a lifetime.

But he never wanted to be another man she regretted. And if she knew everything about him, she would push him away.

After dinner, Julia seemed in no hurry to leave, and he understood her reluctance to be alone with him again. She talked to Lucy and Florence, and he watched with amusement as a little rivalry for the young constable's attention sprang up between the two maids. The girls mentioned the annual harvest dance Sam remembered from his childhood, and how it would take place only days from now. His family always attended in force—could he find a good excuse not to? Julia had never gone to the event as a young girl. How could she possibly attend masquerading as a boy?

The staff began to take their leave. Most had duties to finish up for the night, and he knew Lucy would be turning down their beds and filling their pitchers with hot water.

With the maids gone, Julia briefly met his gaze, then hurriedly looked away as she said her good nights. Sam followed at a slower pace, letting her have the time she needed.

As night overtook the big old house, the rooms grew quiet, solemn, depressing. He imagined a little girl living here with no love or warmth from her family. He thought of his own family, of Lucy, who'd tried to make Julia feel better so long ago; Lucy, who during her interview defended her long-lost brother Sam because she thought she still knew him.

He went into his bedroom first and hung his coat in the wardrobe. He found yesterday's shirt and trousers perfectly pressed and waiting for him. The thought of Lucy taking care of him brought a reluctant smile. Then he looked at the sitting room door, and his smile died. He didn't want to go to bed like this, full of awkwardness because he and Julia had shared things deeper than a kiss.

He opened the door and found her standing by the window. She faced him with determination, as if trying to be brave. She looked thin and sad. Something inside him softened.

He stayed across the room. "How are you?"

"I'm all right—angry, but all right."

"Angry at who?"

"My brother, of course."

Sam didn't know he'd been holding his breath.

She let out her own sigh. "It's not like he treated me well or was my favorite brother."

"But he was your only brother."

Her glance was brief, penetrating, then she looked away. "And I'll deal with my grief and anger my own way. Mostly by making sure he pays for what he's done to everyone, to both of us."

"You can count on me."

This time her gaze caught him and stayed, softening, and beneath the masculine garments and the cosmetics, she was all woman again. "Forgive me," she said.

"Forgive you?" he echoed stupidly. "For what?"

"For making you uncomfortable this afternoon when I—when I tried to—" She broke off, shaking her head. "It was selfish of me." She held up both hands when he would have spoken. "You've told me that you left here because of me, fourteen years ago. You can't possibly welcome such behavior. It made you uncomfortable again, just like my feelings for you did so long ago. You should have explained it all to me before."

He closed his eyes and rubbed the bridge of his nose. "You still don't understand."

Though he wanted to keep a whole room between them, he motioned her to the window and joined her there. He lowered his voice, wishing he didn't have to look into her face, still so beautiful to him under the lifeless hair and shadowed cosmetics. "I should have been specific about my reasons for leaving. I never wanted to be a gardener, and I knew if I stayed, I would have disappointed my father by refusing his profession."

"But you said it was about me," she whispered, looking at his chin and not his eyes.

"Partly, yes."

"I followed you everywhere, made you so uncomfortable."

"Not for the reasons you think. You were only responding to my inability to stay away from you. As you became a woman, I developed this . . . *fascination* for you that I couldn't put aside. I guess my brother Henry used the right word."

Now she stared at him with her blue eyes so intense that he wished she'd look away.

"It wasn't right," he continued. "I was twenty, and you were just becoming a young woman, with the promise of a bright future ahead of you. If I had stayed, I would have had a gardener's cottage, and no name to offer any woman of the gentry."

"I didn't want—"

"Stop. Don't do this. The past is done, and I did it all for a good reason. I found another life, so I made the right decision in the end."

But he couldn't tell her how he still yearned for her. He wouldn't have her accepting less than the birthright she was entitled to. And he was no longer that innocent man, not after everything he'd had to do in the army—not after the way he'd relished it all.

Julia struggled to understand everything Sam was saying. He'd left because she was too young, and above him socially? Then why was he so distant with her now? She well remembered how disappointed he'd been with her behavior in Afghanistan. Her recklessness was most of the reason they were in this mess. How could she expect him to put that behind him? The memories of a young man's emotions were still there, but the older man in him had changed.

It hurt, finally knowing that maybe once upon a time he might have returned her feelings.

And once upon a time she'd wanted adventure, to travel halfway around the world to find it. She didn't want that anymore. She couldn't bear the thought of returning to India, where the memories would be too difficult. She wanted her own family, and Sam wanted his life in the military. She would never follow another man across the world again. She had given up such impulsiveness.

But he stood there looking at her, a good man who wanted to make sure she was all right. She couldn't bear this anymore.

"Good night," she said quietly, and went to her own room.

When she was finally in bed, she stared at the ceiling, letting her silent tears dampen her pillow.

"You most certainly may not review the estate account books." Mr. Rutherford's prominent nose rose swiftly into the air as he gave them each an appalled look. "There would be nothing in there to help you investigate Miss Reed."

Julia sighed as their interview with Mr. Rutherford the steward—the caretaker of the entire estate—proved difficult. He had only returned that morning from London.

He had nothing valuable to contribute to their investigation. She almost felt like doodling as she listened to him drone on about the exemplary character of the Reed family, their long association with this land, and his own family's history with them.

"But if Miss Reed became a traitor because of

lack of finances," Sam said, "this would be a good reason to look at the books."

"Miss Reed received the same allowance she always had, and it was more than generous. She would have had a home here, since it seemed obvious she would never marry."

Julia clenched her fist in her lap. Much as she might have thought the same thing on occasion, she didn't like to hear it so coldly stated.

Mr. Rutherford suddenly turned to her, and she forced a competent, "Yes, sir?"

"Do fetch me a pot of hot tea, Constable. I fear my throat is parched."

Before Sam could object, she shot to her feet. "Of course, Mr. Rutherford. I'll return shortly." Better to play the part of servant than listen to this windbag.

Determined to take her time, she went out the door and into the drawing room. Florence was there, on her hands and knees brushing coal dust from the hearth grate. Julia only nodded and kept on going, casually glancing out each window as she passed.

There was a rider entering through the front gate, and she paid little attention until she reached the next window. Then something about the man caught her eye. He was passing the fountain when she realized that he was wearing the exact uniform Sam was.

He was a constable from Leeds.

For a moment she froze, her heart pounding,

wondering whom to alert first. It would take too long to extricate Sam from Mr. Rutherford without arousing the steward's suspicions. She had to go for Frances herself.

Walking quickly, she entered the entrance hall, and to her dismay, one of the matching footman hovered there. He would be the first to answer the door, the first to inform the new constable that—surprise—Leeds already had two constables here!

It was almost like she was back in jail again, smelling the odor, lying in damp bedding. She couldn't let that happen.

"Harold," she called, glad to have remembered his name. "Could you do me the favor of fetchin' a pot of tea for Mr. Rutherford? He's in the library with Constable Seabrook."

Once the footman had been dispatched, she picked up her pace and followed him down the corridor leading to the servants' wing. She veered off and, after a hasty knock at Frances's sitting room, found the housekeeper at her small desk, the household account book spread before her.

Frances glanced up, frowning at the disruption, but she half stood when she saw Julia.

Julia shut the door behind her. "You have to answer the front door," she said, breathing fast. "A Leeds constable is almost at the portico."

"Oh, heavens," Frances said, darting around the desk.

"Sam told you what to say?"

Frances gave a nervous nod and followed her down the corridor. They arrived back in the entrance hall as the door knocker echoed through the front of the house.

Frances smoothed her apron and took a deep breath, reaching for the door handle. Julia ducked into the drawing room and pressed herself against the wall. Florence, working hard down at the far end of the room, didn't notice her.

Julia held her breath as she heard Frances formally greet the visitor by name.

"Is General Reed at home, Mrs. Cooper?"

"He is in London, sir. May I help you?"

"Just checking up on our investigation of Miss Julia Reed. Has she turned up on the estate?"

"Indeed no, sir. As you requested, I would have sent word to you immediately."

The constable seemed satisfied with that, as if it were all just a formality. When Frances offered him refreshment, he gladly accepted, though asked her if she would pack her generous offer for the road. Thank God it was too early for luncheon.

But this meant that he'd be alone in the hall for any wandering servant to pass by and be questioned. And there was nothing else Frances could do without attracting suspicion.

The constable was right there, on the other side of the wall from Julia. Should she go in and talk to him? After all, she was not dressed in a uniform.

Harold the footman entered the drawing room by the far door. He stopped to talk to Florence amiably, then saw Julia and looked shaken. Julia walked to intercept him, and before she could even speak, Harold glanced at Florence again and wetted his lips.

"Constable, please don't say ye saw Flo and me talkin'. Mr. Jenkins might have me job. Flo's ma and my ma are friends, and . . ."

The poor young man rattled off one excuse after another, until Julia was certain that there was a forbidden romance going on. She frankly didn't care, as long as Harold wasn't going to the entrance hall. She tried to project understanding and camaraderie, all the while straining to hear what was going on in the hall.

She thought she saw movement out of the corner of her eye, and glanced over her shoulder in time to see Frances handing the constable a package. As he tipped his top hat to her and left, Julia went weak with relief.

"Are—are ye feelin' all right, Constable?" Harold suddenly asked.

She gave him a tight-lipped smile. "Certainly. But I must return to the library. Don't worry, it's not my place to say anythin' about what happened here."

They both looked relieved as she hurried

away. The library door was open, and a kitchen maid was just setting a tea tray on a table inside. Julia managed to catch Sam's eye, and he excused himself for a moment as Mr. Rutherford prepared his tea.

Once the kitchen maid had left, Julia motioned Sam farther down the corridor. "A constable was just here."

His eyes hardened. "We have to get Mrs. Cooper."

There was a look about his face that Julia had only seen when they'd been attacked on the road. It made him look like a stranger.

"I found her. She took care of it."

"And he spoke to no one else?"

She shook her head.

"Excellent work, Fitzjames. But now I have to make sure he leaves. Ask Rutherford about Mrs. Hume. That was the only thing we had left to discuss."

She felt a jolt of pleasure that he trusted her enough to handle an interview alone. And then he was hurrying toward the back of the house.

Sam's long stride was another man's run. His every sense was honed on what the constable might be doing. Had he left immediately, or was he even now talking to a stray groom?

He reached the terrace through the conservatory and headed for the stables. Nodding to Tom, the old groom, he slipped a halter on his horse and vaulted up on him bareback.

Tom gaped at him. "Surely ye have time for a saddle, Constable."

"He needs to occasionally be ridden like this," Sam called, ducking as he guided the horse out of the stables. "It helps in emergencies."

By the time he reached the front of the manor, the constable and his horse were past the front gate, heading down the road west toward Rotherham.

Outside the estate, Sam disappeared into the beginning of the trees, parallel to the road. He could catch glimpses of the constable's white trousers through the greenery. Sam felt no emotion, just a single-minded obsession with his target. Nothing intruded, not terrain, not compassion, not scruples. Past each tree, the man's uniform made a perfect target. Sam's pistol was in his pocket, where he always kept it. All he cared about was that this one man was a threat to Julia, that the constable could return anytime and discover them. If this were an Eastern country, Sam could wield justice himself.

Yet why not? The farther they got from Hopewell Manor, the more he considered disposing of the man permanently. The constable could have seen something suspicious and would report it to his superiors. It was better not to take a chance—

And then Sam felt the comfortable grip of his pistol, and he had no memory of reaching for it.

Chapter 15

A shock went through Sam as he realized what he had been contemplating. He brought his horse to a stop, letting the constable plod slowly on his way, out of sight.

Sam had almost killed him, regardless of the fact that this was not a war, that the constable was an innocent man doing his job. The police force would have sent another constable, prompting an even bigger investigation. He dropped the pistol back into his pocket as if it burned him.

The trees were still close around him, and the woods seemed strangely silent. Sam realized he hadn't left the manor since he was attacked in the gardens. He turned his horse about, looking all around him, his hand on the pistol again. He had no sensation of being followed.

Yet he'd left Julia alone. He kicked his horse into a trot until the trees thinned and fell away behind him, then he increased to a gallop.

When he entered the gates to the estate, his brother Henry was there, obviously waiting for him. Sam didn't want to talk to anyone, not when he was this rattled by what had almost happened with the constable, and by the thought of Julia alone, but he had no choice. He swung down off the horse and met Henry's worried gaze, then looked around to see that they were unobserved.

"Did you see anyone near the manor?" Sam asked.

Henry looked taken aback. "Are you worried about your attacker in broad daylight?"

"Julia is alone in there."

"She's not alone; she has the entire staff." Henry glanced at the horse. "Bareback?"

Sam shrugged. "It's always good for a horse to learn to accept commands under any situation. Considering I bought the animal with little time to examine him, he functioned well."

Henry nodded, but was obviously skeptical. "How goes the investigation?"

"Slow. I do have one question for you, though—have you ever seen evidence that the grounds were disturbed in an unusual way?

And I don't mean someone just prowling about."

His brother looked at him blankly. "You mean as if someone besides me or my men had been digging?"

Sam nodded.

"I can't think of an incidence—and you know how particular I am about my work."

There was an uncomfortable silence between the brothers, and Sam knew it was because he was so distracted.

"It's remarkable how much Julia looks like a young man," Henry said. "The way she holds her shoulders, the length of her stride—"

"Keep your voice down, please."

Henry rolled his eyes.

"I trained her as well as I was able to," Sam explained.

"Trained her?"

"We camped on our way here from Rotherham. That's where I showed her how to transform herself."

"You've had to spend a lot of time with her," Henry said slowly.

"Almost a week now." He gave his brother a look that would have cowed any soldier under his command.

Henry only cocked his head. "I used to try and keep you away from her. Don't you remember?"

"It was a lifetime ago. And this is not the same thing at all. She needs my help."

"That's exactly what you said all those years ago."

Sam didn't need to be interrogated by his own brother. His body was still primed for combat, his blood pumping through his veins as if he would need to attack someone to make these feelings go away. Gathering the reins of his control was an exercise he obviously needed. He took a deep breath and strove for tranquillity.

Henry didn't let him speak. "Just because she's running from the law doesn't mean she's brought down to our station."

Sam hated hearing his own thoughts flung back at him. "I know that," he said between gritted teeth. "Henry, I know what I am, and I don't need you to remind me. I have an assignment to do here, and when I'm done, I'll return to my command in India."

"Does she know that?"

"Yes." Or did he only assume that?

Henry sighed and lifted off his hat to run a hand through his damp hair. "I seem to have returned to the part of the worried, careful brother. I hope I'm not offending you."

"You're not. It seems strange to have someone worry about me again."

Henry looked at him as if he saw too much. "Then you've been alone too long, Constable. You've always had people worry about you. Come to dinner."

"No."

"My wife and children don't know you."

"But isn't Ma living with you?"

Henry slowly nodded. "You look very different with the beard."

"But it still has traces of the Sherryngton red. Thank you, but I must decline. I have to get back to the house."

"I'll take the horse around for you." Henry seemed hesitant, frustrated, and sad.

And there was nothing Sam could do about it. He accepted the gesture of peace, and headed down the path to the portico. Until speaking to Henry, he'd been successful forgetting that his mother lived nearby. He'd concentrated on Julia and their life-and-death problems.

But Henry was right—he'd been alone too long.

"Constable Fitzjames?"

Julia was in the library, making notes about her conversation with Mr. Rutherford, when Sam called her name from the hall.

"Yes, sir!"

He entered and closed the door, his expression betraying a moment's relief, then becoming blank. He looked . . . pale.

She came around the desk and approached him, saying softly, "Is everything all right?"

He stiffened, and she could have sworn he wanted to take a step back. A tension vibrated in him that she'd never noticed before.

"The constable was headed back for Rotherham. I let him go." His voice was low, calm—but wrong.

"Why . . . of course you did," she said in confusion. She didn't understand what was going on beneath the surface of his forced composure, but for once she didn't think it was because of her.

"He might return."

"And we'll deal with it if it happens," she answered. "Is . . . something else wrong? Did you see our assailant?"

He took a sudden, deep breath, and some of the palpable strain drained away. He attempted a smile. "No, though I kept watch for him. So how did the rest of the interview go with Rutherford?"

Julia smiled, finally letting her excitement show. "I learned something interesting. Mr. Rutherford let slip that Lewis had questioned him about Mrs. Hume before her death."

Sam perched on the edge of the desk and nodded his encouragement. "What kind of questions did Lewis ask?"

"About Mrs. Hume's health, her stamina, even her daily habits. That must be how he knew that it wouldn't be a total shock should she die in the middle of the night."

"So, the good steward was helpful after all," he said. "And of course his account books will be helpful, too."

She frowned. "But he said we couldn't look at them."

"He doesn't sleep in his office, does he?"

Sam grinned, and with that beard he reminded her of a pirate following clues to his chest of gold doubloons.

Walking closer to him, she smiled, then lowered her voice. "When do we sneak in?"

"*I* sneak in tonight."

"I'm coming, too."

He arched an eyebrow, deliberately looking her up and down as if judging her worth. This tension that she still sensed beneath the surface made him seem . . . dangerous.

God help her, but it was exciting. She quickly reminded herself of her vow to behave.

He said, "I can be quicker, quieter without you."

"We need to stay together. You said so yourself. I just can't lie snug in my bed and let you take all the risks."

Something in his face had changed when she'd said the word "bed."

"These are my family account books," she hurriedly continued. "Unless you plan on bringing them back to our room—"

"We can't risk that."

"Then I'm coming with you. We can read twice as many books together."

He remained silent as he debated. She watched his face; he watched hers. When he finally nodded, she was glad to step away, feeling a lingering heat as if she'd been scorched.

* * *

They finished the last of the interviews just before dinner, and Sam was relieved. He'd suspected Mr. Rutherford might be the only useful subject that day, and he'd been right. A waste of an afternoon, but it had been necessary to keep the staff compliant.

And it had forced his churning emotions back into hiding, where they belonged.

An evening spent with the servants was relaxing, but he retired early, claiming fatigue. Julia's wide gaze followed him out, and he knew with amusement that it might look strange should she constantly leave with him. And besides, she was the center of interest between Lucy and Florence.

An hour later, he heard the sitting room door slam, then an insistent knock on his own bedroom door. He pulled on his trousers and shirt and answered it.

"You must do something about Lucy," Julia said in a soft, angry voice. "And Florence—and Harold!"

Her glance found the open collar revealing his bare chest, and he pulled the edges of his shirt together.

"What did they all do?"

"Lucy is courting me openly, Florence is egging her on with competition just to be funny, and Harold—Harold thinks I'm stealing his girl!"

Sam closed his mouth before his laughter escaped. When he had himself under control, he murmured, "Harold the footman?"

"Who else? The staff isn't supposed to fraternize—"

"That I remember," he said dryly.

She ignored him. "I saw Harold and Florence briefly talk to one another in the drawing room this morning, and you'd think they were worried about execution, the way Harold tried to explain how innocent everything was."

"They could lose their positions," he said seriously.

"I know, I know." She rolled her eyes. "I don't mean to make light of their situation. But Lucy is starting to follow me through the halls!"

"There isn't much I can do about it."

"Tell Frances!"

"What should Frances say to Lucy: 'Constable Fitzjames is a woman'?"

Julia threw up her hands and strode to the window, motioning for him impatiently. He followed, his bare feet sinking into the soft carpet.

"Calm down," he said.

"Lucy expects me to dance with her, and I don't even know the man's steps!"

"Is the harvest dance where it always was?"

"Outside on the back lawn, if the weather cooperates. They have plans for bonfires and musicians and everything."

"Think Lucy will want to sneak you away for a romantic walk?"

She pushed him out of the way and went to her own bedroom. Trying to erase his smile, he held the door when she would have closed it in his face. "Do you think you can handle her for a while longer? She doesn't seem the type to make advances."

She pushed hard on the door, but he propped it open with his foot.

"I'm sorry I said anything at all!" she said.

Forgetting himself, he pushed harder and she stumbled away.

"You'd better leave." Her hands went to her coat buttons. "Or I'm going to start taking things off, and you know how much that will annoy you."

He realized the dangerous game they were playing just in time. He forced his expression to sober. "I'll wake you at two in the morning."

"You must promise. I swear, I'll sleep on your floor if I think you'll leave me behind."

He had a sudden image of the thick carpet in front of the fireplace in his room—and her stretched out on it, naked. He quickly headed for the door.

"I promise."

Sam was awakened from a light sleep by an unusual sound. He sat upright and strained his ears to listen, but heard nothing from the sitting room or Julia's bedroom.

Then he heard it again, a shower of something against the window. It was too hard to be rain. He approached the window and stood to the side, easing the draperies away by mere inches. This time he realized it was a handful of pebbles. Someone was obviously trying to get his attention, but he couldn't imagine it being Henry.

One part of him just wanted to ignore it and frustrate the midnight caller. But the other part of him wanted to let the man know in no uncertain terms that his attempts to lure them outside weren't working.

From the side, he eased his head next to the window and looked down, but he could see nothing. Very slowly, he slid the lock back and pressed open the glass. If the man had scaled the wall, Sam was going to make sure he had a sudden, long fall to the ground.

He peered slowly over the edge, but there was no one clinging to the wall. He had just a moment's warning, a glitter of metal in the moonlight, and he backed away as a knife embedded itself in the wooden sill. He removed it and leaned out the window to toss it back, but all he heard was the dwindling sound of running feet.

He closed and locked the window, then got dressed in the dark. He woke Julia and didn't bother to tell her what had happened. She didn't need the added frustration.

At night, and without candles to light their way, the corridors were pitch-black but for the occasional pale moonlight glimpsed through an open door. One of the footmen passed nearby carrying an oil lamp, but they were able to avoid him. Sam didn't know where the hell he was, and had to rely on Julia to lead him. He had a glimpse of her face with its I-told-you-so expression, but graciously, she said nothing.

After he'd bumped into her twice, she reached back and firmly took his hand. Her skin was warm, dry, and her fingers long. She would know just how to touch—

He forced himself to pay attention to her signals: the tightened grip when she wanted him to stop, and the tug as she moved forward. They hugged walls and crept down the edge of the stairs using the main staircase.

The steward's office was next door to the housekeeper's room, and this was where things got tricky. Sam wouldn't put it past Frances to put herself in charge of the rotation of the patrolling footmen. They had to be very quiet.

As Julia stopped in front of the correct door, he heard her fumbling with the handle. He could have told her it would be locked. Gently pushing her aside, he inserted the key, and the door opened soundlessly. Maybe he should have told her he'd "borrowed" Frances's keys that evening, experimented with them to find the passkey, then put the ring back with Frances none the wiser.

He closed the door behind them and felt his way to the two windows which looked out over the garden. Both sets of draperies were closed. He took a candle, candle holder, and a match from his pocket, and soon there was a small, cheery light on the desk.

Julia just stared at him with a stunned expression.

He'd tell her later that a man like Rutherford would notice if his personal candles were burned lower than he'd left them.

The account books lined a shelf behind the desk, and Sam pulled out the most recent one and sat down in the desk chair to read it. She took the next one, then knelt on the floor beside him to use the candlelight.

As he paged through the book, perusing columns of figures, he grew more and more disheartened by the fact that there were regular small deposits being made every month or so, rather than one large, suspicious amount. He hadn't thought Lewis would be stupid enough to put all his money in at once, but a part of him had hoped Lewis would be careless once or twice.

Julia looked discouraged as she came to the same conclusion.

It would be pointless to travel to London to

Lewis's bank itself. Sam was a wanted man, and without some other solid proof, no judge was going to let him open a military hero's accounts to scrutiny—not to mention the fact that Sam would be arrested before he got near a judge. He reminded himself that he'd known the account books would probably not help him, but it didn't stop the frustration burning a hole in his gut. Every day without solid evidence was a day closer to them being captured and executed. This day was only proving how useless he'd been to Julia.

So now he had to find the money itself, and without a clue, what would he do—dig up every inch of the garden? That would take years. Search every inch of the house, rip holes in the walls? Maybe weeks of effort. And that was if no one stopped them.

For the first time, he wondered if he could really save Julia.

Then he heard the sound of stones against the window.

Julia's head came up in shock, and he held a finger to his lips and blew out the candle. She put her hand on his thigh, and he thought she might be trembling. He put his own hand over hers, then leaned down until her hair tickled his lips.

"He's just taunting us," he whispered. "He won't be foolish enough to try to break in."

"Where are the grooms assigned to watch the grounds?"

"Hopefully walking on the far side of the manor out of danger. Just wait."

Sure enough, no pebbles were thrown at Rutherford's window again, although Sam thought he heard some land on another window farther down the wing. Then there was silence.

Sam let Julia lead him back to their suite, where he was forced to tell her that their assailant had already tried this tactic earlier. Though he reassured her enough so that she went to her own bed, he knew he wouldn't be able to sleep. Despair and anger warred inside him, and after the day's events, he needed some form of outlet.

Chapter 16

Julia lay in bed, eyes aching because she couldn't keep them closed. She should sleep—she *needed* to sleep—but she couldn't forget the fact that they'd lost a major chance to prove Lewis guilty.

The money was somewhere; she had to keep remembering that. But Sam seemed more upset than she was. He'd acted differently from the moment he'd followed that Leeds constable, but she couldn't imagine what had happened.

When at least an hour had passed, she decided to find the book she'd left in the sitting room. At least it would keep her mind occupied. She lit her candle and wandered into the next room, ignoring the window, below which an enemy waited. More than once, her eyes went to Sam's closed door. It drew her until she finally surrendered, and with a sigh, she leaned her head against it, knowing it was the only way to be near him.

But she heard nothing.

Before she could think too much, she turned the knob and peeked in.

The bed was empty.

She resisted the urge to slam the door in frustration. Had he actually gone back to Rutherford's office without telling her?

She quickly bound her breasts and pulled her shirt, trousers, and boots back on. After tucking her hair back under her hat, she blew the candle out and fumbled with her door. Of course, she'd locked it. She found the key, then went off on her mission to find Sam. When she met up with Harold the footman in a dark corridor, looking groggy and stumbling, she sent him to bed, promising to take over for the last hour of his shift.

Sam wasn't in Rutherford's office, and Frances's room was silent. The kitchen was empty, even the library, where he might have worked so as not to disturb her. Surely he wouldn't have gone to visit his brother, not with their attacker lurking on the grounds waiting for his chance to strike.

During a last sweep through the family wing,

she heard an unfamiliar sound, like . . . something soft being struck. She followed the noise down a corridor and found herself at the back of the house, near the conservatory. She could smell the damp earth and the mingled scents of various flowers, and hear the whisper of leaves brushing against each other.

The thumping sound was coming from inside. Stepping through the door, she finally saw the glow of a single candle in the far corner. It cast shadows of ferns and blossoms in exaggeration upon the dark glass walls. Cautiously, she followed the stone path.

As she got closer, the thumps became more rapid, and she noticed a faint creaking. Before turning the last curve of the path, she ducked behind a potted palm tree and squatted down, peering past the trunk. This was an overgrown corner of the conservatory, where vines climbed even the glass, acting like a wall against the outside world.

A rope hung from the ceiling, all but concealed by ivy curling all the way up. A heavy sack hung from the end, swinging out in an arc, then back.

Sam, his torso bare, threw his weight behind a punch that sent the sack creaking away.

Julia knew she should tell him that she was there. But she kept silent, watching him until she almost forgot to breathe.

He held his arms bent in front of him, as if

protecting his chest from an opponent. His skin glistened with perspiration, and his hair hung in damp curls at his neck. His body was smooth and curved with muscle, from the width of his back to the taut indentations down his stomach. She held her hands clenched tight in her lap, and below that, she ached between her thighs, as if her body were trying to force her to go to him.

He watched the swing of the sack, seemed to time his punches, and then threw a flurry of hits that made his muscles do incredible things. She stared at his face in profile, his brows lowered angrily, his mouth set in a firm line, though betraying an occasional grimace when he struck the sack hard. His eyes told her that this wasn't just an attempt to work himself into exhaustion. They were full of frustration and anger and anguish—

And despair?

She stepped out onto the path and went toward him. He was partially turned away, and with a low grunt he launched another punch that sent the sack away. He saw her out of the corner of his eye and caught the sack when it would have slammed back into him.

"Sam."

She whispered his name, wanting to comfort him, to take away the pain, to tell him he was doing his best and that was all she needed. Without skirts, she was able to come too close to him, and suddenly her need to console him transformed into another need.

He was breathing heavily, his nostrils flared, his eyes full of a darkness she didn't understand. There was so much bare skin before her, and she wanted to touch him. Her hands reached out and this time he didn't move away, just closed his eyes when she touched his chest and let her hands slide up and across his shoulders.

He was a man, and she knew what he needed—what she wanted. In this dark, earthy room, there was nothing but them, two people on the edge of disaster, their normal worlds gone but for each other.

She whispered his name again, let her hands slide up into his hair. She pressed herself full against him, and he groaned as he enveloped her in a hard embrace.

"Julia."

Her name on his lips was full of a need she'd always wanted to hear. It drove away the last of her caution. She pulled his head down and kissed him with all the urgency that consumed her, touching his skin everywhere she could reach. His big hands held her to him; his mouth claimed hers. Each swirl of his tongue against hers made her shudder and press herself harder against him. Then he kissed her cheeks, her chin, her neck just below her ear. With his teeth he tugged at her earlobe, and she dropped her head back, baring her throat for the taking. Every exploration of his lips and tongue seemed like uncharted territory, like no man had ever tasted her skin or made her feel so languid with desire. She felt new and whole just for Sam.

"We shouldn't do this," he murmured against the hollow at the base of her throat. "We'll regret it by the light of day."

"Maybe *you* will," she breathed, dangling in his grasp, clasping his head to her chest, "but I won't."

And it was true. She desperately wanted him to need her as she needed him. *Using* each other was not a term that even made sense between them.

She put her hands between their bodies and began to unbutton her shirt. His mouth followed the open path, kissing, licking. After the last button, she pulled the shirt over her head and let him look at the white cloth which wound its way around her body and hid her from him. He met her eyes as he plucked the end of the binding. They stared at each other as he slowly unwound her, pulling the piece from behind her back each time around.

She could barely breathe as she watched her unveiling. Burying the last of doubts about her womanliness, she craved the passion that burned in his eyes for her. Just for her. She'd spent her life regretting that she would never see him like this, and now she wanted to treasure every moment, every sensation, as if it might be her last.

As the bindings seemed to go on forever, he suddenly yanked the rest down to her waist, and she thrilled at his impatience as he pulled it off her and flung it to the floor. Now she was as naked from the waist up as he was.

He breathed her name with a reverence that made her moan. "Such beauty," he murmured, then pulled her backward, deeper between the ferns. The leaves trailed along her sensitive skin like fingers.

They reached a bench she'd long forgotten was hidden here. He sat back and pulled her onto his lap, straddling him. She hugged him to her, felt his mouth between her breasts, his hands slide up over her rib cage to cup her gently. His palms teased her nipples to hardness, then his fingers followed, pulling, flicking, rubbing. Her head fell back as she surrendered to the feelings that swamped her, that made her shiver, that made her full and hot where she straddled him. She wrapped her legs around his waist, and though she pressed hard against him, it only made her ache for what she knew would happen.

And then his mouth covered one breast, taking it all inside with a suction that had her squirming against him, gasping.

"I've wanted this for so long," she whispered, pressing kisses to his hair.

He didn't answer; instead he licked her nipple in a slow circular motion, then moved from one breast to the other until she was breathless, mindless, unaware of anything but him.

She found herself on her back on the bench, with Sam hovering over her with urgency and a single-minded determination. His hands were trembling as he tried to undo her trouser buttons, and she laughed softly and started to help. Then she felt his fingers against her belly, feathering soft caresses lower, lower . . . she arched her back off the bench, wanting more—

"Who's there?" a woman's voice called from across the conservatory.

Sam froze, his hand inside Julia's trousers, close to the heaven he'd always imagined. His wide eyes met hers for the briefest instant before she sat up and pulled away from him.

Damn.

"I know someone's here. Harold? Florence?"

It was Frances. Was she tracking stray lovers in the middle of the night? As Sam searched for his shirt, he realized the sky outside the tall windows was beginning to look less black. Damn.

Julia just stared at him, making no attempt to cover her perfect body. "Send her away," she whispered.

He stopped his search behind a fern and gaped at her. "What?"

"I said—"

"Never mind. Of course. Damn, I can't find my shirt. Wait right here."

Wearing a secret smile that did strange things to his body, Julia leaned back on the bench. Her nipples were hard, the color of pale pink sunsets. She kicked her legs gently, and something about her in trousers and boots seemed terribly erotic.

Damn his sister!

"Blast the shirt. I'll be right back." He picked up his coat and held it strategically in front of him.

He pushed past the ferns back onto the path and came around a curve to find Frances coming toward him, carrying a candle. She stopped, her face astonished, and put her hand on her hip.

"Sam! I thought I was chasing Florence." She looked at his bare chest suspiciously.

"Wherever Florence is, she's not here. You've interrupted my boxing."

"Boxing! You mean prizefighting? You compete in such a barbaric sport?"

"I only use it for training, to keep myself ready to fight."

Again she looked about suspiciously. "How are you practicing boxing in a conservatory? I can barely see anything."

"I have a candle back there for light. Years ago, Lewis hung a sack stuffed with grain from the ceiling." With his thumb, he gestured randomly over his shoulder, hoping she didn't want to investigate. "It's hard to see, with all the ivy climbing up it. I couldn't sleep, so I came to exercise."

For several minutes, she didn't say anything, staring at him with eyes very like his mother's. Eyes that usually saw guilt.

"Sam Sherryngton, I've no time to figure out what you're up to. I have to save Florence and Harold from losing their positions here. But I spoke to Henry, and we're both worried about you and Miss Reed."

He opened his mouth, but she simply held up her hand.

"I don't want to hear it! And you're not a man I can say I truly know and understand anymore. But don't confuse the past with the present. Just be careful where Miss Reed is concerned."

He smiled. "You're a good sister, Frances. You have been incredible and brave through all of this."

She only harrumphed. "We'll see what Harold and Florence think about me when I'm done with them. Now get going."

"I have to put away my equipment first. Good night." He started back down the path, glancing over his shoulder until he was certain Frances had left the conservatory. He slowed down as he thought about Julia, how she'd probably be dressed by now and would soon be hurrying after Frances. And she'd be smart to flee him, with this crazy wildness lurking inside him. He might hurt her with his passion.

He pushed his way through the ferns and stopped dead. Julia reclined on the bench, wearing only an inviting smile. One long leg was bent slightly, and her head rested on her arm. Her skin was warm cream by candlelight, and between her thighs her hair was the palest blond. His mouth went dry; his every rational thought fled with her knowing smile.

She held out a hand to him, and for just a moment he remembered his sister's warning to be careful. But he pushed that thought away, unable to refuse what Julia offered. He stripped off the rest of his clothing, watched her smile deepen with relief. Then he touched her, letting his hands do what his eyes had only done, learning every part of her body. Those long thighs, lean and muscled from her days spent riding; the curve of her buttocks pressed flat to the bench; her rib cage with her breasts perched atop like delicate fruit ripe for his taking.

And he wanted to take her, to enter her swiftly, to claim her if only for this one night. His blood pounded in his ears, his chest heaved with the effort of restraint.

But this was Julia, lost in her few relationships with men, believing herself unworthy of true love and happiness. And he couldn't tell her he loved her, though he did, though he always had. It would only hurt her in the end. He didn't want her pitying him when they had to part.

So he showed her what he felt with his mouth,

with his hands. His tongue memorized the taste of her skin; his fingers worshipped its silky softness. She responded to everything he did with delicate sighs, delightful gasps, and quiet moans. When he parted her thighs, she let him do as he wished, with no maidenly shyness when he stroked her and delved deeper. She was wet for him, and the satisfaction he felt was primal, older than time. He parted her thighs farther, letting one rest on his shoulder so he could get even closer. When he kissed her inner thigh, he felt her languidness revert to tension.

Julia had thought herself experienced, earthy, aware of the sensual relationship between men and women. But with Sam's mouth so high up her thigh, she was suddenly aware that maybe she didn't know everything. She wanted to stop him—and she wickedly wished he would do whatever he wanted.

He stroked her again with his fingers, parting her flesh, making her back arch with renewed, mounting excitement.

And then he kissed her there, and she covered her mouth before her cries could echo through the room. His tongue probed and circled and teased, until her every sense was consumed and exploded, shaking her, shattering her.

He lifted her up, sitting on the bench himself, and once again spread her legs so that she straddled him. But this time they were naked, and his erection was hard between her thighs and his belly. She rocked against him, feeling the length of his penis, watching his face as he shuddered with control.

And then he was kissing her hard, his tongue tasting like her, his breath a whisper of her name. She let her hands explore him, feeling the trembling of his muscles when she kneaded his chest, caressed his nipples, and then took his penis in her hands to absorb its heat and strength.

"Inside me," she said against his mouth. "I want to be part of you."

She lifted herself up and positioned him, and their joining was a final fulfillment. He made her whole in a way she'd never been before, with a sense of destiny. And then he moved and she was riding him, his every undulation touching deep inside her. His hands cupped her backside, his fingers brushing against the cleft between. He lifted her after each thrust, bringing her down faster and faster. She caressed his face, his shoulders, his chest, circling and teasing his nipples until his climax overtook him, his every muscle shuddering beneath her.

She folded him within her arms, waiting for their breathing to ease, their hearts to slow, her mind to function.

Kissing his brow, she held his head against her shoulder, feeling his sighing breath float across her skin and raise gooseflesh.

He looked up and stared at her. She couldn't read his eyes, didn't know whether he was full of regrets or satisfaction. On her part, there was only peace and contentment with the present. The future was not a part of this moment they'd shared.

"We have to hurry." He patted her backside, then set her on her feet. "The staff will be awake soon."

She went down on her hands and knees to look for his shirt, then turned to look back at him when he choked.

"Put some clothes on first," he said hoarsely.

She grinned, but there was no time to disobey him. She brought him his shirt and received a grateful kiss. Soon they were dressed, and the boxing sack tied back against the wall, hidden by foliage.

"You go first," she said, "just in case Frances is still about. You can distract her."

"Good thinking."

He kissed her, softer this time, protectively. She wanted to stay in the safety of his embrace, but she knew she could never recapture the peace. She watched him go, taking the candle with him, then turned away and leaned her head against a tree trunk. She didn't think about their enemy outside. Through the dense foliage, dawn was being heralded by a pale gray sky, signaling a new day.

And with it, another chance to make everything right.

Chapter 17

After just an hour's sleep, they took breakfast with the staff, and Julia noticed that Sam managed to put Harold between them on the bench. She didn't mind, because she preferred to think he was worried that his feelings for her might show. But as the day progressed, she couldn't help wondering. Sam avoided talking about what they'd shared together in the shadowy jungle of the conservatory.

They rode out to tour the rest of the estate, the list of tenants tucked in his pocket. Riding astride a horse showed her that she was tender from her exertions with Sam, so her mind was on their lovemaking whether she wanted to be reminded or not. But always she scanned the grounds, reassured to see farmers in their fields. Their assailant wouldn't dare attack with so many witnesses.

As she'd assumed, the tenants had rarely seen Lewis or her, and some didn't even know they'd returned home. The only good thing about the day was getting the chance to see how much had changed in ten years. Sometimes the countryside seemed foreign to her, after time spent steaming upriver through jungles in India, or on long rides across desert plains. Yet there was a quiet familiarity to the long dirt lanes lined with hedgerows.

In the afternoon, they stopped to eat their picnic luncheon on a hilltop overlooking much of the estate. In the distance, the sun winked off the windows of the manor, as if it were a jewel on display. She remembered solitary walks up this hill during her lonely girlhood. Now there was a new dirt road cut just below the hilltop, a shortcut between two small villages. Occasional travelers passed them, and she felt safe from harm.

She and Sam sat on the bench, this food between them—along with a tension she didn't know how to breach. The sun slid behind approaching clouds, and her mood along with it. She had to say *something*.

After swallowing a bite of her fried chicken,

she cleared her throat. "Your brother Henry had this bench built here for me."

Sam sipped his beer. "Why?"

"I used to walk here a lot, after . . . after everyone had gone."

"It's a long walk."

"I didn't have much else to do. Then I'd sit here and look out over Hopewell Manor, and see all the things I had, but which weren't really mine. Everything is Lewis's—everything but my body and my mind. Those I only give to whom I choose."

He slowly set the bottle back on the bench, and dropped his chin to his chest with a sigh. "But I played with your feelings," he said softly.

"No, you didn't."

"I lost control," he continued, as if he hadn't even heard her words.

"I seem to recall actively participating—in fact, initiating."

"I made unspoken promises to you."

She drew in a sharp breath, confused.

"It makes me no better than those men who seduced you."

Rising anger consumed her. "Do you think I let men have their way with me without my having any say in the matter? That I'm some sort of fragile innocent, guilty of no sin?"

"That's not what I—"

"It's what you implied, therefore it must be

what you think. Yes, my brother has betrayed me, but some of my foolish choices made that betrayal possible." She put her hand on his arm, turning him to look at her. "I live by my choices, Sam. And last night we chose each other for a brief moment of happiness."

"But it's not the beginning of something," he said quietly.

Those words hurt, but they weren't unexpected. He had spent his life keeping away from her, and one night wouldn't change that. "But it's not an ending, either."

"Maybe not now," he said, gripping her hand between his, "but you know it will be, Julia. When you're back to your rightful place, and when I am, too, things will have to be different between us."

"Things are already different. Why must you believe it will make things worse? Can't you enjoy what we have together, here and now?"

"I feel like I'm using you for a brief pleasure that will only cause you pain when I'm gone."

"I don't think we're using each other, not when we're open about the truth. We're not trying to take something away from each other—we're trying to give."

He let go of her and stood up. "And the truth is, you're still seeing me as the boy you used to know. I've changed—Afghanistan changed me."

"Then why go back there?"

Sam couldn't look at her. Spread out around

them was everything her family owned—
including the little plot of land he'd once called
home. Except for the people here, it no longer
felt like home. Home was back in Asia, in the
countries where his best skills could be of some
value. Here, what could he do with these feelings of justice denied, this need to take the law
into his own hands and create the result he
wanted?

He was frightened of himself. How would he
feel, what would he do, when he could no longer
have her? When she was back on the other side
of a line no society woman could cross? No com-
mon soldier could cross, either.

But she was waiting patiently for an answer,
and all he could say was, "I have to return. I have
a duty to my country—and I belong there, not
here."

Her eyes were large with hurt, and it was like
a knife to his chest to know he had made her feel
this way. But then she pressed her lips together
and stood up to face him.

"Sam, for whatever reason, you're holding
something back from me."

He kept his face impassive and said nothing.

"I accept that. But right now, we exist together
outside normal law, outside respectability. You
make me feel . . . alive, and full of hope that together we can uncover the truth, and prove ourselves to the rest of society. I don't want your
guilt, and it's too soon for regret. Just promise

me to take things as they happen, and to know that I am willing to live by that."

She was trying to absolve him of guilt, and she didn't understand how deeply she would have to go. But he couldn't keep turning her away, hurting her even more than he already had. He loved her too much for that.

"I promise."

By the end of the day, they'd finished interviewing the tenants, and discovered nothing new. Sam hadn't expected much, but he still felt depressed. Dinner with the staff was unpleasant. The steward Mr. Rutherford asked when they would leave, now that their interviews were finished. Sam had been forced to explain in front of everyone that the interviews were only part of their investigation. He wasn't about to tell them he was searching the house next, just in case someone decided to get rid of clues. But he knew he wouldn't be able to hide their activities for long. His little sister Lucy had tried to brighten the room by saying she was glad the two constables could attend the harvest dance the next evening. Sam forced himself not to look at Julia, who would surely be blushing at the thought of finding herself trapped between competing girls.

Julia retired first, going up to her notes, or so she told the staff. Minutes later, when Sam finally arrived in their sitting room, Julia was already asleep at the desk, head pillowed in her arms. He studied her innocent face, the way her cosmetics were smudged, the soft, pink lips he'd so recently kissed. She was talented at the illusion of portraying a man, because she certainly looked nothing like one now.

He shook her shoulder, and though she frowned, she didn't awaken. They had had only an hour's sleep the night before, and even he felt exhausted. He tipped her away from the desk and picked her up, holding her against his chest. Her head settled on his shoulder, and the scent of her filled him—not a perfume, of course, but just . . . Julia. He wasn't sure how long he stood still in the candlelit darkness, enjoying the soft feel of her against his chest, the sound of her breathing, her occasional murmurs as she dreamed. When she put her arms around his neck, he wondered if she was dreaming of him. Conceited thought, of course.

He shouldered open her bedroom door and found the large bed turned down invitingly, a single candle lit on the bedside table. He laid her down amid the blankets, then pulled off her boots, unbuttoned her trousers, and slid them down her hips. He left her shirt and drawers on, because otherwise he wouldn't be able to resist crawling into bed with her.

After pulling the covers up around her, he smoothed the hair out of her face and leaned down to kiss her forehead. A sudden sense of danger overcame him, and before he could even straighten up, there was a sharp, painful blow to the back of his head, and the room went dark.

Julia came abruptly awake as something large and heavy fell on her. She recognized Sam immediately, and before she could even imagine how he'd fallen on top of her, she noticed a stream of blood trickle from his hairline and over his forehead. Her breath left her lungs in a soft cry.

And then she saw the other man looming over him, over her. She gasped and tried to move, but Sam's weight held her pinned to the bed. As she pushed at his shoulders, the intruder only laughed and put a hand on Sam's back, holding him down. The man's face came into the candlelight, and he had a black scarf disguising his features, just like when they'd been attacked on the road. He had the kind of flat, black eyes that hid the darkest of evil deep inside, for he looked at her with an awareness that frightened her.

"Miss Reed, why, I'm shocked," he said.

His voice oozed along her spine and gave her gooseflesh. Of course he knew who she was.

"Whatever will I say to your brother, when I've found you dressed as a man and sharing quarters with the gardener's brother?"

She ignored his provocation.

He pulled Sam off her by the collar and

dropped him to the floor. She winced at the loud thump as his head hit the carpet.

The man sat on the edge of the bed, and Julia forced herself not to scramble away from him, understanding that this was what he wanted.

"I know everything," he said.

He examined her face, and she was grateful that Sam had pulled the blankets up to her chin.

"And what do you know?" she asked.

"I've kept a very close eye on you these past years, Miss Reed. Would you mind if I call you Julia?"

She didn't answer, and he laughed silently.

"You have been a very discontented girl. You had a home, warmth, food, pretty dresses, everything a young lady should want. But that wasn't enough for you."

He slid the blankets down to her waist, and she thanked God she was still wearing the shirt and bindings. But that wouldn't stop him, she thought, feeling sick with fear, and so worried that Sam was bleeding to death on the floor.

"You intruded on the general's work in India—"

"I never—"

"You insisted on coming to Afghanistan, when any normal woman would want to stay in Bombay's relative luxury. General Reed had me watch over you, and at first I resented it. But you proved so fascinating!"

She thought about him following her every move, like a dark snake hiding in her shadow.

"You weren't his virginal young sister, you were a well-dressed whore."

She flinched as if he'd slapped her. His laugh was silent, which made his open mouth all the more menacing.

"I followed you every time you slipped away from the encampment, saw you give yourself to one lover after another."

"There were only two." She spoke before she realized defending herself was just what he wanted.

"Only two? And that should absolve you?"

"I don't need anyone's absolution."

"The general would disagree with that. I told him everything." He leaned closer, and his breath was hot on her face. "Well, not everything. I didn't tell him I was often able to watch your entire performance."

She couldn't stop the shudder that wracked her, the nausea that churned through her stomach. "You're disgusting," she said hoarsely.

He shrugged, like a little boy who expected to be forgiven for stealing a biscuit. "Perhaps, but you provided me rare enjoyment in a bleak country. Also, you were the perfect solution."

He paused as if he expected her to respond, and when she didn't, he seemed childishly disappointed.

"It was so easy to use you in the general's

scheme. I made sure he understood that you deserved this punishment. You'd brought shame on the family honor."

"And treason didn't?" she shot back scornfully.

He put his long fingers about her throat and gently squeezed. Her air wasn't quite cut off, but she panicked and tried to pry his fingers loose.

"Watch yourself, Julia. I haven't managed to kill you yet, but I assure you I am quite capable of the deed. In fact, I rather think it will be necessary before I leave this room."

She fought him in earnest, bringing up her knees to hit him in the back, but finding the blankets and his body restricting her movement. She reached to gouge at his eyes, but he held himself above her and laughed.

Her head was pounding; her lungs began to burn with the need to breathe. Her gasping only made him laugh harder. Pinpricks of darkness scattered across her eyes, and she realized she would die, never having exonerated herself, never having loved Sam enough.

Then suddenly the man's weight was gone, and she breathed in welcome air with deep, painful gasps. She came up on her elbow and saw the assailant on top of Sam, struggling to hold him down. There was blood down the side of Sam's face, and he seemed weak as he tried to throw the man off him.

She slid out from under the covers and staggered as she tried to stand. The room went black briefly, but then everything came back into focus. She lunged forward and gave the stranger a hard kick in the back. As he arched in pain and turned toward her, Sam flung him off and the two men rolled together on the floor. She leaned back against the bed, her hand to her painful throat, and waited for an opening to help.

Then the assailant was on his feet, his arm wrapped tight around Sam's throat from behind. Choking, Sam rose up, trying to push backward against the shorter man. Sam's face was red, his wide eyes locked on her.

Julia saw her opening. She kicked hard between Sam's spread legs, her foot connecting with the stranger's groin. He let out a hoarse cry and released Sam, then staggered as he hunched over. When Sam would have rushed him, the man grabbed a knife from its sheath in his boot and held it up menacingly in a shaking hand.

"Stay back!" he said, gasping, as he backed toward the window. He wasn't able to straighten up. "You can't win. The general wants you dead, and I'll make sure it happens."

Sam put himself between her and the knife. "Lewis has sent men to their deaths over this. Don't think you won't be next."

"He's grateful for my help. He'd fall apart without me," the stranger said, his hand on the windowsill. "Don't bother following me, Sherryngton. Until next time."

He laughed silently, stepped over the windowsill, and vanished. Sam staggered forward, but Julia caught his arm.

"Sam, no, your head wound is too bad," she said, her throat tight with pain. "He might kill you."

She was frightened by how weak he looked. The blood stood out on his pale face, mingling with perspiration. But he shook her off and went to the window, pulling back the draperies carefully, and then when nothing happened, peered outside.

"He's gone," Sam said. "I would have thought for certain he'd break a leg from this height."

"Lock the window," she said. "Then lock this door, and I'll go check the other two rooms."

When she came out of his bedroom, he stood in her doorway, watching her. She made him sit down, then poured water into the basin and began to clean his face.

"I can do this," he said angrily.

She knew the anger wasn't directed at her. "Be quiet and let me see how bad the cut is." She separated his hair until she found the lump, where blood matted his hair. The flow seemed to have stopped and she breathed a sigh of relief. "You'll live."

He said nothing. She helped him wash the blood out of his hair into a basin, then very carefully dumped the red water out the window. The whole time he stared at the window with a cold intensity that worried her. Cheerful, kind Sam seemed to disappear behind the old, angry eyes of this . . . soldier.

Finally she stood between him and the window, her hands on her hips. "You're the experienced one—what should we do?"

Like a spell had been broken, he wiped his hand down his face and attempted a poor excuse for a smile. "Never sleep with the doors or windows unlocked."

"We've already been doing that, but he still managed to get in. Will he try to use someone to get him into the house?"

"I don't think so. We've cautioned all the servants. He only wants us, and probably won't take the chance of alerting anyone else to his presence."

"Could we somehow force him to testify against Lewis? If we capture him, surely we can hide him away until we prove Lewis is guilty."

"I'm not sure we can take that risk," he said impassively. "If he attacks again, we might end up killing him before he can hurt us." He stood up, pushing damp hair out of his face. His collar was stained reddish brown with blood. He seemed worried about the danger they were in, but not particularly bothered to be talking about killing someone.

Though Sam would protect her with his life, she didn't like seeing how at ease he was with so much violence. She should be used to it, having been around soldiers for years.

But this was Sam, whom she'd always thought of as a gentle soul.

He glanced down at her with the first real smile she'd seen that night. "That was a pretty close call, that kick you made."

She shrugged her shoulders. "Worried about my aim?"

"It crossed my mind. I would have tried to protect my vital parts, if he had let me."

She tsked and shook her head. "You should have learned to trust me by now."

He looked into her face, and his smile slowly died, and a wilder, more sensual expression lowered his lids, parted his lips. The danger, her sore throat, everything disappeared in a haze of heat that swept through her only because of a look.

Sam's gaze dropped to her mouth. "You need to get some sleep," he said in a husky voice. "But I don't feel that I should leave you alone."

"Then don't," she said breathlessly.

It was as if the combination of fear and danger and the threat of dying all coalesced into a need to feel what it meant to be alive. She wanted him again—she wanted him always.

Chapter 18

Julia reached for him and Sam forced himself to step away.

"We need to keep watch," he said.

He knew she could sway him; he would succumb, though he shouldn't. It was there on her face, the hesitation, the yearning, then the reluctant understanding.

"All right," she said softly. "Don't stay up too late."

"Do one thing for me, Julia. Put a chair on its side in front of the window in your room, and I'll do the same for the other windows. That way, should our friend somehow enter, he'll get tripped up and we should hear him."

He listened from the sitting room as she washed herself. He tried not to hear the dripping of the water, tried not to imagine the cloth touching her skin, but he was helpless to stop his thoughts. He'd assumed that maybe once he'd made love to her, his curiosity and desire would be sated. But if anything, it was now worse, because he knew what he was missing.

It was a long time before he checked in to make sure she was asleep. She was helpless, innocent. Of all the people under this roof, she was in the most danger.

From now on, he couldn't leave her unprotected. He went back inside and barricaded each door. He prepared himself for bed, then brought a blanket into Julia's room and lay down on the chaise lounge. His feet hung off, but he was comfortable enough. He fell asleep watching her face.

In the morning, Sam woke to find Julia staring at him, as she lay in bed with her head propped on her hand. He smiled at her, and she smiled back.

"Worried about me?" she asked.

"Always."

"I seem to require a lot of your worry," she said wryly.

"I don't mind."

"But you used to. You were angry at me in Afghanistan."

"But that's long over with."

She nodded slowly. "You know, you could have slept in bed with me."

His smile widened. "I could have. But then I wouldn't have been thinking about protecting you."

"And that would have been a bad thing?"

Her voice was low, sultry, alluring in a way that was hard to resist.

"For now. Let's get you ready for the day. It's time to search Mrs. Hume's room."

"You're changing the subject," she said with disappointment.

When she sat up, the thought of any danger fled his mind. The shirt she wore was sheer enough for him to see her nipples pointing against the cloth. His mouth went dry, his thoughts became gibberish as his body found the only thing it could concentrate on.

How was he going to keep her safe when he was in this condition? He stood up and headed for the sitting room, calling over his shoulder, "Let me know when you're ready for your cosmetics."

A half hour later, she was seated before him completely dressed but for collar and cravat, and he had himself under better control. As he worked on her face, he noticed the bruises on her throat. He gently touched them and she flinched.

In a low voice, he said, "I hadn't realized how

badly he'd injured you. We should summon a doctor."

Shaking her head, she put a hand to her throat. "No, it looks worse than it feels. I'll be fine. Is there anything you can do to hide the bruises?"

"Cosmetics would noticeably stain your collar. I think the collar itself and a large bow on the cravat should hide it well enough." He went back to painting her face.

"Sam, are you going to tell Frances what happened last night? After all, someone will see your bloody shirt."

"I'm going to burn the thing. And no, no one will know. It will just give him a reason to harm someone else. I couldn't do that to Frances—or anyone else."

After eating breakfast, they went to the governess's old room, with its shrouded furniture and closed drapes keeping the light dim.

"So are Mrs. Hume's things still here?" he asked.

"They were last month. Frances had separated out some personal items she thought Edwin might want—which I'm assuming the police now have."

He nodded. Together they searched through the room, finding nothing more than an old woman's clothes and sad mementos of her husband and child. Nothing that Edwin wrote to his mother implicated Lewis. Sam could hardly have expected to find a pistol dropped beneath the bed, when Mrs. Hume had had no wounds or bruises. She'd probably been suffocated, maybe by one of her own pillows.

As they straightened the room so that it looked just like they found it, he said, "We can't wait to search Lewis's room. We have to do it right now, before his henchman finds and destroys something we could use."

Using the excuse of working through luncheon, Sam and Julia escaped to the family wing of the estate undetected. Lewis's sitting room and bedroom yielded no clues, and they finally had their first success in Lewis's dressing room. There was an unopened crate marked with Indian labels.

Julia stared hard at the crates, memories of the other side of the world haunting her. She shook them off. "What do you think these could be?"

But he was already using his knife to pry open the lid. Straw covered the contents, and they carefully scooped it out and onto Sam's coat. A trunk rested within, and when they opened it, they found several military uniforms folded carefully away.

She sat back on her heels in dejection. "There's nothing here we can use."

"You're being presumptive. We need to search the trunk."

They laid out each set of clothing—coat, trousers, even boots, then she watched as he inspected the trunk itself for hidden compartments. As he was doing his slow methodical search, she began to go through the pockets randomly, trying to forget that her brother had worn these garments. She had to think of them as the clothing of a traitor.

When her fingers encountered something in a coat pocket, she gave a little gasp that had Sam's head jerking up quickly. She pulled out a crumpled piece of paper and held it up.

"Open it," he said calmly.

Her fingers shook as she spread the paper flat on the floor. They both bent over it, and by the light from the small window, they could see Lewis's penmanship—and doodles and dots of ink mixed in.

She held her breath, and stared at the paper as if it were a snake that could bite her.

"That looks exactly like the coded letters he used to send information," Sam said, satisfaction laced through his words. "He must have worked out the code like this. We have it in his own hand."

She let him take the paper and fold it away. She should be happy—this was proof that a court might pay attention to. Her brother had created a code to be buried in her letters and sent to the Russians. If the letter was intercepted by the military, it would simply look like her letter had been misdirected. Lewis had altered the letter with blobs of ink and filled in certain loops, making it seem like she'd doodled as she wrote. With just this single letter, there was no way to read the code. But Lewis had always sent a second letter of hers separately, and this one had tiny dots scattered beneath the words. When you compared both letters, the dots would show which filled-in loop helped form the coded alphabet, and the way to decipher the hidden message.

Sam finally looked up from the paper and glanced at the mantel clock. "We must quickly put everything away. I had no idea how much time had passed."

By the time they had folded each article of clothing away and repacked the crate, they could hear distant voices down the hall. Sam swore softly.

"Surely they'll know eventually that we're searching the house?" Julia whispered.

"But they don't need to know we suspect their master the most. Be ready to move silently."

Always it was Sam encouraging her, Sam who made it seem like everything would be all right. She watched him with his head bent to the crack in the door, his concentration intense. Didn't he ever get nervous? How did he live every day with the knowledge that he might die?

Yet it made every moment of life more precious. She stared at his back, thought of what his body had made her feel. She would never have known such absolute joy, were it not for the situation they were in. How could she hate anything that gave her Sam, even so briefly?

He motioned to her and opened the door. Holding her breath, she followed him into the hall. Terror and excitement bubbled through her, every sense concentrated on avoiding detection. There were open doors down the corridor, and the voices came from there. Women's voices, raised in laughter. Were the maids cleaning?

Suddenly the voices got louder, and Sam opened a random door and ducked inside, pulling her with him, and closed it silently behind him.

She put her mouth against his ear. "But they might be cleaning this room next!" They were both breathing heavily, overheated, and just the brush of his hair against her face made her feel out of control. What was wrong with her?

"We'll wait until they reach the room right next door. We should be able to pass them undetected."

He drew her into the corner, where a wardrobe blocked her view of the door. The shadows seemed to absorb them.

"Do you still have Lewis's paper?" She looked up at Sam to ask the question, but the rest of her words died as she gazed into his eyes.

Julia gasped as he pressed her even deeper into the corner. She could feel every muscle in his body where it brushed against her. Her skin was so sensitive, and she wanted to groan at how little she could control herself. Surely he was only trying to protect her. His hands squeezed her shoulders and moved down her arms, and she barely restrained a moan. Before her endless days with him, she'd been so proud of how she'd reined in her emotions and her impulses. She had long ago decided that she would never do anything that she hadn't given plenty of thought to beforehand.

But ever since her constant exposure to Sam, it was as if every hard lesson she'd learned had been thrown out the window. Her mind and her body were consumed with him. She would be mortified if he found out how much she wanted to pull him down on top of her.

"Don't you understand what's happened?" he said, his breath brushing her face.

She couldn't even remember what they'd been talking about.

"This paper is *evidence* against Lewis, something we can actually use at trial."

"I know, but—"

"And if he's been this stupid once, he'll be so again. We'll find something more."

His body pressed against her lightly, swaying, and she swallowed heavily as if she couldn't remember how. She stared into his face, saw eagerness and satisfaction, and realized that finding a clue had given him a victory that he relished.

Eluding capture had made him even bolder. His gaze slid down her body, leaving her feeling burned in its wake.

She remembered telling him their relationship existed out of time, that she was willing to take things as they happened. She hadn't thought he really believed her. But by the heat in his eyes, the way his thumbs traced circles in her lower arms, he was showing her he wanted her to share in his feeling of triumph.

Her breath picked up pace to match the beating of her heart. He wanted her. Avoiding danger together was intoxicating—but only because this was Sam.

She needed to share everything she was with him. He pushed her hard against the wall with his body, then took her mouth in a hot, deep kiss. Her moan was absorbed by him, her tongue captured by his. He pressed his hands to her face, holding her to him as if he would never let her go. She reveled in the feel of his hard body against her, wished desperately that her breasts weren't so well covered. She smoothed her hands down his chest, felt his heat through his shirt, absorbed the pounding of his heart with her palm.

When she reached his trousers, she flicked open the buttons, felt his stomach muscles shudder against the back of her hand. He kissed her face, then her throat when she leaned her head to the side. He was pulling off her coat as she was tugging down his trousers. She felt his erection fall heavily against her stomach, and she took him in her fist and was rewarded when the breath left his lungs in a gasp. He put his hands on the wall on either side of her, as if he braced himself for an assault he was powerless against.

She had the ability to make him lose himself, and she relished it, dropping to her knees to take him into her mouth.

He was trembling against her, salty and hot and large in her mouth. When she finally pulled back to tease him with her tongue, he lifted her bodily to her feet, pinning her to the wall as he pulled the loose trousers down her body. His face was hard with barely controlled passion, and she loved looking at him.

Suddenly he picked up her legs on either side of him, then buried himself inside her. She was pressed between the wall and his body, held there only by the weight of him inside her, and his hands beneath her thighs. He moved against her hard, and each time he pulled out, his hands were there from beneath, teasing at whatever his fingers could reach, making her mindless and yet aware of his every touch.

Any moment they could be found, and that only spurred her to clutch him harder to herself, to take him deeper, to thrust her tongue within his mouth as if she couldn't get enough of him.

He climaxed before she did, shuddering between her legs over and over until her own desire hovered at the edge, tantalizing her.

And he understood just what she was thinking, just how she was feeling. Though he gasped against her mouth, he continued to support her with one hand, the other reaching between them to caress her. She was slick and hot and so sensitive, still filled with the pressure of him. It only took a moment before the welcome explosion of pleasure enveloped her, consumed her. Only Sam had ever made her feel so alive, so aware of him as the only man for her.

The only man she'd ever loved.

Chapter 19

〰〰

Sam shakily set Julia down on the floor, and watched her stretch the stiffness from her legs. Feeling dazed, he took a hand towel off the washstand to clean her.

"I've made a mess," he murmured.

He knelt at her feet, looking up into her face, wondering what emotion she betrayed with her fond look. In that moment, all he wanted to do was remain a part of her forever.

A forever they'd never have.

He had to stop these morose thoughts, he told himself as he finished with the towel and stared at the smoothness of her belly, the soft curls beneath, and what was hidden there. He could gladly bury his face there, absorb the scent and taste of her again.

But he'd risked discovery to have her, and he couldn't prolong the pleasure anymore. He helped her step into her drawers and trousers, then pulled them up for her. She was blushing when he did up her buttons, as if this were more intimate than what they'd just shared. She was so full of contradictions, so hard to predict.

He stepped away from her to fix his own clothing, put the towel into his pocket, but didn't break their shared gaze. He smiled. "Is this what you meant by 'taking things as they happen'?"

She grinned and stepped back into his embrace. He hugged her for a moment, then released her to go listen at the door. She waited silently behind him, her hand reaching to clasp his.

"They're close now," he murmured, closing his eyes to better hear their voices and imagine the distance. "About to enter the room next to us."

"What good timing."

He looked over his shoulder at her and smiled. "I have an ear for these things."

"Just an ear?" she shot back.

Hiding his laughter, he couldn't help thinking that she was adorable as he used his fingers to blend in the streaks of cosmetics on her face. "Ready?"

She nodded. When he could hear the maids enter the next room, he opened the door, silently closed it behind them both, then crept to the next suite of rooms. He judged how far away Lucy and Florence were from the door, then silently walked past, knowing Julia casually followed him. No one called out to them. Only when they turned a corner did they both let out a breath.

Neither of them spoke until they were safely back in their private sitting room. While she collapsed with relief into a chair, he looked about suspiciously, knowing something was wrong.

Her smile died. "What is it?"

"Someone's been in the room."

"I'm sure Lucy came to clean this morning. And look, she left a luncheon tray."

"That's not it."

He went into his bedroom and she followed in obvious bewilderment. He opened several drawers in the chest. "My clothes have been disturbed. Lucy wouldn't have done that."

Her face paled. "Lewis's henchman?"

He swept past her and flung open her bedroom door, but the room seemed undisturbed.

He turned back to the sitting room and put his hands on his hips. "He came to see what we might have discovered. Luckily, I had my pistol with me. Yours is probably gone."

She shook her head. "I've taken to carrying it in my coat like you do. Didn't you feel it?"

He gave her a slow smile. "I was thinking about what was inside your clothes, not your pockets."

"Do you think he took anything?"

"What was there to take? We had no evidence against Lewis—although we do now. And trust me, if I have to put it somewhere, I'll hide it better than within this room."

"But that man is in the manor. He could be anywhere."

"I don't think he'll risk remaining inside for long. We'll have the footmen patrol even during the daytime. I don't think the henchman will risk hurting anyone else and calling attention to himself."

She shivered. "I never felt safe here as a child, and now it's even worse."

They spent the afternoon going room by room through the servants' wing looking for evidence against Lewis. Their investigation was tolerated by the staff. Julia kept expecting to find a stranger in every room, ready to jump out at them.

They were often completely alone, due to the excited activity as everyone prepared for the dance that evening. The weather had cooperated, so the servants dragged tables and chairs outside. Every time Julia was in a corridor, she was passed by someone carrying lanterns or linens. She had not been allowed to attend the dance when she was young, and the ones in India were so stilted as to be boring.

She felt an ache of wistfulness, especially

when she entered the pantry and saw Sam. When she was young, her fantasies had been about the two of them entering the harvest dance side by side. She'd imagined him bringing her lemonade and then never leaving her side as he gazed at her with admiration and innocent longing. But she was a woman now, and knew that fantasies seldom became reality. A gardener wouldn't have been taught the dances she knew. And she couldn't dance with him now, not when she was in the guise of Constable Walter Fitzjames.

Sam was now on the floor, peering inside a pantry cupboard, though he looked up when she came in. "Where did ye go? I don't want ye wandering by yourself."

"Yes, sir," she said, feeling guilty since she should be worrying about their attacker, not daydreaming about a silly dance spent in Sam's arms. She cleared her throat. "The dance is tonight, sir."

"Perhaps it would be a good time to search the attic," he said nonchalantly, sticking his head back inside the cupboard.

Julia swiftly inhaled, but what could she say?

Then he peered up at her again, a faint smile tilting the corners of his mouth. "But the servants will insist we attend their dance, won't they?"

Letting out her breath with relief, she gave him a crooked smile. "I'm sure they'll insist."

"Especially the young maid Lucy," he added.

Frowning at him, she turned to give him her back, and saw Lucy blushing out in the corridor. Julia stood stunned as the girl laughed and ran away, her arms overloaded with a case of silver.

"Oh God," Julia moaned, and closed the door.

Sam was silently laughing, and she wanted to kick him.

"Maybe we shouldn't go," she said with a sigh. "After all, *he's* around here somewhere."

"We're going. Knowing we're alone in the manor might make him bold."

That night, dinner was a hasty affair, with the noise level raised high as everyone talked at once. Julia found out that family members of the servants would be attending as well, and she saw Sam's face when he heard the news. Would his mother be there? If he was worried, he showed nothing in his expression.

She didn't know why she was so excited, since she'd have to avoid Lucy and Florence most of the time. But the thought of lanterns in the trees and music in the air just made her giddy. She'd been to formal garden parties in London, but she sensed that the Hopewell Manor staff would not be full of the same bland politeness. When she overheard Frances discussing the dance with Sam as they stood before the hearth in the servants' hall, Julia held her breath.

He was playing Constable Seabrook. To her

surprise, she'd begun to hear rumors that the staff believed he was courting Frances and wouldn't miss the chance to dance with her. Lucy and Florence, who didn't often leave Julia's side at dinner, giggled as they watched the housekeeper. Lucy directed an encouraging look at Julia.

Like a coward, Julia lowered her eyes to her cider and took a drink. A big gulp, just like a man.

An hour later, she stood beside Sam in the kitchen courtyard, looking out over the park on the west side of the manor. The lawn sloped down to a grove of trees, twinkling with lantern light now that the sun had set. Colorful streamers gently swayed in the breeze, and a village band of violin, drums, and flute was just warming up. Beneath a pavilion, tables were piled with food and drink.

She sighed. "It looks wonderful."

Sam's face was grim. "It will be an awkward night for us both."

She studied him carefully. "Maybe she won't be here tonight."

"Frances?"

"Your mother," she whispered.

He sighed. "She always comes to the harvest dance, even if she feels poorly."

"It will be full dark soon."

"Not soon enough."

"We can wait until then to go out."

He hesitated, then looked away. "I heard that the Duke of Kelthorpe had musicians at the house party last month just for you."

She felt her face heat with a blush. "He knew I enjoyed music."

"He could have given you music every evening of your life."

Was he wondering about her regrets? There were none, at least not about Kelthorpe. "Music every evening would have become routine. Now, this night, any music I'm lucky enough to hear will take on a new significance. And it will be beautiful because of that."

When he spoke, his voice was husky, strained. "I'm doing my best to make sure this isn't the last dance you'll experience."

"I know you are," she whispered. She reached to gently touch his arm and he pulled away. "Constable—"

"Mrs. Cooper is expecting us both. Shall we go?"

She bit her lip, not knowing what to say. Why did she feel the need to see the villagers in celebration? Was it because her parents had never let her attend the harvest dance? She'd been young, yes, but not as young as the village children who'd cavorted on the grounds while she'd watched from the windows. And then, after her parents had died, there was no harvest dance, nothing to celebrate. The estate had seemed quieter every year, until she could hear her own heartbeat as she wandered the rooms alone. Then she'd had to escape her pretty prison. She couldn't regret that impulsiveness, even now.

While she'd been gone, the servants had brought back the harvest dance, and she was glad.

Most of the staff seemed pleased to see the two "constables" who'd been living in their midst these past few days. Julia had to smile at Frances's continued uneasiness around Sam, although they fell into conversation readily enough. Julia stood beside them and looked around, trying to ignore Lucy, who remained nearby talking to Florence. Harold the footman was on the other side of the tables, watching Florence longingly.

By twos and threes came clusters of people Julia didn't know, and she assumed they were Misterton villagers. Was Sam's family here? But Lucy made no move to join any of the strangers, and Henry had not yet made his appearance.

A cool breeze made Julia shiver. She felt like eyes were watching her from out in the darkness. Their attacker was probably there, waiting for his chance to get the two of them alone. But in this crowd, she felt strangely invincible.

The musicians had finished warming up and now struck up a lively country tune. Partners moved in and out of opposite lines and when Julia saw Lucy and Florence dancing together, she sighed with relief. Sam convinced Frances to dance, and she watched them in delight. After several minutes of watching him move, tall and graceful, bending so gentlemanly to talk to Frances, Julia wondered what it would feel like to dance with him, to have those arms around her out in public, instead of only locked in the secret passion they shared. He was a wonderful dancer—how had she thought he'd be otherwise? A forlorn feeling of isolation swept over her.

Would this be her last dance, her last freedom? They'd found little evidence to convince a jury that Lewis was guilty. But even if she were free, she could never proclaim her love for Sam to the world. It was something only they could share, and only for a brief time. It would have to be enough.

Slowly she became aware of movement behind her, then soft breathing. She quickly looked over her shoulder, but nobody was there. There was a hissing of his breath, and she thought their assailant must be laughing that horrible silent laugh of his. The music seemed to fade into the distance, the voices of the people nearby grew muffled. She could only focus on listening for the man who'd helped her brother put her in jail. Sam seemed so far away, his face smiling down at Frances. The darkness behind the trees was too close. All Lewis's henchman would have to do was drag her ten yards.

And she'd vanish.

Julia stood still, a hot, evil presence behind her. His breathing got louder and louder, and she remembered that he'd watched her with a lover. Had he seen her with Sam, right here in the house?

But no, she was panicking. She and Sam were always careful to be alone. She wanted to call to Sam, but the next dance started, and he remained with Frances.

And she was being a fool. There was no one behind her, and he wouldn't dare draw attention to himself.

Her gaze found the food table, where a line was forming as people served themselves from the assortment of pasties and custards and tarts. She was about to take a step in that direction, when suddenly Lucy appeared before her.

"Good evening, Walter," Lucy said, flashing that Sherryngton smile.

Lucy put her hand through Julia's arm, and Julia stiffened, but certainly did not protest being led away.

"You seemed so alone standing near the darkness of the trees," Lucy said.

"I've never been to a country dance before. I was enjoying watching everyone."

Lucy stumbled over something in the grass, and as Julia helped right her, she could swear Lucy leaned her head on her shoulder.

Oh God, Julia had been rescued from her fears only to be immersed in another kind of danger, one of discovery. She prayed that Lucy took her stiffness as a sign of shyness.

The maid looked up into her face and laughed. "I am such a clumsy thing. Thank you for your help."

Julia just nodded awkwardly.

Lucy glanced away and brightened. "And look, some of my family just arrived."

Julia looked where she pointed, and saw Henry with a young woman and several children scattered between them. "Henry the gardener is your brother."

"You have a good memory," Lucy said.

"I write everythin' down."

"The woman behind them is my mother." Lucy waved cheerfully. "Let me introduce you."

"But surely your family is hungry," Julia said, trying to pull away from the girl's firm grip. "You can introduce me later."

"No, no, Mama was very interested that two constables were looking into details about Miss Julia. She's quite certain you will succeed in proving our mistress innocent."

Julia glanced at her in surprise, but didn't respond. She was being dragged closer and closer to the Sherryngton group, and she reluctantly admitted to herself that she was curious to meet Sam's family again after all these years.

When her gaze met Henry's, he hid his concern well, though he did frown at his youngest sister. That at least made Lucy release her grip on Julia's arm. Lucy performed the introductions. There was Henry's shy wife Sarah and their children, then the twins Abigail and Alice—who Julia remembered playing dolls with—and their husbands, tenant farmers on the estate. Both women were very pregnant. And last was Mrs. Sherryngton herself, smaller than Julia remembered, her red hair faded into white, and her alert eyes examining Julia's face. Sam had her golden brown eyes.

"Good evening, Constable," Mrs. Sherryngton said. "You seem very familiar to me. Were you born nearby?"

Julia tried to speak in her gruff voice, though her heart threatened to jump into her throat. "No, ma'am. I'm from Leeds."

Mrs. Sherryngton hesitated, and Julia tried not to flinch as the older woman shook her head.

"Maybe back a generation or two," Mrs. Sherryngton said. "I have a good eye for faces. It will come to me."

Now there would be *another* person trying to unmask them. She would have to make sure Sam came nowhere near his mother.

Lucy suddenly tugged on her hand. "The constable is going to dance with me, Mama. We'll be back."

"Did the young man even have time to ask you?" her mother gently scolded.

Lucy's eyes were pleading, and at that point Julia would have done anything to get away from Mrs. Sherryngton. Julia nodded and found herself pulled onto the grass dance floor. This was the first time anyone but Sam had touched her hands, and she could only pray that travel and spending time outdoors had roughened her skin and nails enough. And then she remembered that she only knew the lady's part.

"I—I can't dance," she finally admitted when Lucy placed her in position.

"Then just follow me and I'll teach you!"

Julia spent the next fifteen minutes feeling like the most awkward person ever to step foot on a dance floor. Lucy dragged her about, laughing even when Julia stomped on her toes. Julia liked Lucy immensely, and could only hope that when the girl learned the truth, they could still have a friendship between them.

Unless, of course, Julia was returned to jail.

Her morbid thoughts didn't last long during such a festive evening. When Lucy finally let her retreat from the dance floor, Julia found Sam talking to a stranger. Sam motioned her nearer, and she experienced actual reluctance to leave Lucy. She couldn't remember the last time she'd had such fun.

She put on a businesslike expression for Sam, who nodded to her.

"Constable Fitzjames, this is John Keane, the parish vicar here in Misterton."

Julia bowed. "Good evenin', Mr. Keane."

The vicar was a man in his thirties, obviously recent to the post, since Julia did not remember him. He had very kind eyes, and a calm manner which would put any parishioner at ease.

"It is good to meet you, Constable Fitzjames," Mr. Keane said. "Such a terrible time we live in, when a young woman of a fine family can be accused of such crimes."

Julia glanced at Sam, who said, "I've been explainin' our purpose here to Mr. Keane." He turned back to the vicar. "Ye knew the family?"

"I have only been living here in Misterton for the last eight years, long after Miss Reed and her brother had left for the East. But the villagers speak highly of the family, and especially of young Miss Reed. I did have the good fortune to meet the general last autumn."

Julia grew tense, and wished she had her notebook with which to busy her shaking hands.

Sam gave him an assessing look. "How did ye find the general?"

"Quite well. A busy man, without much time to spare, but he missed his home and wished to commemorate his return. He came to me for help."

"And how could ye help?" Sam asked.

The vicar smiled. "I am familiar with commissioning the creation of statues."

Slowly, Sam said, "He wanted to have a statue made?"

Julia stopped breathing. Since when did her brother bypass his staff to worry about something so trivial as decorating the estate?

"In fact," Mr. Keane said, "he originally wanted to commission a statue for the church grounds, a donation in thanksgiving for his safe return to England. But as we spoke, he liked the idea so much he decided to purchase a second one for Hopewell Manor."

"And it's here now?" Sam asked.

"I assume so. I've had the one at the church for months now."

"Thank you, Mr. Keane, you've been so helpful on the family's character."

As Sam and Julia were escaping, the vicar called, "Anytime, sir. Do pay a visit to the rectory when you're in the village."

"I'll be sure to do that, sir."

Chapter 20

❦

Sam tried not to show his excitement as he leisurely led Julia to the edge of the trees, a more secluded spot where lanterns swayed overhead and a breeze rippled ribbon streamers. One swayed against her cheek and he almost pushed it aside himself, wanting any excuse to touch her. Luckily, she impatiently swiped the streamer away.

Softly, she asked, "Was that as significant as I thought it was?"

"It might be," he said, casually looking out over the merry crowd. "I can't believe Henry didn't tell me about a new statue."

"We never asked. Do ye think Lewis intended it for—"

He saw that she couldn't even say the words, that she was afraid to hope again after everything seemed so bleak.

"Do I think he had a different purpose than ornamentation for that statue? That's *exactly* what I'm thinkin'."

"Ye said he had to hide the money somewhere."

"And I couldn't imagine where on the grounds we could even begin to look. And here it fell right into our laps."

"I'm so excited," she whispered.

Lantern light was caught in her blue eyes, dazzling him. Desire surged through his veins, and he was hard in an instant.

He tried to keep his gaze on her eyes, but her moist mouth was almost his undoing. "The way your face looks right now, you make me remember other moments, other touches."

She closed her eyes briefly. "Oh, Sam."

If anyone saw the way he was just staring at his apprentice constable . . . He casually looked about, but no one was watching them.

Sam cleared his throat. "We have to see that statue. I'll go ask Henry about it."

"Oh, but you can't. He's with your mother."

He couldn't help himself—his gaze shot to the crowd, and almost immediately he saw his family sitting at their own table, laughing at the antics of the children out among the dancers. The twins had even come, looking so mature and happy. And then he saw his mother for the first time in fourteen years. She seemed . . . frail, her hair a color he didn't recognize on her. Was that because of him? Did she never stop worrying, as Henry said?

There was a lump in his throat no amount of swallowing could destroy. It had been difficult to stay away from his family, but not half as bad as seeing them and knowing he could not immerse himself in their hugs and kisses.

"I was able to meet your mother," Julia continued in a low voice. "She's as kind—and direct as I remember."

"Direct?"

"She said I looked familiar and asked if I grew up here."

He whistled softly. "If she recognized your features after all these years, she'll spot me in a minute. We'll leave the dance. Will you mind?"

"Mind?" She looked incredulous. "When there's a statue to search for?"

He wanted to grin down into her face, he wanted to hug her, he wanted—everything with her. He would have to settle for seeing her safe.

"But Constable," she continued, lowering her voice even more, "I'm certain I felt someone watching me from the trees."

Frowning, he looked over his shoulder into the darkness. "The grooms have been taking turns keeping an eye on things, but we won't take any chances. We need a distraction. I'll be right back."

Moving into the crowd, he caught his brother's eye and gestured him nearer. Henry carefully positioned himself so that Sam was standing with his back to their family.

"What can I do for you, Constable?" Henry asked softly.

"I need your help. Can you gather everyone and encourage a chase game in the garden? Pretend you hid a prize they all need to find."

"But what will happen when no one finds anything?"

"Say you hid it too well, and *you* find it."

Henry nodded. "Can you tell me why we're doing this?"

"Later. But thank you for your help."

By the time Sam made his way back to Julia, Henry was already calling all the young people together and explaining the game to them. Julia listened with interest, smiling up at Sam.

"How clever," she murmured.

"Thank you." Grinning, he took a lantern, and then he and Julia slipped into the shadows.

The Hopewell Manor garden always felt like his own. His father had devoted each workday to it; he and his siblings had had the run of it. He knew every false crumbling castle, every marble bench, and every grotto. One by one, he ticked off each statue in his memory, carefully searching every stone path. Giggling servants and children occasionally raced past them, but the gardens were large enough for everyone to spread out.

And then they found it. There was a solitary new statue, deep in the heart of the garden, far from any view from the house or outbuildings. It stood in the middle of a rose garden, as if it needed thorns for protection.

"Will it matter if anyone sees us?" Julia asked.

"We're just playin' the game, aren't we? And we got here first."

Her excited face was illuminated by the lantern flame as he held it up high until they were both able to see the new addition to the garden.

It was a statue of a nearly naked woman.

"My brother never struck me as the romantic type," she said doubtfully.

"I don't think there's anything romantic about his choice of the Roman goddess Venus."

"Venus? But surely beauty is romantic."

"She was the goddess of gardeners, and was believed to bring a bountiful crop."

"So you mean Lewis was only being practical?"

"Of course. He thought Venus would be innocuous in a garden."

"She's not wearing much, is she?" she added dryly. "I'm sure he thought she'd be pleasant to look at, too."

He grinned. "Her clothing is obviously

draped to suggest as well as conceal. Let's just hope she's concealing more than nudity. Hold the lantern near the base for me. Perhaps there's a hidden compartment."

But if there was one, he couldn't find it. The base seemed as solid as the statue, though he tested every edge, dug into the earth around its base, and ran his hands over the statue itself. He tapped everywhere, and although the base sounded as if it might be hollow, there seemed to be no way to find out.

They heard a distant laugh before the bushes parted and Florence and Harold came crashing into the clearing. The two servants pulled up short, then released identical sighs of relief when they saw whom they'd interrupted.

Sam grinned. "Ye'd better be more careful. Mrs. Cooper wouldn't take kindly to the two of ye together."

"Thank you, sir," Harold called, grabbing Florence's hand and pulling her into the darkness.

Sam shook his head, and they both turned back to the statue.

"We could just pry it open," Julia suggested.

They stood side by side and stared at the mysteries of Venus. The lantern flame was sputtering now, the oil almost gone.

"And what would that prove? Even if there's money inside, we haven't connected it to Lewis. Damn, but I have to give this more thought."

She yawned, then apologized. "Perhaps we need to talk to Henry? Maybe someone else knows about the statue."

As Sam thought about their assailant, his fists tightened in anger. "Lewis's henchman might yet be the key. I could capture him and persuade him to talk." But not in front of Julia, he vowed to himself. She didn't need to see the lengths he would go to save her life.

"He won't help us."

Sam didn't answer. He only blew out the flame, and in the darkness he put his arm around her shoulders.

"Allow me to be your guide," he murmured into her ear, tugging on the lobe gently with his teeth. God, she smelled so good.

Over the next half hour, everyone gathered back near the dance floor. Henry admitted he must have hid the prize too well, since he knew the gardens better than anyone else. Sam insisted on accompanying him to "verify" the truth, and everyone laughed. But in reality, Sam didn't even want *Henry* alone on the grounds at night. They returned with a little pouch of coins, everything they had between them. Henry surprised everyone by throwing all the coins high in the air, and there was a mad scrabble as all the children dropped down into the grass to search.

Sam watched, smiling, until he felt a tug on his arm.

"Constable Seabrook?"

His sister Lucy stood looking up at him, her eyes wide with worry. He sobered and stared down at her.

"Yes, Lucy?"

"I can't find my sister Frances anywhere," she said, looking over her shoulder in their mother's direction.

Sam's every sense went on alert, and he scanned the crowd. "When did ye notice this?"

"Just now. And she's not in the manor. I didn't want to worry anyone, because I'm probably just imagining things, but you warned about a thief—"

He nodded and took her shoulders to push her toward a surprised Julia. "Stay with Constable Fitzjames. I'll gather some of the men and we'll go look for her in the manor and in the garden. I'm sure she's fine."

"We can search the manor—" Julia began, but Sam cut her off.

"No. Keep watch on the women right here."

Sam's fear seemed to burn a hole in his gut. It took all his composure to keep everyone calm, to explain that Frances had probably twisted an ankle and was just waiting to be found. But he knew that was a lie. Since Lewis's henchman couldn't get to Sam and Julia, he'd obviously decided to try another tactic. The man would be a fool to hurt someone else, but was he beginning to feel desperate?

The men fanned out through the garden, torches and candles and lanterns making it seem like twilight instead of full night. When an hour had passed with no sign of his sister, Sam's fear turned into a hatred so intense he felt calm. The next time he saw the villain, he would kill him.

"Constable Seabrook!"

There was a shout from nearby and he raced through the foliage, knocking aside tall plants and jumping over bushes. Henry and another gardener were kneeling on the ground, and Sam saw the body stretched out next to a pond. His heartbeat went frantic, even as everything around him seemed to slow down. Was she—

"She's alive," Henry quickly said, his smile grim. "Just a bump on the head. She's coming around even now."

More men entered the clearing and Sam pushed them all away as he knelt beside Frances. She groaned and put a hand to her head, but he stopped her. Blood matted her hair.

"Mrs. Cooper, how do ye feel?" he asked softly, pushing a strand of hair out of her face.

She looked up at him with wide, frightened eyes. She opened her mouth, hesitated, then glanced at all the concerned faces. "I—I think I remember tripping."

"Ye've hit your head," Sam said, knowing damn well there was more to this story. But she was being brave and holding it in so as not to alarm the innocent servants.

She gave a faint smile. "So who won?"

There was relieved laughter as Sam scooped her into his arms and rose to his feet.

"I can walk," she insisted.

He didn't put her down.

Julia had gathered the women together, and they all passed the time by cleaning up after the party. Julia felt almost faint with worry, full of guilt that it was all her fault something had happened to sweet, kind Frances, who'd only tried to help.

She was the first to see the bobbing lights that announced the men as they came striding out of the garden. Sam was carrying Frances, who looked annoyed to be in his arms. Julia swayed with relief and leaned against a table.

Lucy stopped at Julia's side and rolled her eyes. "No matter what Frances says, I know she did this to get the constable's attention."

Julia could barely control her giggle, and desperately reminded herself how serious the situation was. In the housekeeper's suite, Mrs. Sherryngton bathed and bandaged her daughter's wounded forehead, while Frances kept insisting that she was fine. When everyone had calmed down, and Henry had taken his mother home, Julia and Sam managed to closet themselves alone with Frances, who rested in her bed.

Julia saw how pale Frances looked. There was

a nasty bruise on her forehead, partially hidden by the bandage.

"I'm fine," Frances murmured when she looked from Sam to Julia.

Sam stood over her, his face cold and impassive, his fists resting on his hips. "You're not fine. Can you remember what happened?"

Julia looked up at Sam. "Maybe this should wait until morning."

"No," Frances said quickly. "I remember everything. There was a stranger on the grounds. He had something black obscuring his face."

Julia closed her eyes and sagged back into a chair. Sam was a dark presence above both women, and she found herself almost afraid of him, as if she didn't know what he was capable of.

"He attacked us before," Sam said in a clipped voice. "I assumed he wouldn't dare do anything with so many people in the gardens, but I was wrong. Forgive me, Frances. It was even my idea to send you into his path. Tell me what he did."

She fluttered a hand. "Don't go blaming yourself, Constable." Even in her injured state, she remembered to use his new identity. "He didn't hurt me. He just . . . wouldn't let me leave. He didn't ask me any questions, just . . . looked at me as if he didn't really have a plan. He covered my mouth when someone came near. He stood behind me, b-breathing in my ear, then he— touched me inappropriately."

Julia gasped.

Sam's gaze froze on his sister. "Did he hurt you?"

Frances shook her head. Then, as a tear slid down into her hair, Julia handed her a handkerchief.

"No, I assure you I'm unharmed. He just wanted to frighten me. He had a message for you. He said that if I'd been a certain woman, he'd have done more to me. He wanted you to know that she won't have an easy death. He meant Miss Reed, didn't he?"

Julia wiped her damp hands on her thighs over and over again, remembering the hiss of the attacker's breath in the trees, trying not to imagine what he planned to do to her if he got her alone.

Sam put his hand on Julia's shoulder. "Frances, did he say anything else?"

"Just that the grooms and footmen won't be able to stop him when he finally comes for you. And then he hit me with something, and I don't remember anything else."

Sam turned away, running his hand through his hair. He suddenly looked tired, and Julia felt his pain along with her own. It wasn't his fault—it was hers. She was the one he was trying to help, risking his own life and now his family's safety. None of this would have happened if she hadn't been so brazen, so selfishly insistent on having her own freedom all those years ago.

They brought Lucy in to keep Frances company. When Julia and Sam reached their suite, he insisted on searching each room before he'd let her out of his sight, including opening each window and looking down. Julia stood in the center of her bedroom, hugging herself, feeling dazed and so very tired.

Sam finally approached her. "I've locked and barricaded the doors, and kept the chairs in front of each window. We're safe."

"Are we? Is everyone else safe? Frances wasn't."

She could see the muscles in his jaw spasm as he clenched his teeth.

"The footmen are patrolling the manor, and the grooms will be stationed around the house. The attacker has warned us; I think that's all he meant to do tonight. Everyone should be safe."

She shuddered, and allowed him to put his arms around her.

"I know what you're thinking," he murmured, "and you mustn't blame yourself. Everything is Lewis's fault, and we'll catch him in the end. We're closer than ever."

"If I'm not to blame myself, then you can't hold yourself accountable either. You're only one man, Sam."

He nodded, but she didn't think he believed her words.

"I don't want you sleeping alone tonight," he said. "Come be with me."

After undressing, she gladly crawled into his bed wearing only a shirt, and let him put his warm, safe arms about her.

In the middle of the night, Sam awoke to find his bed cold and Julia gone. Naked, he ran across his bedroom floor and came to a relieved stop when he saw Julia curled up in a chair in the sitting room, staring at the bare hearth, a single candle illuminating her.

She didn't see him immediately, and for a moment he thought about how isolated he'd felt without her in bed. He knew he'd be sleeping alone again eventually, but now he craved every moment he had with her.

But he couldn't stand to see her looking so sad.

"We never had the chance to dance," he said softly.

She looked up at him and tried to smile, but it was a bleak effort. He walked toward her, holding out his hand. "Dance with me."

She looked down his naked body, and a reluctant smile lifted the corners of her mouth. "I'm sure I've never had such a scandalous dance partner."

"I'm glad to hear it."

She gave a soft laugh and accepted his hand. He took her in his arms and began a slow waltz across the carpeted floor. The candlelight played on her upturned face and her short hair that hung loose and scattered. The pale light cast shadows on the shirt, changing it from opaque to translucent depending on where she danced.

He swept her into a turn to avoid one of the desks, and she finally relaxed and laughed.

"You're very good," she murmured.

He could feel the fluidity in her muscles, the way she moved to music she only heard in her mind. He smiled and just watched her face, glad he'd briefly chased away the shadows.

"Where did you learn to waltz?" she asked.

He moved faster, dipping her through the turn. "Bombay. Officers were in great demand as dancing partners."

"I have a hard time imagining you learning to dance on a woman's whim."

He saw the question she didn't ask. She wanted to know if it was at a particular woman's request.

He grinned. "Nick Wright and Will Chadwick placed a wager that I could not refuse. That's the only reason I learned."

She could not quite hide her relief, and he found himself leaning closer. "Jealous, Julia?"

"I have no reason to be," she said primly.

"No, no reason at all," he said in a low, heartfelt voice.

He picked her up and carried her back to bed, where he memorized every curve of her body, the taste of her mouth, her smothered gasps of pleasure. Would these memories someday give him peace, or only remind him of everything he'd lost?

Julia awoke before dawn, with the first glimpse of contentment she'd felt in . . . years. She was warm and drowsy and safe for the moment in Sam's arms. They lay spooned together, her back to his front.

His arm was draped over her now, his breath warm in her ear. Already his erection pressed into her backside, and she gave a soft giggle and snuggled closer.

"Is something amusing?" he murmured, cupping her breast and tweaking her nipple gently.

She looked over her shoulder to see his eyes heavy with sleep, flecks of gold and brown, full of tenderness that made her ache with regret for the future. She sighed and ignored her sudden melancholia and the thought of empty years without him.

"Nothing amusing at all," she said, giving him a quick kiss on the nose. "What are we doing today?"

"We're going to finish searching the house."

"What about the statue?"

"I'll talk to Henry about it. Looking it over in the daylight might suggest a way to open it that I couldn't find last night."

"Or maybe it's just a plain statue."

"Maybe. But it's too coincidental."

She rolled until she could put her arms around him and snuggle her face into his chest. Sighing, she trailed her fingers through his chest hair. "Waking up like this feels wonderful."

His muscles stiffened slightly, though she knew he tried to hide it.

"It does," he finally answered.

So many words came to her lips, but she wouldn't ruin the moment by saying them. *What are you keeping secret, Sam?* Even held close to his heart, there was yet a distance between them that she had no means to cross. He didn't *seem* to hold her past against her, and she had finally started to let go of her guilt. But when she was free—and she'd begun to believe that such a miracle was possible—what kind of future did she have without Sam? Should she offer to go back to India with him, live life following the drum as an officer's wife, waiting for the day he wouldn't come home to her? And would he even want her there?

She was making herself crazy thinking of the future when the present was all she had. And if part of that present was being able to love Sam, however briefly, she would accept it gladly. She closed her eyes and memorized the feel of his skin on hers, the roughness of his fingertips stroking her arm, the softness of his mouth when he kissed her forehead.

"The day awaits," he said, throwing back the blankets.

She groaned and burrowed closer to his side.

"What if Lucy brings you hot water and finds us like this?"

"You mean if she got past your door barricades? We could trust her with the truth—and then she'd stop following me about wearing a silly expression."

He squeezed her bottom, then gave her a push that sent her to the edge of the bed.

"Hey!"

"Out of my room so I can dress."

"You don't want my help?" She looked pointedly at his erection, which hadn't shown any sign of subsiding.

He laughed and gave her another push so that she ended up on her feet. "We'll have tonight. And maybe we'll have something to celebrate."

She sighed and picked up her shirt from the floor. "We can only hope."

Chapter 21

~~~

After seeing that Frances had recovered, Julia spent the morning following Sam through the family wing, taking notes on what they'd searched.

She had not realized that with so much decorative detail in the plaster walls and ceiling, Sam would feel the need to run his hands over everything. Every room seemed to take an hour, but he wanted to be thorough, in case the statue was a false lead.

They were walking down the long gallery, with its family paintings on either side, when Julia stopped to finish a notation in her notebook. Sam entered the billiard room ahead of her. She was so intent on her work that she didn't hear anyone approach until there was an audible gasp.

She looked up to see Lucy standing not ten feet away from her, staring at her with a stunned expression, then looking over her head. Julia looked behind her and realized she was standing directly beneath her own full-length portrait.

Lucy's face drained of color, and then she dropped her armful of towels and ran.

Julia ran after her. She gave no thought to telling Sam; she just needed to stop Lucy before the maid did. . . . whatever she had in mind.

"Lucy!" she called in a hoarse whisper, but the girl never even looked back over her shoulder.

They followed the dark corridors into the back of the house and the servants' wing. Lucy reached her sister's room, opened the door without knocking, and slammed it behind her. A few seconds later, Julia, out of breath and desperate, halted only momentarily before opening the door herself and stepping inside.

She found Lucy and Frances standing face to face in the center of the sitting room. Both turned to stare at Julia. Frances winced.

Lucy's complexion went red as she pointed a shaking finger at Julia. "You heard me, Frances! That—that is not a man, and he—she looks just like a member of General Reed's family!"

Well, at least Julia hadn't been immediately

recognized. She raised both hands pleadingly. "Let me explain—"

Lucy ignored her. "She's probably one of the old master's by-blows, come to snoop about now that Miss Julia is in trouble!" She rounded on Julia and took a menacing step in her direction. "How dare you! Lying about your identity—pretending to be a constable. Does Constable Seabrook know?" Her eyes went wide. "Is he in on this, too?"

Julia sighed and rubbed her hand across her eyes. Where to begin? This was not something that could be eased over with another lie.

"Lucy, calm yourself," Frances said, her voice as smooth as the quietest violin. "We do not need one of the staff rushing in here curious because of all the noise."

"But—"

"Will you allow me to explain now?" Julia asked with a soft voice.

She was surprised to see tears shining in Lucy's eyes, obviously tears of anger and embarrassment. Julia felt guilty for having caused them.

"Go ahead and try," Lucy said belligerently. "Then my sister will see you thrown into the yard."

Julia lowered her voice and looked plaintively at Lucy. "I'm not a bastard child—I'm Julia Reed."

Lucy's face went strangely blank, and then she

gaped at her sister. "Can you believe what this—"

"It's true," Frances said quietly.

Julia winced and shook her head. Frances had aligned herself with the deception, when Julia had meant to leave her out of it.

Lucy took a step back from them both. "What are you saying?"

"This is our mistress, Miss Julia, and she needed my help, so I've given it."

"You've known, all this time, yet you said nothing?" Lucy demanded, aghast. "You let me—you let all of us look like fools!"

"I warned you to stay away from the constable," Frances said. "But you wouldn't listen. I tried to protect you—"

"Protect me!" Lucy gave a laugh that held no amusement. "You let me believe she was—a man!"

"It was my idea, not Frances's," Julia said quickly. "It was the only way I could remain unexposed as I tried to discover the truth."

"The truth is that you're an escaped criminal who belongs in jail!"

"Lucy!" Frances said in a shocked voice. "That is your anger talking! You know Miss Julia would never have committed such a terrible crime."

But Lucy's tears had begun to fall down her cheeks, and she scrubbed at them angrily with her fists. "My brother is in trouble because of you! What does he think about your lies—"

She broke off, and a startled look crossed her face, which darkened to an ugly crimson. Then she turned and ran out the door.

Julia exchanged a panicked look with Frances.

"Where do you think she's going now?" the housekeeper said.

"I know exactly where she's going."

Julia opened the door and went back down the corridor, trying to keep her pace more normal until they left the servants' wing. Then she started to run, taking the stairs two at a time to the first floor. She saw Lucy at the far end of the gallery only a second before the maid disappeared into the billiard room.

When Julia and Frances crowded through the door together, they found Sam just crawling out from beneath the billiard table, staring in dismay at Lucy's tear-stained face. He rose to his feet.

"May I help ye?" he asked her, then turned to look questioningly at the other two women.

Lucy's stare focused on his face, and Julia wondered if she was trying to see past the beard, past the years that had etched lines fanning out from Sam's eyes, to the amiable big brother Lucy had only known for six short years.

Frances closed the door, and the sound seemed to break some sort of spell.

Lucy licked her lips and whispered, "Are you my brother?"

He betrayed not a single emotion as he glanced at Julia. "What's goin' on here?"

"Stop it!" Lucy cried. "I asked you a question and I deserve an answer!"

He still pinned Julia with his stare, until she almost felt guilty. "She saw me standing beneath my portrait."

Sam took a deep breath and faced Lucy again. His whole demeanor softened, gentled, and his smile held a love that made Julia's eyes sting.

"Yes, I'm your brother."

Julia expected more anger, but Lucy simply flung herself at Sam and began to sob. He folded her tightly in his embrace and just hung on.

"It's all right, baby," he murmured, over and over again.

Frances wiped away a tear and smiled at Julia.

As the truth was slowly explained, Lucy fired question after question at Sam, never letting go of his hand. They told her almost everything, because how could they keep it a secret and allow her to risk her life by saying the wrong thing? But they didn't let her know that Lewis's henchman was nearby, a constant threat.

When Sam finally stopped speaking, Lucy just stared at him for several moments.

"I can't believe I didn't know it was you," she said softly. "Your hair color, your eyes—"

"It's been a long time, and we've both

changed. You've grown into a lovely young woman."

"A *stupid* young woman," she said, blushing.

"Don't be upset, Lucy. My training is such that if you had recognized me, I wouldn't be doing a very good job. Henry already proved that to me."

"*Henry* knows, too?" she cried in dismay.

"Shh!" Frances looked over her shoulder at the closed door. "This is why you weren't told. You're much too loud!"

"I can be quiet! How can I help?"

Sam rose to his feet and looked down at her sternly. "You can help by staying away from us and behaving in a normal fashion. There are dangers all around us, and if we're captured, I don't want you brought to the attention of the law."

"But—" Lucy glanced at Julia for the first time, then looked away. "Surely I can help, if Miss Julia is."

Julia leaned toward her and spoke with deep sincerity. "My life is at stake, Lucy. By helping me, Sam has put his own life on the line, and that scares me more than anything. But at least I know he can take care of himself. Please don't make me worry about you, too! I don't know what I'd do if you—or any of Sam's family—were hurt."

Tears stung her eyes, and she tried to wipe them away with her fingertips before they could ruin her cosmetics. She felt Sam's gaze on her, knew he wanted to comfort her, but would not in front of his family. She understood his motives, though feeling like their relationship was a shameful secret hung heavy on her heart.

He looked solemnly at his youngest sister. "Lucy, remember it is our duty to help Miss Julia."

Julia felt mildly annoyed by his words and tone.

"She is one of our employers, and without her family, our life could have been severe. We should be grateful."

Grateful? Julia was appalled at such submissive advice. She could not imagine why he was going on in such a way. But she could hardly question him in front of his sisters.

To distract herself, she brightly said to Lucy, "Do you know I remember when your sisters and I used to pretend you were our baby doll?"

When Lucy smiled, Frances said, "Not me, of course. I was too often saddled with the real responsibility of watching over you. And you're still a difficult child."

Lucy laughed.

Smiling, Sam chucked Lucy under the chin and walked to the door. "Ladies, I have much left to do today, so I'll bid you farewell."

He left, closing the door behind him, and the three women looked at each other.

Julia found herself the sudden object of Lucy's scrutiny.

"So you've spent a lot of time with Sam," Lucy began slowly.

She willed herself not to blush, and prayed the cosmetics would hide any suspicious color. "He rescued me, and is doing his best to prove my innocence."

"Does he talk about his family at all?"

Frances started to scold her sister, but Julia shook her head. "It's all right. I'll answer that. It's been very difficult to be here and not tell his family who he is. He loves you all so much. We don't want any of you in danger."

"But so many of us know—why not our mother? After all, she hasn't seen her son in fourteen years. And God forbid, if he's killed in this dangerous situation, how will she feel when she discovers that he was so close and wouldn't see her?"

Julia's stomach twisted with sickness and fear at the thought of Sam lost to her—and his family—for all time.

"If my mother knows the truth," Lucy continued patiently, "who is she going to tell, when she so seldom leaves the cottage?"

"Why doesn't she leave the cottage?" Julia asked with concern.

"She's not well. She insisted on coming to the harvest dance last night, but we were all worried for her health. She talks about Sam a lot lately, and I know she feels like she's going to die without ever seeing him again."

Julia walked away from the sisters, looking out the window as if she could see the little gardener's cottage nestled within a riot of colorful flowers. She'd always thought it looked enchanted, with its pretty thatched roof and air of peaceful stillness.

What if Sam's mother was truly ill? If Julia continued to keep mother and son apart, how would she live with herself if Mrs. Sherryngton died?

But Sam certainly would not listen to this argument. He would think his family's safety was more important. Maybe Julia was thinking with her heart, but she felt it was telling her strongly that Sam and his mother should be reunited, regardless of the danger.

"All right," she finally said, turning back to the Sherryngton sisters. "We can't tell Sam to go to his mother—he'll refuse, thinking he's protecting her."

"Then we'll have to trick him," Lucy said, with a bit too much glee.

Frances sighed heavily. "He'll be upset with us for lying to him."

"But your mother will be comforted," Julia said in a gentle voice.

So together they agreed on a plan.

During luncheon with the staff, it took every bit of Sam's attention to focus on staying within his character, rather than dwelling on his unsuccessful search of the house. Lucy and Frances were not in attendance. He overheard that they'd gone to shop in the village together, which made him worried. But at least they were together.

Sam wanted to take out every bit of his frustration on their attacker's face, but he reminded himself that this case was closer to being solved than before. He was beginning to think they'd need Lewis himself to wrap everything up.

After luncheon, in her no-nonsense constable voice, Julia requested a moment of his time. When they were alone in their private sitting room, standing as far from the door as possible, she looked up at him with her big soulful eyes and asked what they were going to do about the statue.

He blinked at her, wondering how she could so easily affect him with just a look. He felt a desperation to be a part of her again, like time was slipping away from them. And it was. These brief moments with her, this enforced intimacy, would soon be gone. Two constables couldn't just remain at Hopewell Manor indefinitely. There wasn't much left to search.

The statue *had* to be the key.

"We need to talk to my brother about Venus," Sam said grimly. "He'll be better able to tell us when Lewis had it brought in, who did the work. Maybe he can discover if the base is hollow."

"Then what are we waiting for? Let's go find Henry."

Sam was disappointed to find out that Henry wouldn't be on the estate for the rest of the day.

He looked back at the manor, fists on his hips, and thought of finishing the indoor searching, but he just couldn't do it, not when there was a statue with hidden secrets.

And nagging at his thoughts was a dark shadow, a question about *why* Henry, who was as dedicated to his work as their father had been, would leave for the day. First Frances and Lucy, now Henry. Was someone in their family ill?

Julia softly spoke some of his thoughts aloud. "Sam, we can't wait another day to find out about the statue. If Henry can help us—"

"I know. Let's walk to the cottage. We'll keep to the main path for safety's sake."

As they walked through the gardens and past the orchard to the gardener's cottage, he constantly surveyed their surroundings. He almost wanted their assailant to strike right now, so Sam would have an excuse to relieve his frustration. Thoughts churned through his mind. Lately, he'd been experiencing the strongest urge to take Julia's hand, to show the world what she meant to him.

For what purpose? he asked himself bitterly. Was he just trying to show everyone that the gardener's son could seduce the daughter of the household?

But he knew it wasn't that. It was Julia herself he wanted to convince, to show her that their brief time together meant the world to him.

Too soon they reached the kitchen garden on one side of his brother's cottage.

He slowed down. "Why don't you go inside and ask Henry to come out?"

Julia had only gone past the gate when suddenly the front door opened. Sam stared in shock as his entire family started spilling out, coming down the stone walkway: Henry grinning; Abigail and Alice wearing sunny smiles; Frances and Lucy looking guilty but pleased; and lastly his mother, who stared at him while tears ran down her face.

Julia gave him a little push. "Go on, they're waiting," she murmured.

This was all wrong, but he couldn't stop himself from taking a few hesitant steps up the path, even as he looked about to make sure no one else observed this startling family reunion.

And then he had his mother in his arms, and Abigail and Alice tried to hug him at the same time, their pregnant bellies bumping him and each other. He closed his eyes and just hung on.

"Oh, Samuel," his mother murmured over and over again.

From behind, Henry laughed. "Why don't we let him come inside, Mama? He still needs to keep his secrets."

Sam grinned down at his mother, who slipped her hand around his arm and let him escort her. When they were all inside and the door was closed, the house was noisy and overly warm with so many bodies—but full of the good smells and sounds of home. Sam knew that Frances, Julia, and Lucy had tricked him into coming here, but he tried not to let himself worry. It was too late for that.

His mother didn't let go of his hand as he answered all their questions. He only told enough not to worry them too deeply, and he promised that he and Julia were close to finding out the truth.

His mother turned to study Julia. "I thought I knew you from somewhere, miss, but never thought you were hiding your *gender*. Certainly fooled Lucy, who has talked of nothing but Constable Fitzjames for days."

Lucy's face went fiery red once again. "Sam taught Miss Julia to hide herself, and she did it well."

Sam grew uncomfortable when his mother looked from him to Julia, then narrowed her eyes in worry. He knew what she was thinking. She'd always warned him that he was too close to the daughter of the household, that he would only get himself hurt in the end.

And she'd been right. But he couldn't do anything else but helplessly follow Julia as long as he was able. She needed his protection.

Yet for her sake, he also needed to put as much distance between them as he could—even if only during the day. With resignation, he let his

mother draw him into Henry and Sarah's bedroom, which had once been her own.

She held his hands and looked up at him.
"Even after all this time, Samuel, you still look at
Miss Julia without the proper respect."

He closed his eyes. "We're friends, Mama. I
can't help that."

"But you always want more than you should
have. And it can only come to a bad end."

"I know, I know. I'm heading back to the army
as soon as I'm finished here."

"Does she know that?"

"Yes."

"You only hurt her by letting her think otherwise."

Hurt her? Even though the cold truth was between him and Julia? Didn't his mother know
how hurt *he* was?

But she was right, and he understood that.
He had to show Julia that nothing could
change between them—even though everything had.

His mother smiled at him. "Come spend time
with us before you leave again, Samuel. You
have been gone too long."

He kissed her cheek and led her back into the
main room of the cottage, understanding her
unspoken worry that she might not be here the
next time he came home. He didn't know what
to do or say, but he couldn't linger here, regretting the past.

Sam turned to Henry. "We need your help in the gardens. Can you come now?"

When the brothers walked to the door, their mother rose too slowly to her feet. Sam winced.

"Samuel, when will you come back?"

"Not until this is over, Mama. It's too dangerous for everyone involved. And two of your daughters knew that."

He glanced at Lucy and Frances, who both quickly looked away.

His mother patted his hand. "It's enough to see you again, to know in my heart that you're alive and healthy. I'll keep you and Miss Julia in my prayers."

"Just don't be whispering those prayers aloud," he said, kissing her forehead.

Chapter 22

The afternoon was full of a mellow warmth and hazy sunshine as Sam, Julia, and Henry stared up at Venus in puzzlement. Henry had tried everything short of using his tools on the statue, and was just offering to fetch those when Julia shook her head, understanding that Sam had something else in mind.

Henry scowled. "But if we don't open it—"

"Oh, we'll see it opened," Sam said, giving a cold smile. "Only we'll be watching Lewis do it. It's time to lure him north."

Julia and Sam closeted themselves in their sitting room the rest of the afternoon to work on the letter to Lewis. She was ready for Sam's demeanor to change this time, and she watched it steal over him in fascination and dread.

Every tender expression on his face, in his eyes, the ones that she cherished whenever he looked at her in private, disappeared. He had a distance, a coldness in his eyes, in his voice when he began to talk about Lewis, about what they would have to do to lure her brother to Hopewell Manor. She always felt at times like these that she was glimpsing Sam the Soldier, a man who had to submerge his good-natured qualities to take on a role that didn't come easily to him.

"We can't write anything about the clues we've discovered in the house," Sam said, "or he'll think it's either us or one of his servants. I'd rather pretend to be a villager, someone who saw him take money from the statue one night."

"But what if the money isn't hidden there?"

He gave her a brief smile. "We'll just say that we saw him take the money, but not from where, that maybe we think he's involved in the crime with his sister. That way we're not claiming you're innocent, which might make him suspicious of *us*. The letter could be from a disgruntled merchant who was owed money for a long time."

"That's all well and good, but what will we do once he gets here?" she asked. "Won't it only be our word against his that we saw him go to the statue?"

"That's why we're going to consult someone beyond reproach," he said with satisfaction. "I'm sending a note to my old spymaster, Colonel Whittington, to ask his advice. He'll know the best way to prove to the government that you're innocent, and that your brother is the true criminal."

Julia shivered at the thought of revealing their whereabouts. "Are you sure he can be trusted? After all, you, Nick, and Will all believed I was guilty."

From across the desk, Sam started to reach for her, then pulled back. "We have proof now, Julia. We can convince the colonel. I'll get Henry to take a letter by train to Lewis in London—"

"But won't Henry be in danger?"

"I'll make him promise to leave the letter without being seen."

"And what about the message to Colonel Whittington?"

"I'll ask Abigail's husband to help us. I remember him from long ago—although I never would have thought my sister would fall in love with him." He gave her a crooked grin. "Can you trust me?"

Oh, she trusted him. But there were clouds in his eyes, hiding his thoughts, and she wondered if she trusted himself.

For two days, while they waited for their letters to work, Julia watched Sam immerse himself in his ongoing search of the manor. During the day he seemed to hold her away, now that the end was approaching. He treated her with a deference that bothered her, as if he were already putting her back on her pedestal as the master's daughter. Their partnership seemed fragile, no longer equal. He actually deferred to her about the order of the rooms they searched, as if her station in life mattered more than his knowledge and experience.

Perhaps it hadn't been such a good idea to re-unite him with his family. She vividly remembered the sad way Mrs. Sherryngton had looked at her, as if she understood Julia's every emotion, and knew Julia would be hurt in the end—when Sam went back to his place in life, his station beneath her.

Whenever she was alone in their suite—behind locks and barricades, of course—she found herself wandering his bedroom, touching the things that were his. To her surprise, in a drawer she found her length of braided hair which she thought she'd thrown away. It hurt her that he'd kept it, even as she foolishly cried tears over his sensitivity. And then she discovered her letters, dozens of them, faded and old and torn—obviously reread many times, but never answered. She was determined to find the right time to discuss them with him.

But not at night. Desperately Julia and Sam came together in heat and passion. But on the second night since they'd sent two letters out, when he suggested she should return to her own bed, she decided she'd had enough.

She sat up in bed and turned to face him, holding a sheet to her breasts only because she knew he wouldn't be able to concentrate on her words if she gave him a reason not to.

When he started to push the covers away as if to rise, she put a hand on his chest. "Wait. We need to talk."

He glanced at her hand, then up the long line of her arm to her face. There was devilment in his eyes, and she knew he would try to distract her.

She pushed him back down onto his pillow, tucked the sheet beneath her arms, and then looked at him with all the seriousness she could muster.

"In a drawer, I found several curious things."

He stiffened and the merriment in his eyes faded away. "My drawer?"

"Yes. You kept my hair and my letters, the ones you never answered. Can you tell me why?"

"I wish you wouldn't have gone where you didn't belong."

"Well, I did. I was sad, and thinking of you, and I just . . . found myself among your things, as if they could give me solace. But all they did was leave me with more questions."

When he said nothing, she felt trapped by frustration.

"I need to understand you," she said softly.

"You're confusing me, as if you're two different Sams, one during the day, and one at night."

He fluffed his pillow against the headboard and sat back. There was a rising belligerence about him that she had prepared herself to do battle with.

He said, "The Sam who comes to your bed is leaving the day's cares behind."

Sighing, she leaned forward. "And that's a good thing. It is the daytime Sam that I don't understand."

"You know what I am, Julia. I'm a soldier."

"And a spy, which seems to me to be a different thing. It's all right if you weren't as good a soldier as you were a spy."

His smile was bitter as he shook his head. "You don't need to see me as either. That's part of the reason I didn't answer your letters."

She was shocked by his statement, as if her life didn't depend on his skills as both. He didn't quite meet her eyes.

"Sam, why wouldn't I be proud of what you do? You're a hero."

"I'm not a hero!"

Sam wished to hell that he could seduce these questions out of Julia's mind, make her think of nothing but their nights of passion. It was all they had left—couldn't she see that? His days were filled with the worries of protecting her, vindicating her, preparing her for when he was gone. She knew the impropriety of a relationship between them, yet still she sought him out each night, and he couldn't refuse her.

But maybe it was time to let her see what her "hero" truly was. Then she'd understand why he needed to return to the army, why it was the only place for him.

"Sam."

She tried to take his hand, but he shook his head. He didn't want to feel the inevitable stiffening of her fingers, the way she'd pull away from him when she heard the truth. He looked into her eyes, so blue and innocent, and knew he was about to destroy the simple faith she'd had in him since childhood.

"You know why I went into the army," he began impassively, "but you don't know why I stayed, or why I became a spy."

"Then tell me," she whispered. "I need to know everything."

He couldn't look at her as he spoke, so he turned to the single candle as if fascinated by the flame. "I was only a gardener when I left England, but soldiering taught me survival, not just in the wilderness, but in the midst of enemies. I liked the challenge, the way after a long day I was too tired to even think." *About you.* "And believe me, I was never poor at it. I was *too* good. The discomforts and the bad food never bothered me. Marksmanship came easily to me, and I seemed to be able to figure out an enemy's mind in a way few soldiers could."

"Why is this so bad?" she asked. "Of course you'd be good at whatever you put your mind to."

He took a deep breath and stared off into the darkness, seeing other lands. "You know what India and Afghanistan are like, the very foreignness of life there. I relished it, relished what I was doing. I enjoyed the triumph of besting my enemy, the reward of the kill—and I don't mean animals. There's something dark inside me, and I had no idea it was there until I was fighting for my life. The killing eventually became second nature to me."

"You were fighting for your life!" she interrupted.

"But did I have to enjoy it so much?" he demanded in a hoarse whisper. His mouth was dry, his heart pounded—he didn't want to tell her anything of this. "I felt like I was turning into the enemy. At least they killed to protect their families, their land, while I was killing for money."

"You were protecting England."

"Stop making excuses for me! You don't know how I felt inside, what I did."

And in his mind he was there again, in the hot, moist jungles of the Punjab, feeling invincible, untouchable—until it all fell apart.

"Tell me," she whispered.

He looked right at her, so she could see the monster inside him. "Another soldier and I were captured. We wouldn't betray our regiment's position, so they tortured my friend to death, forcing me to watch."

He made himself study the shock in her eyes, the way her face paled, committing it all to memory.

"Oh, Sam."

"I escaped, and I killed the commander who'd ordered the torture." He leaned toward her, watched her eyes widen. "And then I slit the throats of all six guardsmen, even though they were only following orders. I made sure they saw who killed them as they died. The final man begged on his knees to live, but he knew secrets they'd tortured out of my friend, secrets that would have to die with him."

He watched a single tear slide from her glistening eyes.

"And when I realized how glad I had been to kill them, how easily I'd done it—" Even all these years later, his throat felt thick and tight, his eyes burned at the memories of what he was capable of. "I hated myself. I spent two days wandering through the jungle alone, trying to get back to my regiment, full of despair. I was determined to resign my commission, to get far away from this bloodthirsty man I'd become."

He stopped, letting it sink into her mind, letting her understand what kind of demons haunted him, had changed him forever from that simple gardener's son.

"But you didn't quit," she said calmly.

He frowned at her. "No. I received word that my father had died. What skills did I have that could earn my family as much money as professional killing could do? But then the Political Department found me. They thought I'd make a good agent. I discovered I could use skill to evade the enemy, rather than killing him. I—I thought maybe I had overcome the darkness in my soul, maybe even buried it for good."

"Sam, why do you berate yourself?" she asked. "You protected your men, protected your life."

"It's still here inside me!" He slammed to his feet and walked to the window, where the darkness could swallow him. "When I followed that constable away from Hopewell Manor, I wanted to kill him for threatening you. I didn't even realize I'd put my hand on my pistol. A few more minutes and I'd have murdered an innocent man."

"But you didn't do it."

"No. But I wanted to." He kept his back to her and sighed. "I didn't answer your letters because you were living in a fantasy world where I could be the friend who rescued you. I had to make you realize that in the eyes of the world we are master and servant. Your parents would have destroyed any letter I sent you, because they understood how things are."

It took all of Julia's will not to cry for Sam's lost innocence. At last she understood his secrets, his worries—his past. And she realized that although she had finally accepted her own past, he wasn't ready to accept and forgive his.

Letting the sheet fall, she got out of bed and walked to him. He flinched when she touched his back, and she wished she could take all his pain away. But she was at a loss as to how to help him.

So she did what her womanly instincts told her to do: she kissed his back, pressed her face against his warm skin, put her arms around him when he would have left her.

She felt like he was a wounded deer, afraid to run, afraid to stay. And then finally he broke away from her and opened the door to the sitting room.

"Go back to your own bed, Julia," he said.

"Sam—"

"No. I said too much, and we both need to think about it."

She walked toward him slowly, let him look his fill at her nakedness.

"You know you can tell me anything, Sam," she whispered.

There was a faint smile on his lips, but it didn't reach the darkness in his eyes. "Go to sleep. You might think differently in the morning."

But she wouldn't. She stood in their sitting room naked, shivering, listening to his door close behind her. How could she help him?

Chapter 23

$\sim\!\!\infty\!\!\sim$

In the middle of the next morning, Julia needed to return to her bedroom. The binding around her breasts was slipping down, and she didn't want to look like her middle was expanding when the cloth dropped. Sam insisted on accompanying her, and she felt more like a delicate flower than a woman whose life was under constant threat.

And was that his point? Logic told her she needed to beware of their attacker, but Sam seemed to have other motives where she was concerned. Was he trying to prove over and over again how wide the gulf was between them?

That he was either a servant or a savage soldier, neither of whom she should want?

But she wanted all of him, his strengths and his flaws. How could she tell him she'd follow him anywhere, even back to India? She didn't want to live without him. And guilty or innocent, what place would she have in England when everything was done?

But she knew him well. He would be appalled by her decision. She would bide her time until she could trust that he'd see the truth.

So she let him walk her back to their room. She thought he almost wanted to take her elbow deferentially, but at least their roles prohibited that. As she opened her bedroom door, she thought she heard the door connecting to the sitting room softly close.

She turned to stare wide-eyed at Sam, but he, too, had heard, for he was already several paces down the corridor. She followed as he flung the sitting room door wide and raced in. She was in time to see him throw himself at the stranger dressed in black, and they both rolled to the floor in a pile. Sam landed several hard blows to his face and stomach. Julia pulled the pistol out of her pocket, but she couldn't possibly shoot at the mix of arms and legs and thrashing bodies.

But she *could* use it for a hard blow to the assailant's head when he was on top. He slumped over Sam, who threw him to the side.

Sam grinned at her, her admiring partner once again.

She grinned back. "Shall we tie him up?"

When they had him bound to a chair, Sam removed the scarf from his face, revealing a receding hairline, and a broad, oiled mustache. He dumped a pitcher of water on the stranger, who sputtered into consciousness. The man struggled for only a moment, and then he glared at the two of them while streams of water ran from his hair. Blood trickled from his nose.

"Hello," Sam said softly. "You seem to be in a bind."

"This won't get you anywhere," the man said coldly. He moved against the ropes and winced. "I won't answer any of your questions."

"And why not?" Sam asked, pointedly putting his pistol on the desk where their assailant could see it.

Julia watched the two men nervously, but her focus was on Sam. Now that she knew his secret worries, she wondered how a situation like this would make him feel. He looked a little wild-eyed, as if he were barely holding himself back.

"You're not going to shoot me," the man said, though he didn't sound very confident. "It will just be another murder on your head. And what would be the point?"

"There would be one less threat to Julia. That's pretty much all I need."

And it was, she saw with shock. Sam's fingers played with the pistol, touching the handle, caressing the trigger, while his face was full of expectation. What was the truth? He was a man gifted at submerging himself in any character. Was all this a ruse to force their assailant into a confession?

Or did Sam truly not care whether the man lived or died?

The stranger was frowning at him. "It's foolish to threaten me for so paltry a reason."

"Paltry? I have impressive evidence against the general—I don't need your testimony."

That was an exaggeration if she'd ever heard one, so she tried to force herself to relax. If they could make him testify against Lewis, it would help seal their case. Sam was a professional; he wouldn't throw aside a witness.

Would he?

If only she knew what to do, what to say.

"If you want to live," Sam continued, "then tell me why I should keep you alive. And please don't malign my intelligence by making me believe I *need* you alive. You've promised to thwart our mission, you've threatened to attack Miss Reed, you've hurt Mrs. Cooper. Those aren't good reasons to keep you alive."

A bead of sweat rolled down the man's temple. "You're not as intelligent as you think. I'm not falling for this ruse."

Swiftly, Sam put one big hand around the front of the man's throat. Julia was startled, and the assailant could only make a strangled protest.

"Ruse?" Sam said softly, his grin manic, his face near his victim's. "I think you misunderstand your importance. I don't care whether you live or die. Miss Reed might."

She tried to catch her breath, shocked at the icy coldness in Sam's eyes when he glanced at her.

"But I can convince her that we don't need you. Not when we already know where the general hid his money."

She licked her dry lips, surprised that Sam would reveal such a thing. To her surprise, their assailant's eyes widened with interest.

"You're lying," the man said. "The general would never be so foolish as to hide something here, where he seldom comes."

"So then he doesn't confide everything in you, does he?" Sam countered.

Julia couldn't tear her gaze away from Sam's face as he picked up the pistol. She held her breath, and even the stranger betrayed a momentary start. But Sam pocketed the weapon and reached for a gag.

"You think about our discussion," Sam said with obvious reluctance. "We'll talk again tonight."

"That's hours from now," the man said. "You can't keep me here all day."

Sam wrapped the gag about his head, effectively ending his protests. "Of course I can. No food, no water—no breaks to use a chamber pot. Tonight, you let me know when you want to convince me why I should keep you alive."

Sam glanced at Julia, and she was uneasy about how excited his expression was, as if threatening a man with death were something he always looked forward to.

"Julia, you continue the search. Please explain my absence to the staff by telling them I'm ill and need my rest. They're not to disturb me or enter the suite."

"Very well," she answered.

Was he sending her away so she wouldn't have to see him come close to killing their captive? She wanted to remind him of the memories that haunted him, the things he regretted he'd done.

But did he regret them? Or did he only wish he weren't the kind of man who could so easily kill?

As she walked to the door, she heard their assailant make several strangled noises deep in his throat. She looked back at his panicked expression. Did he, too, think Sam would kill him? Wasn't that what he was supposed to think?

She stepped out into the hall and closed the door behind her, leaning back against it to listen. She heard nothing at first, then the click of footsteps into Sam's bedroom. She moved down the corridor until she reached his door, then knocked softly.

He opened it, and though he seemed to relax on seeing her, there was a wariness in his expression. "I thought you'd gone below."

"Not yet. Can I talk to you?"

He pulled her inside, then spoke softly. "I don't want him to hear. I'm sorry you had to see that. I've had to play that kind of character before. It tends to make the subject afraid of me."

She nodded and tried to feel reassured. "I just wanted to know what your plans are."

She noticed that he was perspiring, that he seemed tired as he leaned back against the wardrobe and folded his arms across his chest. "I believe I stated them in front of Lewis's henchman."

"So having him wait there all day will make him answer your questions?"

"It might. He's obviously not a soldier and hasn't been trained in hardship."

"What if he won't talk?"

Sam sighed. "We'll just have to see. There are some simple techniques that should make him quite talkative."

She winced.

"You know I don't want him dead," he said. "We need his testimony."

She stared into his eyes, worried that he was prepared to do *anything* to prove her innocence. But did she want that from him? Would she be able to live with herself if he had another reason to feel guilty?

"You're worried about me, aren't you?" He frowned down at her.

She licked her lips, not quite able to meet his eyes.

"You must wish I wouldn't have told you about my past," he said.

"No! Never think that. I just don't want you to have another thing to feel guilty over."

Some of the tension left him. "I promise he'll talk quite easily. I won't deny that it's hard to hold myself back. I could make him talk immediately, but . . ." His voice faded off, and his look was far away. "I don't want to have to do that."

Wasn't that why she was worried? Would he feel no remorse having to torture the man, and perhaps take his life? And then he'd think his soul was beyond hope.

She couldn't let that happen.

Hours later, Sam eventually arrived in the servants' hall for supper, settling in to talk to Frances, and Julia was able to leave easily. He let her go with a wave, because now that their assailant was captured, he had less reason to fear for her.

As she climbed the stairs, she felt distant, even numb. But not uncertain, never that. They had some evidence now, and with Lewis coming, and even Colonel Whittington's help, she could hope to be exonerated.

The door to the sitting room was locked, but she had the key to her own bedroom. She heard the man's muffled sounds as she walked to the sitting room and stepped inside.

His red face quickly turned to face her. Again, he tried to speak, but his words were garbled behind the rag. He was tugging frantically on the ropes now, and she could see blood at his wrists. He'd been bound for over eight hours, and there was a desperation in his movements and a wild look in his eyes.

When she stepped closer, he stilled, glancing repeatedly behind her as if he expected to see Sam. She gave him a cold stare and went past him into Sam's room, emerging with a long-handled knife.

He watched her warily.

"I'm not like other women," she said softly, menacingly. "You know how I lived my life in the East, how I traveled through jungles and over mountains. I was given this knife during a tiger hunt by the Maharajah of Benares. And I'm an expert with it."

She lunged at him with the knife, and then buried it into the wooden chair between his thighs. He gave a hoarse cry and tried to rear back.

"Now listen to me carefully," she said. "I'm letting you go."

He blinked at her, and she could practically

see the workings of his twisted mind. He would agree to whatever she said, lie to her face, then break his word to try to kill her. He was, after all, a murderer.

But she had another plan, one that wouldn't make her into a cold-blooded murderer like he was.

"There are conditions," Julia said. "You are to leave Hopewell Manor immediately. You will speak with no one. I make no guarantees where Sam is concerned. He wants to kill you." She had no qualms about lying. "You also have my brother to worry about. I'll make sure he knows that you wanted his money more than you wanted to serve him."

She undid his gag and pulled it away. "Do we understand each other?"

The gag had stuck to the corners of his mouth, and she watched him try to moisten the parched skin.

"The general won't believe you," he said hoarsely.

"Won't he? It will be very easy for me to make sure a sum of money is missing." Well, it would be if she knew how to get *at* the money. "Are you saying that you don't want your freedom?"

He was squirming now, staring at the door. "How do I know this isn't a trap, that your lover isn't waiting outside the door to kill me?"

"If he wanted to kill you immediately, you'd already be dead." She lifted the pistol out of her pocket and looked at it thoughtfully. "I suggest you get as far away from here as you can. My brother was careless, and he's left enough evidence to incriminate himself. We already have the government on the way." So, these were a few half-truths. "Do we have an agreement?"

He was wriggling frantically now.

"I assume you need to use the chamber pot?" she asked.

He groaned. "Why are you doing this?"

"I have reasons you don't need to know. Do we have a bargain?"

He finally nodded, and she sliced the rope binding his hands and stepped away. He frantically tugged at the ropes on his ankles, while she trained the pistol on him.

When he stood up, she smiled. "There's a chamber pot in Sam's room. Allow me to escort you."

She didn't leave him for a minute. Afterward, she kept the pistol aimed at him as she followed him through the house, quiet now as the evening wound down. They avoided the servants' wing. He walked stiffly, obviously still sore from the bindings. He appeared somehow meeker, as if he thought she'd really rescued him from a bad end. This made her even more wary. She waited for her chance. She followed him to the stables, where, hiding the gun, she sent the tired groom to his bed and let the stranger saddle a horse.

Then they looked at each other. He suddenly lunged at her, but she was prepared. She shot him, and he fell backward, blood streaming from his upper arm. He groaned and rolled side to side, and she stood over him. He'd fallen right into her trap.

"My aim was true," she said softly, her pistol pointed at him. "I could have killed you, but I didn't. Leave here now. I'll be waiting if you return."

He managed to mount the horse, cradling his arm, which hung uselessly from his shoulder. With a snarled curse, he rode away into the darkness.

Chapter 24

Sam was feeling rather relaxed, knowing that his enemy was confined and no longer creeping about the manor. When Julia left for a moment of privacy, he felt confident she'd be fine, and it didn't even occur to him that she hadn't returned until Frances pointedly yawned an hour later. He wished his sister good night, and as he walked up through the dark house, he thought about Lewis's henchman, and what would need to be done.

Truly, he didn't imagine the man would be able to take much pain. Julia was worried about nothing. But if it took more effort, she would just have to realize that the man was her enemy, that certain things needed to be done for good to triumph.

The door to the sitting room was unlocked, and this gave Sam pause. He hadn't thought Julia would want to see their assailant again until they'd gotten all the information they could out of him.

He swung open the door and came to a complete stop. The chair was empty, the ropes scattered on the floor.

Where was Julia?

He already had his pistol in hand, and he kept a wary eye on Julia's open bedroom door, while he approached his own. His room was empty. Still hearing nothing, he crossed the sitting room, led with his pistol, and entered Julia's room. Nothing. He forced every bit of panic from his mind. He was just heading out into the corridor when he practically ran over Julia. She smiled at him warily as he caught her arms and steadied them both.

"Thank God," he murmured, pulling her inside the room for a quick hug. "He's gone, and I thought he'd taken you." He couldn't quite seem to catch his breath, and he filled himself with the beautiful sight of her.

She had a strange look on her face, as if she were uncomfortable as well as wary. Then she inhaled a deep breath that ended on a sigh. "I know he's gone."

"Were you following him?"

"No. I let him go."

Sam stared at her, not sure he'd even understood her words. "What did you say?"

"I let him go. I even shot him in the arm when he came after me again."

He was so stunned that he barely noticed the anger in his voice. "You let our only witness go? What the hell did you do that for?"

She raised her chin in the air, though she trembled with emotion. "I won't let you have any more nightmares of the things you wish you didn't have to do."

"You're saying you did this for *me*?"

Her eyes glistened with unshed tears. "You hated yourself for some of the things you'd had to do in life. I didn't want you to feel that way because of me."

He was stunned to realize that she had risked her own life, maybe even given up her freedom, all to protect him. He was overwhelmed at her sacrifice, unable to imagine what he had done to inspire such a gesture from her.

But in the end, it was his dark side that she had feared would emerge. He feared it, too. He turned his back on her and paced to the window.

"Sam," she said pleadingly, "don't you see that you have to come to terms with what you had to do to survive? It doesn't make you a horrible person."

He tried to ignore her words. "All we have now

is the hope that Lewis will come," he said coldly.

"He will. He won't risk losing the one reward he had for treason."

Sam turned to stare at her white face and softly said, "Let's hope you're right. Because if he doesn't, we might have to resign ourselves to leaving England and our pasts behind."

That night, Sam insisted that the footmen keep patrolling and that he and Julia barricade themselves into the room. He claimed Lewis's henchman was even more dangerous now that he'd been shot. But Julia was confident that she'd dealt him a wound that rendered him useless, at least for a couple days. But she didn't bother Sam with her opinions.

The next afternoon Lewis Reed's arrival was heralded by his groom, who came ahead to alert the household. Julia, just sitting down to luncheon, closed her eyes with relief. She felt nervous, shaky, and so full of hope. She exchanged a meaningful gaze with Sam, while the staff erupted around them. Mrs. Bonham and the kitchen maid went running to prepare a meal for the general, as Lucy and Florence were sent up to ready his suite. Julia quietly followed Sam, who was catching up with his sister in the corridor.

Sam caught Frances's elbow and leaned near her ear. "Don't mention us if you can help it."

"Did you know he was coming?" Frances demanded.

He nodded. "We'll keep out of the way. If he demands to see us, say we went into the village for the day."

Julia thought Sam's eyes were full of secrets as he looked at her. Had he forgiven her? She'd gone to bed alone last night. She had thought she was helping him, but his furious silence had been a shock to her. None of it mattered as long as he was safe, and able to heal instead of adding another sin to whatever mental list he kept. In the face of his anger, she had wanted to shout out her love for him, to prove that he was worth any sacrifice to her.

But she'd been afraid of his pity.

Julia and Sam spent the rest of the day in their suite, receiving occasional reports from Lucy on Lewis's whereabouts. Lewis had asked to see the constables investigating his sister, and when Frances told him that they were in the village, he'd insisted on seeing them when they returned. Sam said he would go to Lewis alone.

Julia found herself too nervous to read as the evening approached. She could only pace and think about how close they were to proving the truth. She was still so angry at everything her brother had done to her, but she was also full of pity and sadness at what he'd allowed his life to become. What if he recognized Sam? Would her brother try to kill him?

But Sam seemed unconcerned, poring over their notes, distant and polite. She wanted the old Sam back, the one who understood her every thought, who treated her with gentleness and love, even though he would never say the words.

Lewis spent much of the day alone in his bedroom, but for dinner taken in the dining room with the silent company of his footmen. Lucy claimed he seemed distracted, and hadn't asked any questions at all about the household.

In the evening, Sam went down to meet Lewis in the study, and Julia sat with her back against their sitting room door, listening for any sound in the quiet house. She kept expecting raised voices, shouts, even a gunshot. But there was nothing. When she heard footsteps in the hall and Sam's low voice at the door, she let him inside and hugged him.

He hugged her back. "You're trembling," he murmured into her hair.

"What did you expect? I thought you might try to kill each other."

Sam shook his head in bemusement. "It was the strangest interview. He seemed very distant and troubled. He didn't recognize me at all, barely looked at me, in fact."

"I'm not surprised. That beard really disguises you. You're very good at what you do."

He grinned wickedly.

She held up a hand. "None of that, now."

"Oh, all right." He nodded and sat down in a chair. "I think he was worried that I, as a constable, might recognize his guilt. He seemed to only want assurances that I had discovered nothing new about you, and that you hadn't turned up to cause trouble."

"And that was it?" she said in amazement.

"That was it. He was already thinking about the night ahead, and what he had to do."

"Oh, Sam, I'm almost afraid to see him."

"Don't be. It's almost over."

After Lewis had retired for the night, Julia and Sam stationed themselves in a guest room across the hall from the master suite. She found herself pacing again, but Sam sat beside the door, which he'd opened a crack so he could peer into the hall. He never moved, he never spoke, and she knew it was because he didn't want to alert Lewis. But she desperately wanted Sam to hold her, to tell her that everything would be all right.

After midnight, Lewis emerged from his room carrying a shuttered lantern. Sam followed him at a discreet distance, and Julia followed Sam. Lewis made every attempt to be quiet, as if he thought one of the household servants might be the blackmailer. He trod lightly down the stairs and out the front door.

The wind had picked up through the evening, and she smelled moisture in the air. Shivering, she followed both men down the darkened paths deeper into the garden. She was glad to have Sam to follow, because she didn't think she could look at her brother without feeling sick. He was her last relative, and he'd betrayed her for money.

She kept her senses alert for Lewis's henchman, just in case he knew his master had come and might need him. But after the way she'd incapacitated him, and the fact that he'd failed to kill her, she assumed that he wouldn't want to face Lewis's reprisals.

Lewis hardly needed the lantern to guide him. He knew these grounds as well as she did. He led them straight to the statue of Venus. As she and Sam had arranged beforehand, they separated and circled to different sides of the statue. Lewis opened the shutters on his lantern and set it on the statue's base.

Clutching the pistol in her pocket, Julia stared at the anxious face of her only brother. His skin was puffy, lined with age in a way she hadn't noticed just months ago. His sandy blond hair looked faded and unkempt, as if he spent a lot of time running his hands through it. She told herself to feel relieved that they'd been right about him all along—instead she was sick with worry.

Lewis ran his fingers in a pattern over one edge of the base, then pulled open a door. Julia held her breath, waiting to see if their assailant had returned, but she heard nothing.

Sam stepped into the small circle of light, his pistol in his hand. "Hello, Lewis."

Her brother gasped and moved his hand toward his pocket, but Sam quickly said, "Don't. After all you've done, you know I won't hesitate to kill you."

Julia moved out from behind the bushes, and Lewis turned his head and saw her. He looked puzzled for a moment. As he recognized her, his expression registered shock and disbelief. They stared at each other with a lifetime of incomprehensibility. Then she pulled out her own pistol, and his shoulders sagged.

"You're the constables," he mumbled.

"Julia," Sam said calmly, "please remove his weapon from his pocket."

She didn't want to touch him, but she trusted Sam's aim more than she did her own. She left her pistol on the ground so her brother couldn't reach it, and approached him briskly, trying not to show the effort it took to hold her tears back. Lewis remained still as she patted his pockets and removed a single pistol. She stepped away quickly.

"Lewis, sit down on the path," Sam said, gesturing with his pistol.

Lewis waded through the ferns and rose vines and sat down heavily, his hands resting in his lap. Julia once again aimed her pistol at him, while Sam held the lantern near the statue's base.

"Is it there?" she asked, her stomach taut with nerves and suppressed hope.

Sam reached inside, and she watched him drag a portmanteau to the edge of the compartment. He opened it and stared inside, then looked at her.

"There's money here—a lot of it. Gold, too."

She heaved a sigh and started to tremble with relief. But she reminded herself that it wasn't over yet. She kept the pistol trained on her brother. She was waiting for his belligerence, his protestations of innocence, but he looked exhausted.

"I didn't mean it to be like this," Lewis said brokenly.

If he expected her pity and compassion, he wasn't going to get it. "You didn't want me executed, Lewis?" she said with sarcasm. "You didn't think implicating me in treason might bring about this result?"

Still not looking at her, he said, "I never thought it would be this difficult. I thought—I thought I would be able to live with myself, because of the way you'd disgraced me."

"*I* disgraced *you*?"

He went on as if he hadn't heard her, as if now that he'd started, he couldn't stop. "I didn't know about your behavior at first. I just . . . used your letters. It was harmless—I didn't think you'd ever even know what I'd done. I only told the Russians our troop strength, something they could have figured out on their own in time. I was going to save Hopewell Manor. That was all I ever wanted. Doesn't that count for anything?"

He looked up at her plaintively, as if his good

intentions should negate his methods and the result. She pressed her lips together to keep from interrupting him.

"And then I was told Lieutenant Lawton became your lover. I was . . . appalled by your wanton behavior. You'd always been a creature to tolerate, because I had no choice. But that was—that was too much."

"My mistake was born out of anger and loneliness," she said softly. "You did things out of hatred and indifference. What kind of a man are you to sentence thousands to their deaths, and then blame me?"

"They weren't supposed to die!" he cried. "I never thought the information could be used that way!" He clutched at his hair frantically. "When I heard—when I realized—it was too late. I was sick about what had happened."

"But not sick enough to admit what you'd done," she said.

"I had the estate to protect! Where would you live if I lost it?"

"Me?" she cried, raising her arm so the shaking pistol was aimed at his face. "You were thinking of yourself, not *me*! You were thinking of yourself when you killed all those people to keep your secret. And then you made me look guilty!"

"They weren't good men, the ones who died!" he protested. "They knew too much."

"What about Mrs. Hume? Did that frail old

woman somehow threaten your plans? Wasn't she just a way to get me to travel north to her son?"

His whole face seemed to spasm as his mouth worked silently. "I didn't know—I didn't mean—she was going to die soon anyway!"

"You bastard!" She took a step toward him, holding the shaking pistol in both hands.

"Julia." Sam said her name quietly, calmly.

Lewis didn't say anything, only lifted his chin and closed his eyes.

"I won't kill you, Lewis," she said, "though you obviously want me to put you out of your misery. Too much a coward, even at the end, aren't you?"

He covered his face with his hands. "Don't you understand?" he mumbled. "I never thought the government would execute a woman. Doesn't it matter that I've only used the money on the estate? I never gambled or spent any on whores. I haven't slept, I can barely eat—"

"Shut up!" she said fiercely. "We could have solved our financial problems another way. Selling the London town house would probably have taken care of everything. But it was your selfish pride you sold yourself for. Sam, can you please gag him so I don't have to hear another word?"

By the time Sam had him gagged, and his hands tied behind his back, Julia's whole body was trembling uncontrollably. She felt disgusted and sick at what Lewis had done in the family name. She started to put both pistols in her pockets to be sure she didn't accidentally set them off, when Sam stopped her.

"Keep your pistol on him for a moment. I need to close the compartment in the base of the statue. Although I think I can open it now that I saw how it was done, I'm going to try to keep it unlocked for now."

She nodded, her gaze on her brother. Lewis swayed as he sat, his head drooping, his whole frame showing dejection.

When she glanced at Sam as he pushed aside rose vines to approach her, he was watching her worriedly.

She waved away his concern. "What are we going to do next?" she asked.

"We have to keep Lewis hidden until we hear from Colonel Whittington. He'll know the best way to handle this."

"So where are we going to put him? I suggest in a privy somewhere."

Sam smiled. "We can't risk holding him in the house. I don't know how long it will take the colonel to get here. That old gardening shed where we spent our first night will do."

She nodded and fell into line behind him as he grasped Lewis's arm, lifted him to his feet, and tugged him along the path.

In the shed, Sam set the lantern on the bench, and she saw that he'd already prepared the little building to house her brother. There were now several sturdy chairs, and all of the debris had been swept aside.

She watched him tie Lewis into a chair, exhausted to her bones in a way that made her feel a hundred years old. Yet Sam moved with a calm efficiency that set her wondering. Had she done him a disservice by letting their assailant go? Perhaps Sam could have proven to himself that he had changed. Instead, she'd taken away his every choice—as if she didn't trust him. Was that how a woman in love was supposed to behave?

She was tired of questioning her every motive, her every thought and word. She so desperately wanted this over, so she could sleep in peace.

"Sam, would you mind if I leave? I'm not sure I can look at him anymore tonight. I promise I'll take a shift guarding him first thing in the morning."

Sam glanced at her and arched an eyebrow. "Are you sure you want to leave me alone with him?"

His words pained her to the depth of her soul. How she had hurt him, when he'd given up his very life to help her.

"I trust you," she whispered, hoping he could see in her eyes how sorry she was for everything.

Sam felt the tightness in his chest ease, and he smiled at Julia. "Get some rest. We'll be fine."

After she'd gone, he stared at the door for a moment. She finally knew everything about him, and yet she still trusted him to keep her safe, to prove her innocence. Maybe he wasn't the same man anymore. Could that man who'd found satisfaction in the duties of a soldier now find something else to live for?

Chapter 25

Colonel Whittington arrived the next afternoon, distracting the staff from gossiping about where Lewis Reed had disappeared to. The colonel entered the house on crutches with a brisk speed that belied his age. Sam had told Julia that he'd lost his lower right leg to an infected wound in India. Sam had also promised she'd be able to trust the colonel to help them. Yet she still couldn't dismiss her fears of discovery. What if the old man refused to believe them? What if he'd summoned the police?

She stood beside Sam in the entrance hall, watching several of the colonel's retainers hover about him making sure he was all right.

The old man's white mustache twitched with outrage as he waved them all away. "Go on, go on, see to the luggage."

Harold the footman followed the servants outside.

Colonel Whittington smiled as Frances stepped forward to introduce herself.

Then she gestured to Sam and Julia. "And these gentlemen, Colonel, are Constable Seabrook and Constable Fitzjames."

Bless her heart, Frances was protecting them to the end. Julia tried to smile at her, but her lips didn't want to behave. She was beginning to worry she'd lose her lunch, all in fear over an old man.

Colonel Whittington looked them both over carefully. Julia retained her manly bearing as Sam limped forward and held out a hand.

"Colonel Whittington, it's good to meet ye, sir."

"Likewise, Constable," he said dryly, as though he knew they had to keep up appearances. "Now, I do believe I cannot wait to begin our discussion."

Sam smiled. "Sir, a walk in the garden will help answer all your questions."

The colonel only nodded and followed Sam. Julia barely kept herself from looking out the front door to make certain the police weren't waiting. She was so close to freedom that the thought of losing it at this late date was frightening. She reminded herself that even if she was vindicated, she would have nowhere to live, no money to support herself—but she would be free, and she trusted herself to survive.

Yet she couldn't help being afraid as two soldiers who were waiting at the door fell into line behind them. Surely they were only safeguarding the colonel.

Sam led Colonel Whittington straight to the shed, and the soldiers stationed themselves outside. Lewis was right where Julia had left him less than an hour ago. She had spent the morning in the shed with him, organizing her notes for the colonel, ignoring her brother's occasional stirrings and sighs. The gag had been a blessing.

Now Sam left the shed door open, so the sun could illuminate Lewis's bedraggled form. Colonel Whittington halted on his crutches, then slowly sat down on a chair, never taking his gaze off the prisoner.

The colonel's smile had disappeared behind his terrible frown of disapproval. "Sam, please ungag the man so that I may speak with him."

As soon as Lewis's mouth was free, he began to protest his innocence, as if his confinement had made him realize the consequences of what he'd admitted to last night.

"Do shut up," the colonel interrupted coldly. "Sam has written to me about everything you've done. I know there are witnesses to put you at the scene of an old woman's murder, and I know

why you did such a terrible thing. There are
other men who worked for you, plenty who died
for you, others who will testify about these
deaths. I know about your access to the methods
used to betray British soldiers to the Russians
and your deliberate betrayal of your sister to
save yourself. But mostly there is your sudden
windfall of money and the lengths you went to
in order to hide it. Is that everything, Sam?"

Julia practically danced on her toes in ner-
vousness as she listened to the recitation of
Lewis's sins. Oh God, the colonel actually believed her and Sam. Would she finally be free?

"It's not quite all our proof, Colonel," Sam
said, "but it's enough for now."

Lewis opened his mouth, and the colonel
thundered, "Silence!" After a pause, the colonel
resumed speaking in a normal tone. "I do believe, though, that we are facing a dilemma."

She put her hand on the tool bench to keep
from sagging to her knees. Had she been foolish
to believe that justice would win out in the end?
Maybe the colonel could at least free Sam, and
he wouldn't have to be dragged down with her.

"What dilemma, sir?" Sam asked.

"The Crown cannot allow itself to be embarrassed by making the news public that a British
general betrayed his country."

Lewis sat up straighter, even as Julia covered
her face with her hands.

"But we also cannot allow Miss Reed to suffer

for crimes she did not commit. General Reed will be exiled from England. Miss Reed, for the sake of your family's—and the Crown's—reputation, we will have it known that the general is on an extended journey in the government's service."

"But if we're not able to establish his guilt," Sam said, "then who—"

"You're so impatient, Mr. Sherryngton," the colonel interrupted. "I don't remember that being one of your failings."

Julia knew that Sam was only worried for her. She watched her brother, expecting him to appear elated with his good fortune when so many others had suffered terribly. But what he had not been offered was money to allow him to live a comfortable existence, the reason he had committed treason. Nor had the colonel offered protection from the enemies Lewis had made. Her brother appeared dazed.

Colonel Whittington absently rubbed his maimed leg. "As for the treason itself, we will blame it on a man who was involved in the crime, but who is now dead: Edwin Hume."

Julia thought of Edwin, her governess's son, who'd taken money to cover Lewis's crimes and become a drunkard in the process. In the end, Lewis had had him killed and tried to make Sam look guilty. She should feel relieved that she would be cleared, but she was just so sad for all the people who'd died.

"Colonel," she said, "what about Sam's part in this?"

"He's an innocent man, Miss Reed. He was trying to protect you from your brother's manipulations. He will be exonerated as well. You both will be free to return to your lives."

She stared at Sam with wide eyes. He would be free to leave her and rejoin the military. Would he take her with him? She had nothing else, nowhere to go. But could she bear knowing he helped her only out of pity once more?

"Sergeant Hammersmith," the colonel called in a louder voice, "do come see the prisoner to my carriage. We'll be escorting him all the way to the coast. Untie him, as we don't want his servants to talk."

Julia tried not to listen as Lewis pathetically thanked the colonel for his life. She didn't watch as the two soldiers led him outside, knowing she would never have to see or think about him again.

"Shall I get the hidden money for you, sir?" Sam asked.

The colonel sighed with distaste. "There *is* that blood money to deal with. I'll send the sergeant back to retrieve it with you."

Julia spoke up. "I imagine you could use the money to help all the families who lost someone in the massacre at the Khyber Pass. Maybe those sixteen thousand souls would rest easier."

Sam smiled at her as the colonel nodded.

"A good idea, Miss Reed. You do have a sensible head on your shoulders. And it seems you were able to carry off a difficult disguise at a time when many other women would have fallen apart."

"It was all thanks to Sam, sir."

Sam looked uncomfortable at the praise. "Colonel, what about Hopewell Manor?"

She smiled and looked away. She appreciated Sam's thoughtfulness, but she was done waiting for events to carry her along. She would make her own future, and God help her, she would tell Sam she loved him, and hope for the best.

The colonel laughed. "Seems I'm getting forgetful in my old age. Of course the estate will need an owner. After all you've suffered because of the Crown, Miss Reed, we can only give you small recompense by offering you Hopewell Manor."

Hardly breathing, she put a hand to her chest and stared at the old man. "This—this manor is to be my . . . home? Are you certain you don't mean until Lewis's heir is established?"

"If there is an heir, he will eventually be compensated should General Reed die," the colonel said mildly. "Do you accept our offer, Miss Reed? The Crown will make certain that all in the land know that you're innocent."

She wiped tears from her eyes. "Yes, Colonel, I gladly accept, and you have my thanks."

"I only wish that we could promise that Lewis Reed will suffer for what he's done."

"You took everything away from him, sir," she said. "He'll suffer."

"And perhaps his enemies will save us the trouble of having to keep watch on him," the colonel added.

Julia didn't know how to respond to that, and didn't want to waste another thought on her brother. She could only look at Sam now, feeling hope straining at her chest. She had a place to belong, but without Sam, it was a hollow victory. He stared back at her, but she couldn't read his expression.

The colonel cleared his throat. "Hmm, seems I'm no longer needed here." He looked from Sam to Julia with a twinkle in his eye. "I imagine you two have much to discuss."

Sam smiled. "Thank you, sir. I knew I could count on you."

"Should have counted on me from the beginning," he grumbled, shaking his head.

Julia kissed his cheek. "You have my everlasting gratitude, Colonel. I do hope that someday you will do me the honor of allowing me to call upon you and pay my respects."

"Why, of course, Miss Reed. My daughters are about your age."

"I have recently met them, sir, and they are fine women who must make you proud."

If he knew that his daughters had aided Nick, Sam, and Will in putting her in jail, he did not say. He only smiled at them both and left the shed.

Looking back over his shoulder, the colonel called, "Take your time, Mr. Sherryngton. Sergeant Hammersmith can wait for you to lead him to the money."

"I won't be long, sir."

Sam stood in the doorway and watched Colonel Whittington leave. Julia stepped beside him, letting their shoulders brush. They silently looked out on the garden in all its lush beauty. The seasons had changed while they'd been preoccupied with proving their innocence. The occasional dry leaf blew by them on a brisk breeze that hinted at colder nights ahead. But right now the sun could only shine on them.

Nearby, the manor—*her* manor—waited. She would never have to leave. She could sell the London town house, and use that investment to make the estate flourish. Every dream she'd ever had was finally coming true—except one.

As she gathered her thoughts about how to approach Sam, he took her hand.

She turned and looked up at him, at the sun on his bearded face. She wanted him to shave, so that she could see the Sam she remembered—and the incredible man he'd become.

"You could use a gardener," he said softly.

The hope she'd suppressed now burst open within her, spreading her wide smile, finally freeing her at last. She took both of his hands in hers and faced him. "I already have a gardener. But I could use a husband."

He closed his eyes and pulled her against him. She held him close, then looked up into his beloved face.

"I love you, Julia, I've always loved you. I spent my life thinking I could never have you, thinking society kept us apart, when all along it was me and my own doubts. But you know everything now, and yet still you trust me."

She touched his lips, wanting to shush his words, but he only kissed her fingers, then held them against his chest.

"Would you trust an old soldier to try retirement?" he said. "I never had a plan for what I would do when I left the army. I guess I thought death would take me first."

"Sam, don't say such a thing!"

"I never considered the future except for seeing you free. Do you think you can put up with me as I try to discover myself as a civilian?"

"Oh, Sam, I love you so!" She stood on her tiptoes to kiss him.

He pulled her inside the shed and shut the door. Against her mouth, he whispered, "We can't have the servants seeing their new mistress like *this* for the first time."

She kissed him over and over again. "Their new mistress and *master*."

"Good God, what will my family say to *that*!" He shook his head ruefully.

"They'll be as proud of you as I am."

Then she kissed him, telling him without words that he'd been in her heart for a lifetime.

The two "constables" left Hopewell Manor, their work finally over. A week later, when the news of her innocence had been in every newspaper, Julia and Sam returned home. He'd shaved his beard. She'd bleached her hair, managing to put it up with pins and disguise its length with flowers. To wear a corset and dress again should have felt restrictive, but the appreciation and desire in Sam's eyes made her feel so very feminine and beautiful.

After somehow acquiring a special license—she thought Colonel Whittington might have had a hand in that—they were married in a private ceremony with only the staff and Sam's family in attendance. Julia had never felt so welcomed and loved by his family—the only real family she'd ever had. Now she was one of them, beloved in Sam's eyes.

Epilogue

"**W**hen is that baby going to be born?" Nick Wright demanded, pacing in the sitting room.

"It's not even your baby," Sam said, smiling. "Julia is doing just fine."

Will Chadwick put a hand on Nick's shoulder. "It can take forever. When we had our daughter in Italy—"

"Oh, stop going on about that!" Nick pushed him away and sank down on the sofa. "Yes, yes, you're the first father among us. But Sam will be a father today, and I'll be one in a couple months, and—I don't feel very well." He put a hand to his stomach. "Getting shot was easier."

Will harrumphed. "Oh, please. As an earl, you'll have dozens of servants surrounding your wife. You won't even have to be there."

"Not be there!" Nick thundered.

Shaking his head, Sam walked over to his bedroom door, softly knocked, and went inside. Julia was sitting up in bed, her lovely face full of concentration, but she spared him a smile. Sam's mother was helping with the birth, so he felt confident everything would be fine. A woman who'd had seven children would know what to do in any situation.

Jane Chadwick, the newly experienced mother, was pouring a glass of water for Julia. He was so glad she and Will had decided to return to England for a brief visit, before they were off on their next adventure together. Charlotte Wright, Nick's wife, was seven months pregnant, and she wore a look of peace and anticipation. She brought Julia a wet cloth for her face.

Sam looked at these three young women, once enemies, now united by marriage and friendship. He had never imagined his life would turn out so wonderfully. He was at peace, and his memories no longer haunted him. He had Hopewell Manor to run, his wife and family and friends all around him, and soon a baby to love.

And the baby had decided on sooner rather than later. The women tried to shoo him away, but he stayed near Julia as she gave birth to their son, whom she'd already insisted on calling Samuel.

After holding his son and kissing his wife, Sam left them to sleep and rejoined his friends.

Will grinned when Sam came back to the sitting room. "A boy, Jane tells us. Congratulations! You'll enjoy being a father."

"So how did she handle the laboring?" Nick asked with concern.

Charlotte rolled her eyes. "You act as if *you* have to feel the pain."

Nick took her in his arms. "No, but you do, and that's worse!"

"Enough," Sam said, laughing as the two broke apart. "We need a toast." When they'd all had a glass of wine, he raised his. "To new friendships, new families, new love." He looked at the door behind which Julia lay peacefully sleeping. "And to a love that began long ago and never died."